HARD GLAMOUR

Glamour Series Book 1

MAGGIE MARR

✤ Created with Vellum

BOOKS BY MAGGIE MARR

The Hollywood Girls Club Series

Hollywood Girls Club

Secrets of the Hollywood Girls Club

Hollywood Hit

Hollywood Girls Club, the Series

The Eligible Billionaires Series

Can't Buy Me Love

One Night for Love

A Christmas Billionaire

Last Call for Love

Running from Love

Eligible Billionaires Books 1–5

Eligible Billionaires: The Travati Brothers

A Forever Love

A Billionaire for Christmas

A Convenient Arrangement

A Forbidden Love

Eligible Billionaires Books 6-9

The Powder Springs Series

Courting Trouble

The Christmas Wish

Candy Cane Lane

The Glamour Series

Hard Glamour

Broken Glamour

Fast Glamour

Easy Glamour

Luxe Glamour

Impossible Glamour

Coming Soon: Vicious Glamour

The Hollywood Hitmen Series

Beck

Coming Soon: Jax

The Wonderful Love Duet

Wonder F*ck

Mister WonderFULL

Wonderful Love

This book is dedicated to Nealie Harrison.
You are my forever friend and the sister I always wanted.
All my love,
Stinky

CHAPTER 1

LANE

I WASN'T SUPPOSED TO BE IN LOS ANGELES. I wasn't supposed to drive halfway across the country for a job in entertainment and live in a city where I knew absolutely no one. This wasn't supposed to be my summer. No, I was supposed to take the summer corporate job in Kansas City. A summer job that would pay enough for my tuition and books for the next year, a job that nearly guaranteed me a permanent gig when I graduated college. A job I should have been thankful to get, a job that any responsible, Midwestern girl from Brokesville, with no backup plan, would get down on her knees and thank the good Lord above for providing.

I didn't take that summer job. In fact, I'd burned a gargantuan bridge by declining, but getting into my Jeep and driving to an adventure was the first time I'd felt alive in months. The first time I didn't feel numb. I pressed the accelerator down and whipped around a curve on Oak Canyon Road. The guy at the front desk of my motel had told me I'd get a great view of the city if I wound up this road. I hit the brakes and made a quick right onto a turnout. I jumped from my black Jeep and felt the familiar crunch of gravel under my boots. A breeze whipped my hair and I pulled a caramel-colored strand behind my ear. I settled my hands on my hips and looked at this giant monster of a city. L.A. Out there... way out there, but not too far, where the sky merged with the sea, was the Pacific. I was a landlocked girl from the middle of the country and this was a helluva sight.

My best friend and roommate, Emma, had called going to L.A. for the summer the Big Risk. I bit down on my bottom lip and shook my head. Emma, with her sweet periwinkle-blue eyes and corn-silk hair and a surgeon for a mother and a CEO for a dad, couldn't begin to understand why I would want to risk everything and go to Los Angeles. Here's the thing Emma didn't understand, couldn't understand: the Big Risk is not that big when you have nothing left to lose. That's how I'd felt this past semester after my mom died. I loved Emma, she was my best friend, but how could she understand? She had the perfect life with a whole lot of money and a great family. Me? I had nothing and no one left. At least not in Kansas. Maybe this summer in Los Angeles was a Big Risk, but I wanted into the world of entertainment. I wanted to make movies. I wanted to live in California. I wanted to feel alive and whole. I wanted so much more than a girl from Kansas should ever want.

My heart pounded. My internship at CTA was an

opportunity I'd chased down for myself, a big opportunity that would hopefully lead to another big opportunity that would lead to another and another and another. Until someday Los Angeles might be my town. I cupped my hand over my aviator sunglasses and took one final scan of my summer home. Then I hopped into my Jeep. I had the entire summer to explore L.A.

꽃

THE WINDING ROADS BACK DOWN THE HILL circled and curved and circled again. I leaned forward, trying to read the street sign on my right. I'd driven by the big white house with a Mercedes and a BMW parked in the drive three times. I pressed the brake and stopped in the middle of the road... shit. I was lost. The sun sank in the west, and even with my sunglasses on, the harsh light blinded my eyes. I pulled hard on the wheel of my Jeep and turned left. There had to be a way out of this maze of streets and back to my motel—I just hadn't found it yet. I sped down the road.

Orange-and-white barriers closed off the way I needed to go. Three giant white semitrucks lined the road I needed to drive down. I could back up, turn around, and try to find my way back to my motel by going the other direction, but I wasn't sure where I was. My fifteen-year-old Jeep didn't have power steering, much less GPS. Instead, I pressed the clutch and pushed the stick into first gear, then wove around the barricade. The sun beat into my eyes. I swiveled my neck to get a good look at the giant white semitrucks.

There was a planet logo and a studio name painted on

the cab doors of the trucks. My heart kajolted in my chest. These were production trucks. Someone, somewhere on this street, was making a movie. I craned my neck to the right and lifted my foot from the brake, and my Jeep rolled forward. In front of the last truck was a giant RV. Was there a star inside? Someone I'd have seen on the big screen? My eyes widened and my heart beat faster. This was the very reason I'd shucked my golden opportunity in KC and taken the Big Risk. I wanted to be part of this world. I wanted to make movies. To work with people who made movies. For me, movies were magic.

Metal clanged and I slammed my foot onto the brake pedal.

"Hey! Watch where you're going!"

Standing beside my Jeep with his eyes burning fire was the best-looking guy I'd ever seen. His white T-shirt strained over his chest and his black hair blazed in the sun. His arms were thick with muscle, and a giant tattoo wound over his forearm to where his hand was balled into a fist. The same fist that he'd just pounded onto the hood of my Jeep. His bright blue eyes pierced through my window. His full lips pulled tight. He walked around to my side of the Jeep.

Up close he looked even better. Hot little flashes pulsed over my skin. His cheekbones were high and cut hard. His golden skin was perfect, flawless, his body muscled and tight under his clothes. With so much masculine perfection so near, I could barely breathe.

"D...d...do? Do I know you?" I stammered out. He looked so familiar. That face. My eyes dropped down to his neck and roamed over his body.

"Do you *know* me?" He shook his head and rolled his eyes up toward the sky. "Oh, sweetheart." He crossed his arms and the muscles in his forearms flinched. "There is no way that you don't recognize this face, is there?" He pointed at his own mug. He looked at me like I'd fallen out of the sky from an alien planet.

Did I know this guy? Did I recognize his face? I could sit here all day and watch his muscles tense. He waited and finally he pressed his face forward with a bored expression. "Even as good as you look, you've got to come up with a better line than that."

A better *line*? Behind my sunglasses I squinted. What the hell? Did this guy think I was picking him up?

"You"—he pointed his finger at me through my open window—"nearly ran over me."

I should have apologized. I could have apologized. I would have apologized if this guy wasn't behaving like such an incredible ass.

"Maybe you shouldn't walk out into the center of the road without looking," I said and flipped my hair over my shoulder. I cocked my eyebrow. He was the jerk, I was just a driver.

"Maybe you should pay attention to where you're going instead of craning your neck at a film set." His voice grew louder with each word. "There are barricades all over the street so some no-name person like *you* doesn't run over someone like *me*."

Someone like *him*? I fought the urge to shove the stick into reverse, back up, then ram it into first, hit the accelerator, and let this asshole know just what it would feel like for this no-name someone to run over his ass.

"Dillon, baby, are you okay?" From the left, a bleached-blond California bimbette ran into the road and grasped his arm. He didn't look at her or even answer. She ran her hand up his bicep and over his shoulder. Her eyes turned to me and shot me the smoldering bitch-look.

"This is a closed set," he said, his tone so sharp it could make you bleed. "Do you know what that means?"

I ground my teeth. I was new to L.A., but I wasn't stupid.

"Dillon, baby, let me call security." The girl whipped her cell phone from the back pocket of her barely there short-shorts. I was surprised she could stand up straight without those fake ta-tas pulling her forward.

"Leave it, Denise," he said without looking at her. He sharpened those blue eyes on me, then left Denise on the edge of the street and walked right up to my Jeep window. The muscle in his jaw flinched. He was so close I could feel the heat of his breath. He was even more handsome up close—if that was possible. How *was* that possible? He smelled like mint and something so very… male. "A closed set means you're not supposed to be here."

I thanked God I had on my sunglasses so he couldn't see the wide-eyed attraction racing through me. I'd never been so affected by a guy. Even with his anger and his smoldering look, something so crazy inside me wanted to lean forward, clasp my hands to his face, and plant my lips on his. He wasn't nice, he was a big jerk, but this guy was all kinds of sexy. He latched his gaze on me and paused for the tiniest second, then jerked backward away from me and away from my Jeep.

"So back this heap of shit up and get out of here." Again he folded his arms over his chest as though he were king of the world and the bimbette reattached her body to his side.

He was going to watch me leave? Make sure I was gone? I didn't like being ordered around, and I definitely didn't like being supervised as though I was a child.

"I can handle it," I called and shoved the stick into reverse, grinding the gears.

"Sounds like you can handle it," he said and smirked.

"I can," I yelled. My heart hammered in my chest and a tiny bead of sweat rolled down the back of my neck. I looked out the windows. A small crowd had gathered on the edges of the road. All of them watched me. They stood there and laughed at the hick in L.A.

I pressed the accelerator, and my Jeep jumped forward and died. The crowd around me laughed.

"Are you kidding me?" the guy yelled from where he stood. He held up his hands and smiled, looking at his audience. "No surprise she almost hit me, this chick can't even drive."

My face flushed red and my breathing shortened. Humiliation carved a giant hole in my chest.

"I can so drive," I yelled. "I just finished driving two thousand miles."

"Oooo," he said and raised both of his eyebrows and that smirk, that god-awful smirk, crawled across his face. He took four steps forward and bent in front of my Jeep.

"No wonder!" he yelled to the crowd as if he'd just found the answer to life's biggest question. "She's from *Kansas!*" He nearly bent double with laughter. Laughter directed at me, my driving, and where I was from burst through the crowd.

"Yo, Dorothy, you a little lost?" he called, amping up the crowd.

I slammed my foot onto the clutch, then turned the ignition on my Jeep and fired up the engine. I wouldn't give any of them an opportunity to laugh again.

"My name's not Dorothy." I stared into his eyes. I would never forget that face. I would never let anyone like him ever make me feel this humiliated again. "It's Lane," I yelled. I slammed the accelerator and my tires squealed as I laid rubber to pavement. I flipped him the bird and hoped I would never, ever, meet that jerk again.

DILLON

"CAN YOU BELIEVE SHE FLIPPED ME THE BIRD?" I called out to Ryan, my costar on the film. He walked beside me toward my trailer.

"Bitch nearly runs your ass down, and then you're the one that gets flipped off?" Ryan looked at me over his sunglasses. "Nice tits, though," he added. Ryan was always willing to notice a good rack.

"Yeah, nice tits," I called. "Later." I laughed off the whole thing and bounded up the steps to my trailer. I was a damn good actor. I slammed shut the trailer door.

What the hell!

My heart exploded in my chest and I scrubbed my hand over my forehead and through my hair. I'd seriously almost bitten it because of some chick from Kansas. *Kansas!* That wasn't how I was supposed to go out. Not the legacy I wanted to leave. I could see the headline in

Variety now: Dillon MacAvoy Tornadoed by Kansas Driver. I paced up and down the length of my trailer. I'd definitely never thought I'd die because of some tourist who didn't know how to drive.

But those eyes. I was pissed, but I wouldn't forget those eyes. Fire and ice—her look burned. The color was ocean blue with flecks of green and brown that glimmered in the setting sun. Good thing I'd never have to see that face again. Wow. And that tight little body under a tank top. She definitely didn't look like she was from Kansas.

"Dillon? Baby?"

I spun around. Denise climbed the steps of my trailer. She was pulling the halter string over her shoulder. Her tits were huge, but they were seriously fake.

"You want me to make you feel better?" A coy smile wrapped around her lips as she played with the snap button on her short shorts. Denise was easy. A little too easy.

I didn't feel it. I didn't really want it. I'd already tapped it a few too many times. She was getting the wrong idea. The idea that we were regular, that we were a thing. We weren't regular and we didn't have a thing—I didn't want either.

I turned away from her. "Thanks, babe. Not now." I headed toward the back of my trailer. She'd get the hint and return to her double-banger on the other side of set, or better yet, she'd head home. She'd gotten a little too clingy in the last week. Monogamy, relationships—not my scene.

The trailer door slammed shut and Denise was gone. Good. It was time to start hitting something new, something different. I didn't want Denise to get the idea that I would ever settle down. I didn't have the time or the inclination. I was too busy taking care of my little brother and my career. Plus, settling down with one woman didn't go with my image, and my "team" had spent a lot of time cultivating my image. An image that was supposed to make me the next big box-office sensation. An image that wasn't too far from the truth. An image that was easy for me to maintain as long as I continued with the never-ending string of fabulous-looking women who wanted to hang on to my arm.

My phone beeped and I slid it from my back pocket. Webber's name flashed across the screen.

"Hey, man," I said. "What's up?"

"What's up?" Webber's tone sounded more serious than usual. "What's up, is I need an answer on those four offers you have for those films. If you don't read the scripts and tell me which film you want to do within the next seventy-two hours, the studios are going to pull all the offers."

I sat on the edge of the couch. There was a two-million-dollar offer attached to each of those scripts. I ran my hand through my hair. That money could take care of me and my brother for a long while. I couldn't let this kind of opportunity slip away.

"Shit, I don't know," I said. The muscle under my right eye twitched.

"Have you read them?"

I bit my bottom lip and cocked my eyebrow upward. I hated reading scripts. "No, I haven't."

"Has your reader read them?"

Webber didn't know? My gaze bounced around my

trailer. My eyes landed on the stack of thirty scripts next to the couch. I had the same thirty scripts at home.

"No." I sighed. "The reader is gone."

"Again? The reader is gone again?" I heard Webber cover the phone. "Get me Human Resources next," he yelled. "Dude, you have to stop sleeping with your readers. You bang them and then they quit. If you won't read the scripts, then someone has to read them."

"They get all gooey and clingy, and man, I can't be around that shit. Find me a guy."

"Working on it, but until I do, you have *got* to read the scripts. These are major action films with some serious money offers. The Steve Legend script is at the top of the pile. You do realize what starring in a Steve Legend film would do for your career?"

I leaned back on my couch, covered my forehead with my hand, and closed my eyes. A Steve Legend film would *make* my career. He was box-office gold in action films.

"Legend is looking for the next big action star. That's who he wants as his costar for this film. Every actor in town between the age of eighteen and twenty-four is begging for this role, and you have the offer. You! Legend came to you." Webber's tone was hard-edged but had a tremor of panic. "Am I making myself clear on this?"

"Yeah, I got it," I mumbled.

"You've worked too hard to let an opportunity like this slip through your fingers—read the script."

"That's what I pay you ten percent for, isn't it?" I said. Why the hell did I have to read scripts? I wanted someone else to tell me if the script was good or not.

"I do read the scripts that come with offers. Every one of them. But, man, I can't accept an offer if *you* don't read the script and want to do it. I read the Legend script it's good, but you have to meet with Legend and you can't do that until you read the script."

Webber was right. I settled back onto the couch and slung my feet up onto the coffee table and crossed them.

"What about your brother?" Webber asked.

"Too busy," I said, "working *your* agency."

"Right." Webber's voice trailed off. "Okay, I'm sending you coverage from our intern on the Steve Legend film. Read the coverage. This is a big movie, man."

"Yeah, okay." I wanted to work. I needed to work. I just didn't want to have to read five scripts a night to be able to work.

"Also we need to schedule a call with Boom Boom. I want to go over publicity for the premiere of *Mission Ranger*. It's your first film, man, we got to get as many eyeballs on you as we can. Get those teen queens salivating. They buy tickets, baby! Those girls see a movie two or three times. That is your audience. If they love you? You are golden. You only get your first time one time, right, my man?" Webber laughed. "And you never forget it."

"Damn." I shook my head. "That seems like forever ago." *Mission Ranger* had been my first role in a film. The shoot had wrapped in February and the film would finally premiere in July.

"So first read the Legend script, then we'll schedule the meeting with Legend, and we'll also schedule a call with Boom Boom for this week. Got it?" Webber asked.

I nodded. I had my orders from my agent, and before the end of the week I would get more orders from my publicist, Boom Boom. I sighed. These were good problems to have. I was a working actor. A working actor making money who could take care of his kid brother.

"Get me a reader," I said. "One that will stick. Someone ugly or with a penis."

"Dillon, you're running thin over here. You've fired four in three months."

"Just find me one," I hammered into the phone. "Preferably one I don't want to have sex with."

CHAPTER 2

LANE

I MIGHT HAVE BEEN STRAIGHT OUT OF THE FLY-over states, but I wasn't a moron. I definitely didn't appreciate the looks or the attitude being shot my way. I stood in the center of the human resources department in my new suit and my new heels with my new bag and my new haircut, expecting to start my new job.

"What do you mean my job is gone?" My fingertips tingled and my heart jolted in my chest. I stared wide-eyed at the blonde behind the human resources desk. She settled her chin on her hand. She looked bored. My problem was definitely not her problem. A part of me wanted to reach over and shake her.

"A client needed a summer internship for his brother."

"But you have something else for me, right?" My voice grew louder as the idea of what was going down sank into my brain. "I just drove two thousand miles for a summer job." I crossed my arms over my chest. "I need the money."

Her eyes slitted and she tilted her head. "It's an *internship*," she said. "You don't get paid for an internship in entertainment." Her eyes roamed over me and my sixty-dollar suit like I was a hick from Hicksville, USA. When was the last time this little girl had ever paid for anything on her own? Her HR assistant gig wasn't paying for those Loubies on her feet, which were peeking out from under her desk. *Damn*, those were some great-looking shoes.

"What kind of company doesn't pay a person for summer work?" I asked.

"The kind of company that gets five thousand résumés a week." She rolled her eyes toward the ceiling as though she was educating a Neanderthal and not someone who'd just locked down her third year of college. She resettled her gaze on me. "Who do you even know to get in here?" she asked as though there had been some tragic mistake other than CTA giving away my internship to some overindulged rich kid and me believing my internship would be paid.

Who did I even know? I cocked my hip to the side and sucked in my cheeks. Little Miss Attitude was not so great at HR. "A friend of my mom referred me," I said. "But I nailed the Skype interview."

"Who's your mom?" She twisted her blond extensions between her finger and thumb, suddenly interested that maybe I was somebody she should know.

A piece of my heart broke with the word *mom* on her lips. Who *was* my mom? She was my world—had been my entire world—with her wild, curly golden hair and bright blue eyes, eyes that always seemed to smile even when things were remarkably bad. Tiny pinpricks of heat started at the backs of my eyes and I swallowed and forced myself to concentrate on the entitled girl in front of me.

"That's not important." I cleared my throat and looked around the gray room full of cubicles. "Is there anyone else I can talk to? You know, about a *real* job?"

I'd rolled into L.A. on gas fumes and grabbed a bed and a shower in a Best Western. I didn't know a soul in Los Angeles. I had approximately seventy dollars to last me until my first paycheck, and I dearly hoped one of my coworkers needed a roommate for the summer. Call me a gambler, call me a risk-taker, call me crazy—I'd been called worse—but when I found out I'd gotten the gig for the summer at CTA, the biggest entertainment agency in L.A., I didn't think twice about hitting the road from Lawrence for my opportunity of a lifetime. Especially after the hell of the past year. The only problem was that it appeared that my "opportunity of a lifetime" had evaporated.

"You can talk to Nancy," the blonde said and jerked her head toward the door. "She's the head of HR, but she won't have anything for you either. Not if you *need* money."

A flush blossomed on my neck and bloomed on my cheeks. Who didn't *need* money? Oh, right, rich kids with trust funds and parents that stole other kids' jobs. Yes, I was one of those people that needed money. No daddy to bail my ass out, no mama with a trust fund to pay for my entire life. I had to actually work *and get paid* to have clothes, a car, a place to live, and even school.

"Take a seat. I'll see if she has time."

Half a day later, after meeting with two other people,

both of whom seemed grandly perplexed that I would assume my internship was paid, I had no job, no internship, and in twenty-four hours most likely no place to stay.

"You coming to work in the mailroom?" I looked up at a tall guy with shocks of ink-black hair that sprung out in odd angles from his head. He had on thick-rimmed glasses, and under his suit jacket he wore one of those graphic tees that looks shabby but costs the same amount as my books for a semester. He pulled a thick manila envelope out of a loaded mail cart.

"Don't think so," I said and settled my head onto my hand. Nancy, her assistant, and some guy from Business Affairs were on the other side of her office door, still yakking about what to do with me.

He set the envelope on Nancy's assistant's desk. "I'm Choo," the guy said and held out his hand.

"Choo?" I asked. Maybe I hadn't heard him right.

"Choo," he said again and nodded.

I leaned forward. "Is that even a name?" I asked.

A wide smile broke over his face. "Girl," he said and rolled his eyes, "I like you."

I smiled and tilted my head. "I like to be liked," I said. "I'm Lane." I took his soft palm into mine. "Lane Channing."

He settled one fist on his hip, and examined me from my shoes to my hair. "You're not from around here," he said and tapped a finger to his lips.

"That obvious?" I asked. I would have been annoyed if I wasn't so tired. "I just spent three days driving two thousand miles to discover those people gave away my job."

"Job? Or internship?" Choo asked.

"How come everyone knows the difference but me?" I sighed. "Internship, okay." I cocked one eyebrow skyward. "An internship that, now that I know all the definitions, I wrongly thought was a job." I jiggled my foot and looked away from Choo and toward Nancy's closed door. "I was so excited to get the gig, I didn't even ask. Then I went and based my whole summer earning potential on my inaccurate definitions. Now I am all kinds of screwed."

"But you're gorge," he said and planted his hand on his hip. "Super gorge, and baby, that can go a long way in this town." He wiggled his eyebrows and I had to laugh. This boy was funny. Anyone who could make me laugh when I was broke, without a job, and nearly homeless was okay in my book.

"You should come out tonight," Choo said. He slipped his phone from his back pocket. "Digits."

"Choo, after my day, I can guarantee I won't be fun." I gave him a warning look. "Plus I got no bills, you hear me? Not a dime."

"Don't worry about the money." He waved his hand as though money could never be any concern. "And it doesn't matter if you're fun or not, L.A. is." He plugged in my number. "Besides, you might find a job."

"At a party?" I asked.

"Lane, this is L.A., that isn't even strange." He tucked his phone into his pocket and grasped the handle of the mail cart. "Nice to meet you, Lane Channing. I'll text you about tonight."

"You too, Choo," I said and watched him sashay his way down the hall.

Half an hour after meeting Choo, Nancy didn't have any good news.

"We've filled our internships for the summer," she said. "I'd put you in the mailroom where you could get paid, but we're overstaffed." She tilted her head to the side and lifted her shoulders. "Sorry."

I bit down on my bottom lip and fought the urge to yell or cry. I didn't want to cry in the office of the head of HR at the biggest talent agency in Los Angeles because I was already humiliated by the assumptions I'd made about my internship. I didn't want to yell because of the next thing I had to ask her.

"If something comes up," I said, looking directly at Nancy, "*anything*, would you let me know?"

She nodded and slid her business card across the top of the desk. Over the day, Nancy had heard my long, sad story and knew I needed a job. "I'm sorry," she said. "For the misunderstanding. I'm sure you'll find something."

I stood and forced my lips to smile. "Thank you," I said and clutched her card.

I walked to the street and turned the corner. My air conditioner had crapped out in Nevada and my ancient black Jeep baked in the California sun. I didn't look forward to climbing into that oven. Then I saw it, fluttering on the windshield, taunting me.

"No, no, no, no, no!" I said with each step toward my car. I yanked the paper from beneath the blade. "Eighty-seven dollars for a parking ticket!" Tears welled in my eyes. My heart rate spiked and a large lump choked my throat. Not only did I not have a job, but I also now owed the city of Los Angeles eighty-seven dollars, which was seventeen more dollars than I currently had.

DILLON

"YOU CAN GET THE FUCK OUT OF MY WAY," I growled as I hauled the missile launcher over my shoulder and pointed. "Or I can blast a path through your ass."

"Cut!" Hunter Fabian called. The bell rang and the entire crew started to clap. "Brilliant, Dillon, absolutely brilliant." Hunter's British accent was lighter since he'd lived in Los Angeles for closing on twenty years. He lifted his baseball cap from his head and looked around the set. "We're done for today, people."

"You were so good!" Denise squealed. She clipped across the set and grasped my bicep, which looked filthy and charred, thanks to the makeup department. Denise's scenes had filmed early in the morning. Why was she still here?

"Yo, man, nice job today," Ryan called from the top of a tank he'd been pretending to jockey. He, too, was rocking the hard-core dirty-military-man thing going for today's scene.

"You look so sexy when you're sweaty," Denise cooed.

I pulled away from her. I needed to get clean and get it through this chick's head that while it'd been fun, it'd been nothing but that.

"Dillon," Hunter called from behind the monitor in video village, "can we chat?"

I nodded and headed toward my director. Blond hair curled under the edges of his ball cap. He stood, hands on his hips and a smile crinkled his suntanned face. Hunter was solid. This was his third action film and he was definitely making bank for every studio he worked with. I handed one of the crew my "rocket launcher" and stripped the fingerless black leather gloves off my hands. "Thanks," I said to the guy who took both.

I ambled over to Hunter. He now sat in his director's chair, his aviator sunglasses reflecting an image of me.

"You are doing a kick-ass job," he said. The crew who usually congregated around him had scattered. I settled into the director's chair beside him. "I see big things for you. Huge. And I mean that."

I smiled. I needed big things. I wanted big things. I wanted them fast. I didn't know how many opportunities I would get to work in films. According to my team, I should grab every role I could, at least until my first film premiered in July. Then we'd have a better idea of how to manage my career. I would either take flight and be huge, or I could land with a giant thud. Having Hunter tell me I was doing good work and that he thought I had a future in film made me feel a little less anxious about my career.

"Thanks, Hunter," I said.

"So what do you think of the Steve Legend script I sent you?" Hunter asked.

My throat tightened and my heart beat faster in my chest. I looked past Hunter to the now-empty set. I didn't want to meet his eyes; I didn't want Hunter to see the guilt I felt over not doing part of my job—the part I loathed, reading scripts, but still a part.

I cleared my throat and gave him a slight nod. Damn, I wished I had some sunglasses.

Hunter's hopeful expression fell. "Dillon," he said and his eyebrows furrowed, "The biggest action star in the world is considering you for his costar—don't tell me you haven't yet read the script?"

I bit down on my bottom lip and finally met Hunter's gaze. He collapsed back in his chair.

"Dillon, do you want this Steve Legend film?"

My throat grew tighter and I nodded.

"Then don't give Steve a reason to tell you no." Hunter scrubbed his hand over the back of his neck. "I really went out on a limb for you with Steve." He leaned forward. "Read the script. Meet with Steve. Convince him you're the right guy for this role."

My palms were moist. This was not an opportunity to mess up. Steve Legend scripts didn't happen for every actor. I cleared my throat. "I've been having some problems with my readers." I pressed my knuckles into the palm of my hand. I looked past Hunter to where the crew now rolled the tank away from the set.

"So I hear," Hunter said. The corner of his mouth lifted into a smile. "Sounds like you need a bloke for a reader."

I nodded. "That might fix it."

"A big offer came with that script," Hunter said. He pointed at me. "I told Steve that I only wanted you in the role. *The Legend Returns* should be your next picture. Every actor in town wants this role. Don't let this opportunity slip away simply because you don't love reading scripts."

I nodded. I liked working with Hunter. He'd worked with the biggest and the best. He knew how to film "Blow 'em up and Shoot 'em down" movies and those were the movies I wanted to do, where a big star was made. Getting the costar in the next Steve Legend film would be the biggest thing to happen in my new career. Working with Legend was like him giving me the nod.

"I'll have an answer for you by Monday," I said to Hunter. And I would, even if I had to read the damn script myself.

He slapped my shoulder. "Great. Thanks, Dillon. Hope it's the answer I want."

I stood from the chair. I needed a shower and obviously some reading time. I didn't want to get the reputation of being difficult or a pain in the ass or somebody who wouldn't read or respond to an offer. Those could be career-killers.

I also needed a little stress release. I looked toward my trailer where Denise was lingering. She twirled her hair and her hips and talked to Ryan. She lifted her hand and touched the side of his hand. Please let her be moving on —I was tired of hitting that. I needed to get off, but not with Denise.

"Hey, Dillon," Denise said and her hand dropped from touching Ryan's arm.

Ryan's gaze glanced over to me and I could see the questions. He wondered if he'd been caught or if he could have the okay. One of the wardrobe mavens walked up to Denise and tapped her on the shoulder. Denise turned toward her and I leaned in close to Ryan. "Dude, she's all yours," I whispered. "Enjoy."

I slipped around the edge of my trailer and up the stairs. Once inside, I peeked out a window just in time to see Ryan and Denise walk away with his hand settled on her tight little ass. The tight little ass that I had already tapped.

CHAPTER 3

LANE
<hr/>

"SORRY, CHICKY. YOU NO PAY, YOU NO STAY."
Haroom tilted his bald brown head and planted his hands
on the front desk.

I glanced at the two suitcases and duffel bag at my feet.
I pressed my fingertips to my eyes. "I just need one day." I
pulled my cell phone from my purse and scrolled, praying
that someone had called—anyone. The only message was
the same one that was always there. An old message that I
could never delete that was from my mom, telling me how
proud she was of me and how she wished she could help
more. I looked up at Haroom. "Please," I said. I glanced at
the guests milling around the lobby. "Just one night."

"A dollar for every time I've heard that and this place
would be free." He shook his head and his lips thinned.
"Your company decline your card. No money not funny. It
is time for you to be going now."

My stomach growled. Nancy had ordered me lunch, but that had been a long time ago. After paying for my one night at the motel with cash, I only had twenty dollars left, which I'd set aside for gas. Twenty dollars that I wouldn't touch no matter how hungry I got.

"I can't let you stay. I cannot turn away paying customers for a deadbeat like you."

"A deadbeat like me?" I slammed my hand to my chest. "I've been looking for jobs—I put in seven applications today. If you'll just let me—"

"No, chicky. No can do. Either you pick up that bag and head through those doors, or I'll be picking up this phone and you'll be staying for free tonight somewhere where the nice men with handcuffs and guns won't let you leave."

I got the message. I hoisted my duffel up over my shoulder, tilted my rolling bags, and turned toward the door. At least I had my Jeep. That rattletrap was the only thing between me and homeless. Plus I needed my car to keep looking for a job.

I couldn't afford the parking rate at the motel and I'd already experienced the handiwork of the L.A. Parking Authority, so I parked three blocks north and three blocks west. I figured that was the safest place to leave my car. I'd needed a neighborhood that wasn't too far and didn't have meters. I'd had to hike a mile each way to find one.

I lumbered down Franklin Avenue. Shame settled in my gut. A deep, hollow feeling. I was a fool. Embarrassment over how stupid and naive I was heated my belly. I clenched my jaw and rolled my shoulders back. I held my head up and let my brown hair bounce around my back. None of the people driving by in their BMWs and Bentleys and Range Rovers had any idea I was stone-cold broke and homeless. Let them think that I was some posh young executive. My throat choked tight. I was such a fool. I'd thought my career was on the rise, but instead I had crashed and burned. I turned the corner and walked up Whitley. I stopped.

Where was my Jeep?

My heart thwapped hard against my ribs. My fingers tingled as panic crept up my spine. I walked to the end of the street and looked up at the green street sign. This was definitely Whitley. I walked up the street and back down the street, dragging everything I owned with me. Then up and down each street three streets each way. With every step, a bigger hole tore into my heart.

What an absolute idiot I was, stuck in Los Angeles, no money, no job, no place to stay and now—no Jeep. Darkness chased the sun. I dropped my duffel on the curb and sat next to the spot where my Jeep had been parked.

"What am I going to do?" I mumbled. Life wasn't easy and life wasn't fair, and I was a get-off-your-ass-and-make-something-happen kind of girl, but today… today I'd been handed a crystal vase full of shit. Shit that not even I could spin into roses.

My phone rang and I scavenged through my purse. I pulled it out and pressed it to my ear. Please God, let it be someone who has a job for me. I looked out at the street that didn't contain my Jeep. Not that I could get to a job.

"Hello," I said.

"Lane?"

The voice was familiar but at first I couldn't place it.

"It's Nancy." She took a deep breath. "Nancy Tyson, from CTA."

"Hi, Nancy!" I said a bit too enthusiastically and bounced to my feet. "How are you?"

"I'm good." She hesitated and I heard papers shuffle. "So listen, Lane, there's this job—"

"A job?" I interrupted, excited about the prospect of not being homeless and broke. "At CTA?"

"Not exactly." I could hear the frown in Nancy's voice. The hesitation and the pause. "But the pay is really great."

DILLON

"BRO, YOU TOTALLY OWE ME. I SO COMPLETELY saved your ass."

My little brother seemed to always think that I "owed" him for something, even though I'd been the one saving his ass since we were kids.

"My ass?" With my phone pressed to my ear, I jumped down the steps of my Star Wagon and walked toward my bike. I glanced to the far end of my trailer to where a black-haired actress I'd played a scene with earlier that day stood chatting up a grip. "Isn't that backward, little brother? I've been saving your ass since I was nine and you were six. Ever since you let loose with the little fact that you preferred Barbie to GI Joe and accessories to ammunition." I nodded my head toward the raven-haired beauty and smiled. She wasn't as smokin' hot as the girl in the Jeep from the day before, but she'd be okay for tonight.

"Whatevs," my brother said with a tone that implied my saving him when we were kids was way past being owed back. "I heard that Worldwide is about to pull your offer for the Steve Legend film."

My stomach clutched and panic hit me hard in the gut while I maintained my I-want-to-bang-you smile for the girl waving good-bye to the grip and hello to me. She sauntered toward me in her barely there shorts.

My career was just getting liftoff. If a director like Hunter Fabian and an actor like Steve Legend wanted me in their next movie and went out on a limb for me with the studio, I at least had to show enough respect to read the script.

"Hunter was pissed!" my little brother continued. "I got to listen to the call in Webber's office."

The actress I wanted for tonight now stood before me. Her eyes were dark brown and her skin was this luscious mocha shade. "You listened to the call?"

"Webber does that sometimes. How else am I going to learn to be an agent? Assistants listen to *every* call."

"Right, but that's Webber's assistant," I said. I reached out and let my finger run over the actress's arm. What was her name? Lilah? Lola? Lisa? I couldn't remember and it didn't really matter. "You push the mail cart, remember?"

"Not much longer, bro. I'm getting my first assistant desk soon. And I believe it will belong to Webber."

"That's a good thing," My eyes roamed up over her high heels and killer legs to her tiny shorts that barely covered her ass. Her shirt played peekaboo with her belly button. I got to her tits and then up to her face. She cocked an eyebrow and I wiggled mine to let her know I liked what I saw. My brother continued to yammer in my ear.

She reached out her hand and I wrapped my arm around her. Without a word, I settled her onto the back of my bike. "You'll get the inside scoop too and be able to read the scripts I don't want to read," I said to my brother as I smiled at the girl.

"Hell no!" he said. "You're not Webber's only client— you're not even his biggest. You need a reader. And that is how I have just saved your ass—I found you one."

"Is she ugly?" I asked. I mouthed, "What's your name?" to the hot sweet thing I would soon hammer.

"Lola," she mouthed back. I nodded and handed her a helmet. I climbed onto the back of my bike. "Or does she have a penis?"

Lola tilted her head at that question. A smile broke across her face.

"That is weird, even coming from you," my brother said. "but neither. She's untouchable."

"Untouchable?" I turned the key to the bike. I leaned back and relaxed into Lola. She had some seriously nice tits, which now pressed into my back. "She must be some shit-faced type of ugly," I said.

"Nope. Not it."

"Is she a dyke?"

"Hey!" He yelled into the phone, "No derogatory gay comments. You've got family."

"Look, I know you're gay. It doesn't bother me," I said and smiled. I loved my brother. I loved busting his chops. I mean, he was gay, but he was still a guy. I glanced over my shoulder at Lola. While my brother loved guys, I loved having sex with women.

"Asshole," he said, but I could hear the smile on the other side of the phone.

"Okay." I laughed. "But what is it? What's wrong with this girl?"

"You'll see once you get here."

LANE

THE ESCALADE SWEPT UP THE STREET AND pulled to a stop in front of me, my duffel bag, and my two suitcases. How pathetic did I look wearing a rumpled sixty-dollar suit and sitting on a curb in Los Angeles? The driver jumped from the front of the car and swung around the back to where I now stood. He was older with dark hair and deep-set eyes. He was thick and broad and looked like he could lift a monster truck with his bare hands.

"Lane Channing?" he asked.

I nodded.

"I'm Bob," he said. He grabbed my bags like he was lifting an empty paper plate and tucked them into the back of the Escalade. I wasn't sure what I'd signed up for, but I knew the only choice I had was sleeping on a curb in Hollywood or getting into the car.

Bob opened the back door. "Miss Channing," he said and tilted his body forward as though he was helping the Queen of England and not an-almost-homeless-girl from Kansas.

"Thank you," I said. I scooted into the back of the car.

Bob fired up the engine and ripped down the road. I watched through the window as houses of the rich and famous flew by. The road curved and winded, then the car slowed and Bob turned left.

Nancy had been right, based on the neighborhood alone, this gig would be like no job I'd ever had.

"Your employer is an important client of the agency," she'd said into the phone. Her voice had nearly trembled when she said it. "A very important client. I wouldn't even be offering you this job if your name hadn't been brought to me by someone very close to this client. Someone…" She paused and chose her words carefully. "A person the client listens to and respects."

"But what am I supposed to do?" I asked. She hadn't really told me my job duties or what this important client of the agency wanted from me. "Scrub toilets? Clean floors? What the heck does this bigwig muckety-muck want me to do for my pay?"

"Wellll…," Nancy said and stopped speaking. "Well, Lane, I think that those questions are the questions that your employer will be best able to answer."

"And who is this guy?" I asked. I plucked grass from the ground and let it drop through my fingers.

"Again, Lane, I can't disclose much. I can say that, well, CTA and specifically this client's agent would consider it a favor if you could keep the job for the entire summer."

"What does that mean?" I stopped dumping grass onto the ground.

Nancy cleared her throat. "What it could mean is that you would have a guaranteed paid spot at the agency as an agent-trainee when you graduate next spring."

My fingertips tingled and my heart beat faster in my chest. A guaranteed job, in L.A., at the biggest agency in Los Angeles, really in the world. My ticket into entertainment? This was exactly why I'd wanted the internship this summer so that I could meet some people, make some connections, impress someone enough to offer me a full-time job once I graduated.

"You'd put that in writing?" I asked. She had given away my summer internship, what's to say she wouldn't give away my job?

She paused. "Yes," she said, and I could hear the smile in her voice. "By that very question I know you will be an asset to the agency."

I smiled too. This was good news. Then I squinted... "But I have to survive whoever this client is and do whatever it is he needs me to do for the *entire* summer to get the offer? Right?"

"Right," Nancy said.

"Nothing illegal? I won't go to jail?"

"I think not," Nancy said. "Although there could be some other *challenges* with this client."

Challenges? I could take challenges. I liked challenges, especially when those challenges ended with a guaranteed job.

"If you're interested, he'd like to meet you tonight. Where can I send the car?"

Bob pressed the accelerator and we started to climb. We passed a dozen houses, all big and beautiful but set way back from the street with a cozy type of vibe. The fading light hit the wall of a house tucked into the Hollywood Hills.

"What the hell?" I said and pressed my face to the glass. Whoever the muckety-muck was, he sure had a great house.

CHAPTER 4

LANE

BOB STOPPED IN THE CIRCULAR DRIVEWAY. HE opened the back door and I slid from the Escalade. A wave of exhaustion swept through me. I kept getting pummeled with emotional ups and downs today. The front of the house was deceptively cozy because when I entered through the front door, the foyer was huge. Twin staircases wound their way upward from the foyer to the second floor. I took a deep breath, letting the air settle my nerves and hopefully whisk away my exhaustion. I certainly wasn't in Kansas anymore.

The tippity-tap of claws on hardwood scrambled across the floor. I turned. Four dogs scampered toward me. Three giants, one that was nearly bigger than me, and a tiny, itty-bitty mutt of a dog scrambled over and bumped into my legs.

"Hey there." I bent forward and gave the mass of

wagging tails and slobbery mugs pats and scratches. "Who are you guys?" The brown-and-white giant licked up my cheek. He looked like a St. Bernard. "Aren't you a good boy," I said. I grabbed the side of his face with both hands. Whoever owned this house couldn't be all bad with pups like these.

"Lane Channing, you are the best-looking female I've seen today."

I turned toward the vaguely familiar voice and the dogs pranced in delight. This time I couldn't stop my jaw from dropping open.

"Choo?" I'd met this guy today in the HR department of CTA for all of three minutes, and now he was luxuriating in a big house in the Hollywood Hills. He leaned against a doorframe on the far side of the foyer, his arms folded across his chest.

"As you live and breathe." He pulled his shoulder from the wall and walked toward me. "They like you." A smile carved into his face. "You said you needed a job." He reached for my purse, which in my stunned state, I'd dropped to the floor.

"But..." I didn't understand. I was so confused. I'd been walloped all day. I'd actually been feeling again, I wasn't numbed out, but I wasn't sure that numb wasn't better for the type of day I'd experienced. "Do you work here?" I asked.

"I *wish* it was only work." He waved his hand as though inhabiting the house and dealing with everyone else who inhabited the house contained the same annoyance as shooing mosquitoes. He walked between the twin towers of stairs and I followed, as did the four-pack of fur and paws. "Nothing that simple," Choo said. He turned left into another giant room with wood paneling, deep chocolate-leather couches, a flat-screen TV, a pool table, arcade games, and a giant, ornately carved bar. The dogs hopped onto the couches and settled. "This"—he waved his arms at all that surrounded him—"is family."

He dropped my purse on a barstool and stepped behind the bar. "What are you having?" he asked. His eyes roamed over my gaping face. "Something pretty strong from the way you look."

I climbed onto a barstool. "This..." My eyes roamed around what was only one giant room in a large, beautiful house. "*This* is where you *live*?"

Choo nodded.

Either Choo or his parents were rich, but it still didn't explain why I was here. My eyes wandered around the room. The whole room screamed "made for men." My mama always said you could tell if a woman lived in a place because of three things: cleanliness, pictures of family, and flowers. This place was clean—spotless—but there were definitely no flowers and no photos.

"How about a Choo special," he said and dropped some raspberries into a glass. He muddled the berries and pulled out the vodka. A few moments later, he pushed the drink my way. "That will make everything better."

I took a long swallow of my drink. "That," I said and smiled over the rim at Choo, "is fabulous." The anxiousness careening through my belly smoothed with each sip.

"Everything I do is." Choo smiled. With a drink in his hand, he led me through sliders into the backyard. All four dogs ambled behind us.

I stopped and stared. The house was fabulous, but this

view, the view behind this house... "It's... it's amazing," I breathed.

"It's pretty killer," Choo said. He settled onto a couch not far from the infinity pool, then leaned forward and lit two candles and with a remote made the fire in the fireplace spring to life.

I took another gulp of my drink, got a good look at the view, and sat down in the chair next to Choo. The lights in the pool, the candles, and the fire created a little circle of light. I could see Choo and the dogs, and if I looked to my right, I could see the glittering lights of L.A. Choo patted the black lab with one hand. The itty-bitty dog that was a cross between a Chihuahua and some sort of terrier hopped into his lap.

"This is Kong," Choo said and ran his hand over the tiny pup in his lap.

I smiled. "As in—"

"King Kong." Choo nodded and smiled. "He may be little, but he has a big personality. That's Scorsese." Choo patted the black lab now curled beside Choo on the outdoor couch. "And Spielberg." He nodded toward what had to be a shepherd-collie mix. "And the one warming your feet."

I glanced down at the giant brown, black, and white dog who tilted his head toward Choo and then looked at me.

"Yeah, you buddy," Choo said. "That's Bernie."

"I like Bernie," I said and rubbed his head. "He's keeping my toes warm. What kind of dog is he? A St. Bernard?"

"Burmese mountain dog rescue." Choo looked around at the pack. "They're all rescues. It's kind of our thing."

Our?

I really needed to know what the our meant, and why I was here, and what I would be doing for work. If not for the Choo special being halfway finished, anxiety would again be pummeling my chest.

"I…" My eyes roamed over his face. "I don't know what to say. I'm so confused." I reached down to stroke Bernie's head. I bit my lip and looked at Choo. "Why am I here?"

"Because we need you." He waved his hand at the pack of four. "And from what I heard today, you need us."

I definitely needed a job and a place to stay, but I still wasn't sure what Choo was offering me. "You want me to take care of your dogs?" I asked. "For the summer?"

"I know." Choo sighed. He puckered his lips together and settled his elbow onto the back of the couch and his head onto his hand. "Not a great title for a summer gig. We'll have to come up with a better title than dog-walker," he said. "What about you also read some scripts and we call you a development intern and the dog-walker can be on the side?"

"Development intern? But… wait." I pressed my straw through the ice in my glass. My mind spun through the varying scenarios. "You push the mail cart at the biggest agency in town." I looked up. His eyebrow quirked with interest. He wondered if I could figure out this puzzle. "Just like everyone else in this business when they start out? Right?"

Choo nodded. "Smart girl." He crossed his ankle over his knee and waited for me to continue.

"And you're offering me a job at a production company." I was trying to make intelligent guesses. "Not *your* production company." The straw danced on my lips as I spoke around it. "Maybe your dad? He has a production company, right? Or your mom?"

"You were on track until the mom and dad part," he said. He set his drink on the table in front of him and stretched his hands over his head. I noticed the rainbow-flag tattoo on his wrist. His eyes followed mine. "You knew, right?" He asked and tapped the rectangle with his finger.

I bit my bottom lip. "I thought maybe... but I didn't want to assume."

"Assume away, my pretty little girl from Kansas. This flag is the very reason the job I'm offering you can't be with my parents' production company... Well, that and they live in Idaho." Choo traced the edges of his tattoo with his finger. "They threw me out of the house when I told them."

A shiver crept through my body. "Oh my God, Choo. How old were you?"

"Sixteen," Choo said. "They let me back in when I agreed to get deprogrammed." His gaze locked with mine and while his face seemed relaxed—as though he'd come to terms with his parents' betrayal and abandonment—a sadness permeated his voice, a thick sorrow over what he'd lost.

Choo's gaze rolled upward as though he searched the heavens for some kind of answer. "I went to one of those places that tries to de-gay you. I did that three times." He let out a little puff of air, closed his eyes, and shook his head. "I tried to de-gay myself for my parents." The color fell from his face with the memory. "Then, when I finally accepted who I was and realized there was nothing wrong with me..." Choo took a long breath. "Well they threw me out."

My fingertips covered my lips. I took a ragged breath. The idea that a parent's love could be conditional on Choo being who his parents wanted him to be, was so foreign to me. That his parents wouldn't accept him for who he was? Being gay was simply how Choo was born.

He rolled his lips inward and resettled his gaze onto me. The corner of his mouth raised a hint and so did his eyebrow. "I'm sure someday I'll tell you every single sordid detail, but suffice it to say without my older brother's love and acceptance, I'd be homeless. There'd be no way for me to go to college." He shifted his shoulders and swept his feet up under himself. "I actually was homeless for a little while."

I shivered. I'd been homeless for an hour and the desperation that had clenched me and shook me—at sixteen? I closed my eyes, thankful I'd had my mom and her unfailing love for as long as I had.

"Anyone ever call you Dorothy?" Choo asked, changing the subject, his voice lighter, almost playful.

Heat fired up my body and flushed my neck and cheeks.

"Once," I said. My back teeth ground with the still-too-fresh memory of me stalling my Jeep in front of the entire cast and crew of a movie production. "The guy who called me Dorothy was kind of a jerk."

Why did everyone in L.A. think me being from Kansas said something about me? Something that I wasn't sure was true or fair or even right. Their assumptions made me feel small. Like everyone thought I couldn't understand what went on in the rest of the world because I'd grown up in the middle of the country.

I shook off my feelings and continued with the puzzle. "So it's not your dad, and it's not your mom"—I pressed my lips together—"is it your..." All four dogs shot upward and their bodies and tails wiggled with joy. They bounded across the patio and grass to a different doorway than the one through which Choo and I had emerged.

An outline of a man angled through the door. He bent forward and patted each pup. I couldn't clearly see him through the darkness, but he scrubbed their backs and ears and even scratched two bellies. He couldn't be all bad if he loved the dogs that much. He kneeled down onto the grass to pet the tiniest one. He stood, picked up Kong, cradled him in the crook of his arm, and walked toward us through the dark.

His bare feet broke into the circle of light created by the flickering candles. Then the fingers of the hand he had hooked around the loops of his low-hipped jeans. I looked up his bare arm with the long tattoo...

My heart picked up speed in my chest.

His arm hugged the pup to that broad, thick chest. A broad thick chest that seemed to strain against his white T-shirt in a familiar way.

A low tingle threaded through my spine and something hard settled in my stomach.

Finally, his face was the last thing to emerge into the circle of light.

My heart pounded in my chest. I swallowed. My jaw locked and my gaze latched on his face.

He had a beautiful face. Blue, quicksilver eyes with long lashes, full lips, and a sharp jaw. It was the type of face I'd never forget, even if it wasn't attached to the biggest jerk I'd ever met. A face I really had never ever wanted to see again.

He crinkled the skin around his sparkling blue eyes. His gaze went from Choo, back to me, back to Choo, back to me, and he shook his head like he couldn't believe what he saw. Finally his gaze locked on Choo.

"What the hell is Dorothy from Kansas doing in my backyard?"

"My name isn't Dorothy," I said. I set my empty drink on the table in front of me. My lips pressed tight. *His* house? *His* yard? My breath shortened and my heart pounded in my chest. "My name is Lane."

"Lane, Dorothy, what the hell? Like I care?" He shrugged one shoulder and didn't look at me when I spoke. He kept his eyes locked on Choo and waited for an answer.

"Wait, he's the jerk?" Choo waved a finger from me to the guy standing across from me who obviously thought he was some kind of big badass. "You two know each other?" Choo's eyes widened. "Dillon, you know Lane, and Lane, you know Dillon?" He shook his head, completely perplexed. "How could you two know each other? You"—he pointed his finger at me and narrowed his eyes—"just got to L.A. yesterday."

I was thankful for the darkness. My cheeks warmed and I knew they were bright red. I didn't want to relive my embarrassment from the day before as the hick from Kansas who couldn't drive a stick shift and got humiliated in front of the entire cast and crew of some film.

"Dorothy nearly ran over me," Dillon said and turned his steely gaze to me, "on a closed set."

"You walked into the middle of the road—"

"On a closed set."

"Without even looking—"

"On a closed set where there were barricades—"

"Besides, I didn't even come close to hitting you—"

"How the hell would you know?" His eyes cut through the darkness at me.

Those eyes. I could barely breathe when I locked onto those eyes.

"You were too busy craning your neck like some looky-loo gawking tourist who'd stumbled onto a film set and had never seen a production truck."

I slammed my jaw closed. Yesterday I had been a looky-loo gawker who'd stumbled onto a film set and had never seen a production truck, but I wasn't a tourist.

"I'm not a tourist," I said. I tried to gather a shred of pride, which would save me from the humiliation that again burned a hole in my chest. Humiliation that clamored beside fear, because if this guy—this Dillon—was the person I was meant to work for... I would soon, once again, be homeless and unemployed.

"This is too good!" Choo said. He leaned back into the couch and clasped his hands over his mouth. The edges of his giant grin showed around his hands.

"Again, little brother, with limited patience, I ask," Dillon said, and turned his hard gaze to Choo, "what is Dorothy from Kansas doing in my backyard?"

Little brother? My eyes flew from Choo to Dillon and back to Choo. They were so different, but as I examined both their faces I could see a tiny resemblance around their cheeks and eyes.

"Lane," Choo said and reached his hand toward me, "has graciously agreed to help you with your conundrum."

"I don't *have* a conundrum," Dillon growled. Kong scrambled in Dillon's arms and Dillon gently settled him onto the patio.

Choo's eyes grew serious and he leveled his gaze on his brother. "You *do* have a conundrum, Dillon. You have thirty-four scripts and four dogs. You have an offer for a Steve Legend film which is about to be pulled"—he cupped his hand around his mouth and mock whispered —"and in case you didn't know, you have a growing reputation of being impossible to work for."

"This is bullshit." Dillon ran his fingers through his ink-black hair. His bicep curled tight. I couldn't pull my eyes from the black tattoo that licked around his muscled upper arm. I forced my jaw to remain closed. I didn't like this guy—he was arrogant and self-centered and seemed to be one of "those" guys who got everything he wanted all the time. Even with the irritation of what type of guy Dillon was and how he'd humiliated me the day before, I couldn't rip my eyes from his arm.

"Just find me a damn reader," Dillon said.

I looked up at his lips, and his jaw muscle flinched.

"I did," Choo said and waved his hand toward me.

Dillon's hard eyes landed on me. He started with my feet, no longer covered by Bernie, and worked his way up my bare legs and onto my still-rumpled suit. It was like his eyes were touching me and peeling away my sorry clothes as he examined me. He stared at my neck and I felt the pulse of his gaze over my throat and jaw. My breath grew short when his gaze locked on my eyes. I flipped my hair over my shoulder and straightened my spine, pursing my lips to show my utter distaste for Dillon and then gave him my hardest coldest stare.

"Naw," Dillon said as his eyes hammered into mine. "She's not gonna work for me."

My heart crumpled in my chest. I'd been completely checked out and told I wouldn't work out? Part of me wanted to crawl under the table and cry, but another part of me wanted to jump up and bust this arrogant prick in the nose. Even if it was a really good-looking nose.

Dillon turned away from me, tilted his head, and let his hands roam across his chin as if thinking.

I fought the urge for a moment, and then my eyes landed on Dillon's ass. Even if he was impossible, he had a great ass. He turned back around to me and to Choo. He opened his mouth to say something, but his gaze locked on me. He cocked an eyebrow and the edge of his lip fish-hooked upward. I'd been caught. I'd been caught staring at Dillon's incredible ass.

I jerked my eyes downward and again silently said thanks for the darkness around me as my cheeks flamed red. I wished for another Choo special.

"There's nobody left," Choo said. "You've tapped out all of L.A. for development interns. Nancy said the agency isn't sending you another one. Besides, I like Lane. And they like Lane." Choo pointed to the pups. Kong hopped into my lap like he was an exclamation point to Choo's statement. Scorsese and Spielberg each took a seat to my left and right, and Bernie resettled on my feet.

Dillon looked up at the sky, his annoyance at me and at the fact the dogs actually liked me evident on his face. "Has she ever even read a script? I mean, she's from

Kansas," he said again for the thousandth time, as though my home state were a stain that couldn't be washed away.

"There's nothing wrong with Kansas," I said. "At least there they teach people manners." I quickly shut my mouth. I'd just insulted my potential employer. I was staring down homeless and unemployed with a missing Jeep and only $15.75 in my purse. Now really wasn't the right time for my lippy mouth to get away from me.

"Dillon? Baby, where are you?" A voice called from the edge of the yard, near the door that Dillon had walked through.

"Oh, please." Choo shook his head and let his gaze of disgust rake over his brother.

"What? She's in the film."

"Another gold digger with claws," Choo whispered.

A gorgeous girl with light brown skin and ink-black hair stepped into the circle of light. She ran her hand up Dillon's arm and chest and molded her body to his. Kong squirmed in my lap and then tensed. She stopped snaking her arm up Dillon's side and her eyes latched onto me with a cold bitch stare. "Who is *she*?"

Kong growled and let out a solid, mean yap. I already loved this dog.

I put my lips to his ear. "Shh," I said. He turned and gave me a lick on the chin.

"Cut it, Lola," Dillon said and extracted her arms from his body.

Lola crossed her arms over her very big, very round, and I what I thought was probably very fake, chest. "Who's your little friend?"

The emphasis on little and friend made it clear that Lola considered me farm team to her very big league.

"I'm Lane," I said.

"She walks the dogs and reads scripts," Choo said and stood as though the discussion between the brothers as to my employment and position was closed. He reached for my hand and Kong hopped off my lap but stayed planted by Bernie at my feet. "Come on, Laney." Choo pulled me upward and closer. He whispered in my ear, "The quality of people has dropped waaaaaay below my tolerance threshold."

I fought the smile that wanted to curve over my lips at Choo's comment and glanced toward Lola, who'd resumed her "he is mine" display by hanging all over Dillon. She could have him. From where I stood, they were made for each other.

"We have places to go," Choo said. "Let me show you your room."

"She's living here?" Lola asked Dillon.

Choo held my hand and pulled me toward the sliders. All four pups clattered along beside us. I didn't dare look over my shoulder and catch what I knew had to be Dillon's very hard, very cold stare.

CHAPTER 5

<u>LANE</u>

"THIS IS YOUR ROOM," CHOO SAID.

He flipped on the lights and all four pups bounded onto a giant four-poster bed. I stood in the doorway and gaped at the space. My best friend, Emma, had a big, beautiful room like this at her parents' house, but I'd never had so much space just for me. To the left there was a desk and a couch and two little chairs. Behind the work area was a wall of windows. Beyond the glass, L.A. glittered in the night. This was the same view as the backyard. A glass door led out to my own private balcony. I peered through the balcony doors. Outside there was a chair and a lounger and an umbrella to shield whoever sat on the balcony from the Los Angeles sun. You could see the giant swimming pool in the backyard. On the far bedroom wall was a fireplace. The room was painted a light, creamy gold and the woods were a rich brown. The door to the walk-in closet was open and my bags were already settled just inside.

"There are flowers," I said. There was a vase full of light pink peonies on the bedside table and also on the dresser.

"Every girl needs fresh-cut flowers," Choo said. He sauntered across the hardwood floors to the door on the opposite side of the room. "When I heard from Nancy that you said yes, I asked Mathilde to get some. You'll love Mathilde," Choo called. "You'll meet her tomorrow."

I followed Choo and let my fingertips trail over the lush, heavy silk comforter on the giant bed. Gray and bright blue with silver threads interwoven through the fabric, the comforter was exotic and luxurious and looked like it should be in a very expensive hotel.

"And this is your bathroom," Choo said. He flipped on another set of lights.

I pressed my fingertips to my lips. My wide-eyed expression stared back at me from the giant mirror. I turned from my reflection to Choo. A smile broadened his face.

"I've never seen such a big bathroom."

White and Tiffany-blue tiles decorated the wall. Giant, fluffy white rugs lined the marble floor. Dozens of bright white towels were folded and hung from silver towel holders. A glass-walled shower that could fit me and the dog pack was on the far side of the room beside a deep marble tub with a window view. A white marble sink with threads of gray and silver running through the stone and a vanity with a little silk-tasseled chair and glamour lights around the mirror completed the room.

"Feel that." Choo placed his bare foot on the marble tiled floor just inside the door.

I set my much smaller foot beside his. "It's warm!"

"You like?" Choo asked and gazed at my reflection in the mirror. "It's the girliest bathroom in the house, so I thought it should belong to the only girl who lives here."

"I... I..." I turned to Choo and looked up at him. "I don't know what to say. I mean, you don't even know me. I don't even know you. Why are you doing this for me?"

"Why not?" Choo said. He crossed his arms over his chest and raised one shoulder. A smiled curved over his lips, but his eyes held hints of melancholy, maybe even sadness. "I like you, you need a job, we have a job. I know I'm going to totally enjoy hanging out with you this summer." He walked across the room and plopped on top of my bed between Scorsese and Spielberg. "Plus, now I get the additional pleasure of torturing my brother all summer. Please." He waved his hand toward me. "You're heaven-sent."

I glanced one more time into the bathroom, not yet sure if it would truly be mine. I flipped off the lights. It was pretty obvious that Choo's brother, Dillon, loathed me. He had decided that I wasn't the girl for the job. I walked to the bed and climbed up the two tiny steps and plopped on the bed between Kong and Bernie. Kong immediately resettled into my lap.

"Choo..." I thought about my words while I stroked Bernie's head. "I don't know if this will work."

"Lane, I am never wrong." Choo scratched behind both of the dog's ears. "Look, if it makes you feel better I read your résumé. Nancy had already checked your references. You've already been preapproved by the agency. You're doing me, the agency, and that jerk outside that I call a brother a huge favor." He leaned forward toward me. "I promise you, if you can stick out this gig for the next three months, the agency will totally owe you. You'll definitely be able to get any gig in town."

My heart fluttered in my chest. This summer job, reading for Dillon, could be my way into the entertainment industry. Bernie lifted his head, made a sleepy sound of satisfaction, and dropped his mug in my lap beside Kong. I considered my options while my hand stroked through his thick fur. I'd taken the Big Risk so that I, a girl with next to no connections, could wedge her size-seven shoes through a crack in the Hollywood door.

"We have so many scripts that need to be read. So many. And obviously way too many dogs. I'm at the agency twelve hours a day. Dillon is on set twelve hours a day. We need someone here."

"You mentioned Mathilde?"

"Great housekeeper, phenomenal cook, not a dog walker and and *habla* very little *inglés*." Choo bit his bottom lip. "Look, you obviously want into the business. And this is a great way to get there. You'll be reading scripts all day. Yes, you'll have to walk the boys a couple of times a day." Four pairs of eyes looked at Choo as though they knew he was speaking about them. "But the rest of the time you'll be here with Mathilde, reading some of the biggest movies in town."

This job, this place, seemed like an opportunity I needed to grasp with both hands. An opportunity that satisfied all my needs: a job in the industry for the summer, a job in the industry next spring, after I graduated, if I survived this job, a paycheck, and a place to live.

But... the opportunity came with a giant snag and that giant snag was downstairs with a bimbette pressed to his side. The guy I'd be reading for seemed to totally hate me, or at the very least seem to think I was a worthless nobody.

"What about Dillon?" I asked and now stroked Bernie's belly.

"He's really not that big of a jerk," Choo said.

I looked up through my lashes at Choo.

"Okay, he wasn't that big of a jerk before all this happened. And he won't be as big of a jerk once he gets used to it... at least I hope not.

"Wait? So all this is new? How did this happen...? I'd wondered why if Dillon is such a big deal how come I'd never heard of him."

"Because he's the *next* big deal. Or everyone seems to think he is." Choo rolled his eyes up toward the sky and shook his head in disdain at that idea as only a little brother could. "He's got two films in the can and he's filming his third. *Mission Ranger* releases in July, *White Heat* in September, and *Offend and Defend* he's shooting now. Based on those films, he's getting offers, but the public doesn't know him yet. If *Mission Ranger* does great, then his career is set, but if it tanks..." Choo shook his head and scrunched his nose. "Let's just say my brother, right now, needs to keep booking the roles, at least until *Mission Ranger* hits."

"He's on his third film?"

Choo nodded. "In six months. Before that he got plucked from campus and tagged for an Armani underwear ad. Wham, bam, thank you, ma'am. Six months later, he's the next It boy in Hollywood."

I pictured a nearly naked Dillon with only tighty-whities. Heat flashed through my body. Those arms, that chest... his abs and hips and ass... every inch had to be just as tight. Heat flushed up my neck. I'd see where that tattoo ended... I shook my head and jerked my thoughts back to now and away from the naked images of Dillon that my brain was creating.

"Wow," I said. "That would be one wild ride."

"It has been. We've both gotten a little carsick a couple of times." Choo scooted to the edge of the bed and let his feet drop to the floor. "So you'll stay?" Choo's eyes seemed to plead for me to say yes. Choo thought he needed me here, I didn't yet understand why, but I definitely needed the job, and a place to live, and a paycheck.

The four dogs leaned against me. They loved me. And Dillon loved them. How bad could a guy who actually rescued animals be? I would be reading for Dillon, but that didn't mean I had to be around him. Plus, what choice did I really have? I didn't even know where my Jeep was. I slowly nodded and a small smile stretched across my face.

"Awesome!" Choo said and hopped off the bed. "I'll let you get settled." He stopped and turned. "Do you see that giant pile of paper over there? Next to the desk?"

I swallowed and nodded.

"That, my lovely Lane, is why you're here." He flashed me a smile. "Grab a script, come downstairs, and I'll fix you another Choo special."

DILLON

"WHAT THE HELL IS THAT?" I SAID AND POKED Choo in the shoulder as he ambled down the stairs.

He turned his smart-ass look at me, the one with a smirk and a cocked eyebrow. The one that, before they threw us out, our parents used to say was identical to my smart-ass smirk—no wonder Choo's look nearly drove me off the rails.

"That is your new reader," he said. He looked like he'd just solved the biggest problem in the world. He leaned forward his voice low. "And I was right," he said. "Totally untouchable."

My heart slammed into my ribs. I reached my hand to the banister.

Yeah, Lane was untouchable, but in a totally different way than I'd expected. She wasn't ugly or gross or disgusting. Choo knew me so well. Lane was completely untouchable because she was too perfect.

"Not even you are depraved enough to tap that. I knew it the first time I saw her. You may be Mr. Tough Action Man, but I know you, big brother, I do."

Choo was right. She was too good, too pure, too innocent—exactly what I'd want for a forever kind of girl, but not what I wanted for now. I wasn't ready for forever. I wasn't even close. Not now. Not anytime soon. Not with the image that Webber and Boom Boom and even I had spent months developing. Not when I was so close to getting my career launched. Not when I had Choo to get through college.

I had rules with women. One of them was not messing around with purity. If a girl wanted to throw herself at me, who was I to say no? Especially the easy lays that inhabited L.A. I was quickly becoming a trophy for some of those girls—they wanted to sleep with an actor, especially an actor on the rise. I could walk into any club and walk out with nearly any piece of ass. Perfect. No problem. Those were a different type of girl, those were the type of girl that Lane Channing wasn't. I could tell just by being in the same room with her. But I could also tell that she was gorgeous, and rules or no rules, I didn't need her in my space all the time.

"Won't work," I said. "I need a guy reader."

"You have over thirty scripts someone has got to read and an offer on a Steve Legend film that will get pulled on Monday if you don't give them an answer."

I shifted my weight from my right foot to my left. Why did my brother have to be such a pain in my ass and be right?

"She's smart and she needs a job."

"I don't want her in my space." I searched the room with my eyes. "I don't want anyone in my space, why is that so hard to understand?"

Choo pushed past me to the bottom of the stairs. I followed him to the foyer. "Look, I don't have time to do the reading and the dog-walking. I found a solution; deal with it."

"I don't want to deal with—" I glanced up toward the top of the stairs. My heart thwapped in my chest. She wore a dress, if you could call it a dress, more like a long shirt. Her legs gleamed. From where I stood, I could see way too far up her thigh to the tiny patch of lace at the top of her leg. I tried to pull my eyes from her, but I couldn't. Rules or no, I was so completely and utterly screwed.

CHAPTER 6

LANE

THE NEXT MORNING I MET MATHILDE. THE kitchen smelled like fresh coffee and something warm and sweet—and bacon. God, I loved bacon. My stomach grumbled and reminded me that yesterday I'd had a salad and four Choo specials.

"*Buenos días, señorita. Mi nombre es Mathilde.*" Her face was like a gentle hug and a smile raced across it. "Sit and eat before you walk the pups." With the mention of food, my stomach rumbled again. I sat at the place fixed for me, and Mathilde filled my plate with bacon, eggs, fresh blackberries, and a warm scone. She set the meal before me and then fixed my coffee. I wasn't used to being waited on, but when I asked to help, she shushed me and waved me back to my seat.

"Choo said I feed you and help you," she said and smiled. "You are too bony. You need to eat."

I would have agreed with her if I wasn't so busy shoveling food into my mouth. I ate like a girl who hadn't seen a hot meal in days.... Well, I was that girl. Once I finished my breakfast, I found four leashes, four scripts, and a long note from Choo on the center island. I had my orders and a set of house keys. No vehicle to transport me and the pups to Runyon Canyon, one of their favorite places, but we could walk—it was only a mile.

"Okay, so look," Choo said over the phone, "be careful of rattlesnakes at Runyon Canyon."

"Yeah, right," I said and laughed, but when Choo didn't laugh back I wondered if he was serious. "You're kidding, right?"

"They lose a couple of dogs every summer at Runyon from rattlesnake bites. Just don't let them off their leashes all at once. They get too brave when they're all running around without leashes. They do better two at a time."

Runyon Canyon was a giant, steep-hilled park with scrubby brushes, a dirt trail at what looked to be a near-ninety-degree angle, rocks, and trees, set high in a residential neighborhood. Choo's safety warning in mind, I stopped at the bottom of Runyon, looked up at the brilliant Los Angeles sky, and then started up the steep incline. The pups trotted with me. I wasn't brave enough yet to set any two of them free. Runyon was packed with runners, walkers, and dogs, all of them huffing and puffing up the never-ending hill. The dirt path wove around bushes and through scrubby trees. We turned around giant rocks, forever climbing. My thighs started to ache and I gulped for air. The dust was a reddish color. Kong trotted next to my feet and Bernie loped by Kong. Scorsese and Spielberg tugged at their leashes, straining to run up the hill. Those two were strong and impatient. I pushed forward. By the end of this walk, I'd have my workout done for the day.

I reached the third turn, and I bent down and unsnapped Scorsese and Spielberg. The duo ran three feet ahead but then stopped and looked back at me, Bernie, and Kong. I was pretty sure they weren't going to take off without us, so we started the stiff hike to the very top. Runners passed me and while I was in pretty good shape, the way they were pushing and sweating and panting impressed me. Near the top, I looked up and just ten feet beyond us was a familiar broad chest with a familiar tattoo.

I stopped and took a deep breath. A bolt of energy zipped through my body. The heat that coiled in my belly and spread between my legs contained a kind of want that I'd heard about but not experienced. My breathing shallowed as my eyes roamed over Dillon.

A light film of sweat glistened across his chest. The sun heightened the shadow under his six-pack, the existence of which I'd speculated on just the night before. No wonder he'd been plucked from a college campus to be an Armani underwear model. His hard, muscular thighs, his chest, even his flatiron stomach, all of it meshed together to make a perfect body—really, absolutely perfect. So perfect it barely looked real. Looking at Dillon with his sweat glistening perfection made breathing difficult. I struggled to pull my eyes from ogling his body. I was thankful, once again, for my sunglasses.

I'd overheard Choo and Dillon talking late last night. I

didn't hear the exact words but could pretty much tell from the tone that I wasn't exactly wanted. I needed this job. I needed to last through the summer as Dillon's script reader and get my offer from CTA. Being physically attracted to Dillon wouldn't help, but I could control my physical feelings. I might agree with the world that Dillon was sexy, but I didn't really *like* Dillon. So far, all I'd seen of him was a self-involved jerk. Granted, I did really adore Choo, and I did adore the pups, and all five of them seemed to think Dillon was A-okay, but I still wasn't sold on Mr. Dillon MacAvoy. It would take more than his all shades of sexiness plus a little brother's love and the abject devotion of four rescue dogs to convince me that Dillon was anything more than the narcissist who'd humiliated me in front of an entire film crew.

That little memory, the memory of my humiliation at the hands of Dillon, threw a bucket of cold water on my physical desires. The heat scorched out. Scorsese and Spielberg barked. They'd caught sight of the gorgeous man dripping sweat not far from us and bounded up the hill, wagging their tails. Bernie and Kong both pranced by my side once they saw Spielberg and Scorsese's reactions. Bernie looked up at me and whined.

"I know," I whispered over an exasperated sigh. "Mr. Perfect is here. Come on."

Looking at Dillon was like looking at chiseled perfection. His body was thick with muscle. He wore shorts that were slung low on his hips. Dillon bent down and patted Bernie and Kong. He turned his face toward me. A giant smile burst across his face. My heart hiccupped.

"Morning," he said.

"Hi." My smile was hesitant. I shifted Kong and

Bernie's leashes to my right hand and pushed a loose strand of hair behind my ear. All four dogs were a wiggling mass of joy around him.

He stood. I forced my eyes to remain on his eyes and not wander across that thick chest or down that lovely hint of hair that whispered below his six-pack to underneath his shorts.

He cleared his throat. I'd failed to control my roaming gaze. His lips hitched up on one side. I'd been caught, a second time, checking him out.

Scorsese and Spielberg sniffed the grass just to the left of the path. Women in shorts and tank tops kept sliding their eyes to my near-naked boss and whispering behind cupped hands. Dillon's effect on females was undeniable—even I, who'd witnessed his penchant for jerkiness, went noodle-legged at his sweat-glistened chest. He wasn't super famous yet, but he had graced a giant billboard on Sunset Avenue sporting nothing but his tighty-whities and his giant package. They either recognized him from the Armani ad or simply couldn't keep their eyes off this gorgeous man.

I couldn't blame them. I couldn't control my own eyes, so of course they wanted to let their gaze roam up and down his arms, chest, and—Dillon turned toward the grass where Scorsese and Spielberg stood—his ass.

The tiniest gasp escaped over my lips. A light film of sweat decorated his back and his tattoo wound its way around his muscled arm, over the V muscle of his back, and past the waistband of his shorts. Where did that tattoo end? I licked my bottom lip and pulled it between my teeth. Heat pulsed through my body. That beautiful, firm, globe of an ass was right there. I fought the urge that hit me to reach out and grab that gorgeous ass.

"Scorsese! Spielberg!" Dillon called.

A redhead in a neon-pink jog bra and a brunette in a white tank top tittered behind cupped hands when they heard Dillon call out the names.

"Cute names," the redhead cooed and cocked her eyebrow in a come-hither look.

Dillon's megawatt smile breached his face. He reached out his hand to me without looking at me or speaking; instead, his eyes ogled the girls' asses as they walked by.

"Leashes," he commanded.

I stood there and ignored him.

His ripped his eyes from the two retreating females. "I asked for the leashes," he said, his tone impatient.

"You didn't ask," I said and let Bernie pull me toward the grass. "You didn't say may I please have the leashes. You barked 'leashes' like I'm supposed to know what that means."

He opened his mouth to speak but then stopped. He turned his head toward the view of Los Angeles, sighed, and then turned back. "Lane, may I please have Scorsese and Spielberg's leashes."

My heart thwapped in my chest. He was going to fire me for sure, but I deserved to be spoken to in a polite tone. I lifted the two leashes and he took both from my hand.

"Thank you," he said and snapped one to the collar of each dog.

He turned and we fell into step with each other. Kong, Bernie, Scorsese, and Spielberg all trotted just in front of us.

"You found everything this morning," Dillon said. "Did you meet Mathilde?"

I nodded. "She seems nice."

"Did she feed you?"

I nodded again. "So much food. Does she do that all the time?"

"Why do you think I run up and down Runyon Canyon every morning?" Dillon tipped his chin toward me and flashed his smile.

I looked away from him and toward Bernie and Kong. The power of that smile was cataclysmic. Being the focus of that stellar smile was like being thrown in front of Klieg lights.

"We have a little bit of a language barrier," I said.

"It's tough. I'm guessing you don't develop Spanglish skills in Kansas."

I slid my eyes toward him. This was the first sincere, non-derogatory comment he'd made about me being from Kansas. I searched his face for some sort of sneaky look that showed he was teasing me, but there was nothing on his face.

"No *habla español*," I said. "That is the limit of my Spanish."

"Mathilde understands a ton of English," Dillon said. "She just doesn't speak it very often."

"How long has she been with you and Choo?" I asked.

"Since we rented the place, which was right after I booked my first film."

I nodded. We bounced along. He stopped, bent down, and let all four dogs off their leashes. They jumped with glee. Choo had told me never to let them all off their leashes, but I figured since they were Dillon's dogs, he knew what to do with them.

"How long have you been doing that?" I panted out. I really needed to work out more. Dillon's body glistened with sweat, but he wasn't out of breath from the steady climb.

"What?" He shot me a puzzled look.

"Rescuing dogs?"

He tilted his head and gazed at me, then looked back at the happy pack of four just a few feet ahead of us. "Nearly my whole life," he said. "I couldn't keep them until I had my own place." He scratched his neck and his hand drifted down across his chest and finally to his side.

I kept my mouth closed and reminded myself not to drool. I needed to at least pretend I didn't think he was the most gorgeous man I'd ever spoken to in my entire life. Besides, his ego was too big for a girl like me, plus I was certain I was two speeds below his normal gear where women were concerned.

"Did you have a dog?" he asked. "Growing up?"

I nodded. "Petunia."

"Good name," he said. "I got my first dog when I was eight. Dallas, a beagle puppy." His gaze jerked from Kong to me. "My dad shot it."

My eyes widened with his words. My heart thudded against my chest and a hollowness lodged just beneath my ribs. "W...why would—"

"He caught him in the neighbor's chicken coop, so he killed the dog."

An ache pulsed through my body for the little boy that Dillon had been when his father killed his dog. I couldn't begin to understand what kind of father would shoot his son's pet.

"According to my dad, everything is disposable, even things that are alive."

I clenched my jaw and bit back the words I wanted to say about Dillon's father. "Do you... do you still see your dad?"

The muscle in his jaw flinched and he stared beyond me into the distance and didn't meet my gaze. "Not anymore," he said. "Sometimes I hear from our mom."

He didn't offer more about his parents. I remembered Choo's words from last night. Dillon didn't mention how their parents had tried to deprogram Choo and finally tossed him out into the street. Dillon also didn't mention that he'd saved his brother and was now putting Choo through school. Instead, Dillon kept walking. I chewed my bottom lip. He was all of a sudden a whole lot less of a jerk than I'd originally thought.

We rounded the corner to the top of Runyon and approached the highest spot on the path. "You close with your family?" Dillon asked.

My inside crumpled with the word *family*. I'd only ever had one person in my family. Hot tears plucked at my eyes. The benefit of feeling numb was that when someone said an innocuous word like family—a word that for most people brought feelings of happiness and joy—if you were numb, you could just shrug and you felt nothing. But I was less and less numb every day, and the feelings that swirled through me weren't always easy to control.

I turned to Dillon. "My mom died last year," I said. "And I've never met my dad."

He nodded. His gaze remained on mine. I liked how he

reacted. He didn't apologize; he didn't act like he didn't know what to say or was afraid of what I'd told him. Instead, he looked at me in silence and waited. He seemed to be watching me and waiting for me fill the silent space, to see if I had something I needed to say.

"I miss her," I whispered. I turned out toward the overlook. All of Los Angeles lay at my feet. A breeze whispered across my face. My heart hurt with the thought of my mom. Her blue eyes, her blond hair, that laugh that I would forever hear in my mind that made me think of wind chimes and warm breezes, her smile. The fact that even as she lay in a hospital bed with tubes sticking out of her, she made me promise to chase my dreams no matter how long or how far.

"She lived out here for a while," I said. "In L.A." I looked to my left where the L.A. skyline cut upward into the blue sky. The ache in my heart lodged hard and deep. I wanted to imagine my mom my age, standing here, on top of Runyon Canyon, looking out at the view. My gaze traveled across the horizon toward the blue of the ocean. "She loved the beach." My throat thickened around my words. We'd meant to go to the beach, together, someday, but the time to someday had run out for us. "She used to tell me stories about all the time she spent there." My voice quivered and Bernie walked to me and nuzzled my hand.

I took a giant breath and closed my eyes. The hard lump in my throat was there and was at this moment the only thing that prevented me from screaming. Screaming out "why?" There wasn't an answer, not a good one. All that remained of my mom was me and my memories of her.

I turned my face from the view of L.A. and looked at

Dillon. He watched me. He was really listening. There was an earnest intensity on his face, as though what I was saying was important to him.

I hitched the corner of my mouth upward into a false smile. "Probably not what you expected to hear on your walk this morning." I rolled my gaze toward the sky. Suddenly I felt stupid and exposed. Vulnerable and embarrassed. Why had I just totally laid out my life for Dillon?

He nodded. "Unexpected, yes." He turned away from the view and started down the long canyon hill.

Great. I'd just convinced Dillon that his brother had hired an unprofessional, emotional nutjob.

Downhill was much easier than uphill. While embarrassment still coursed through me, my breath was more even. Women walking by ogled Dillon and kept checking him out. I noticed they would actually turn around after they passed him so they could check out his ass.

"Does that get old?" I finally asked.

"I don't even notice it," Dillon said. "Anymore." He turned his face toward me. "Until you point it out."

"Sorry."

He called for the dogs and put leashes on all four. He handed me Kong and Bernie's leashes. He'd been silent since the top of the canyon. I hoped I still had a job.

When we got to the flat area at the bottom, he turned his head to me. "You got those four scripts?"

I nodded. Bernie and Kong jerked hard to the right and I stumbled.

"Gotcha." Dillon's hands caught my shoulders and a jolt of electricity whizzed through me.

I looked into those intense blue eyes. He was right in front of me. He still held my shoulders. My gaze roamed down over his chest. I could smell the salty sweat on him. He smelled like outdoors, and wind, and grass, and God that sweat would taste salty on my tongue.

Salty on my tongue?

I jerked my head back from staring at Dillon's chest. I was considering licking the sweat off my boss's chest. Thank God he couldn't read minds. I peered into his eyes, and his wicked smirk decorated his face. Or could he? I stepped backward and turned toward the pups. They slobbered and slurped from a bucket of water. Once they finished, Dillon walked us toward the canyon gates.

"Where's your Jeep?" he asked and scanned down the street.

I bit my top lip and twisted Kong's leash around my wrist. "I don't know."

Dillon scrunched up his face and looked at me as though I had half a brain.

"I parked it on Whitley and when I came out of my motel, it was gone," I said. "I haven't had time to track it down."

Dillon's brow furrowed. "How did you get here this morning?"

"We walked," I said.

Dillon jerked his head back and then shook it. "That's farther than the loop at Runyon."

"But not nearly as steep," I said. I twisted the ends of all four leashes around my hand.

Dillon dug into his pocket and pulled out a set of keys. "Black Range Rover." He pointed and I spied it three cars down. He held out the keys and dropped them in my hand.

"How will you get back?" I asked.

"Same way you got here." He put his hands on his hips. They were beautiful hips with little round muscles just at the edge. "So, listen," he said and turned first back toward Runyon and then looked at me, "would you read that script, *The Legend Returns,* as soon as you get back to the house? It's on the top of the pile."

"Sure, of course," I said and chewed my bottom lip. So maybe I wasn't getting fired just yet. Maybe Choo had convinced Dillon to let me stay on as his script reader slash dog-walker for a little while, or at least until I could gather enough money to find my own place. Kong pranced around under Bernie's legs, and I knelt down and scooped him up into my arms.

Dillon took two steps back from me. "Once you're finished reading the script, come by the set."

I whipped my head toward Dillon. "The set?"

Panic clutched my belly and a feeling of dread flooded my body.

"Yeah, the set." Dillon stopped walking and stared at me. "Where I'll be the rest of the day and most of the night. I need to know what you think of that script. The director on this film is doing it next."

"Can't I just e-mail you what I think?"

Dillon shook his head. "Naw, I don't want to read about it, I want to talk about it."

"I'll call," I yelled out toward Dillon as he turned to run back up the hill. He was running up Runyon Canyon again? What was he, a masochist?

"I need to see you when we talk about it. I do better in person. I can't understand you the same way over the phone."

"What... wait..."

"Just read the script, Dorothy, and come to the set," he yelled and then trotted up the dusty path.

A queasy feeling snaked through my belly. Easy for Dillon to say, he hadn't been the laughingstock of the entire cast and crew the last time he was on set.

CHAPTER 7

DILLON

I SAT AT THE TABLE IN MY TRAILER AND WENT over my lines.

Ryan grabbed another beer from the fridge in my trailer. "Want one?"

"No, man, thanks." I glanced at the clock above the windshield. It wasn't even noon and Ryan was already suckin' 'em down and playing *Halo* in my trailer. There was no way I could get through the scenes for today if I was drinking, but Ryan played his character half in the bag most days.

He plopped down on the couch, cracked open the beer, and took a long gulp. He pulled the earphones back onto his head and continued blowing away everything that came at him on the flat screen.

I tried to refocus on my lines, but when I tried to read, all I saw was a pair of blue eyes and long caramel-colored hair. What the hell was I thinking? I shook my head and tugged at my hair. I'd actually been interested in what Dorothy had told me this morning. I'd wanted to listen. I'd wanted to hear about her, about her life, about her past. This was bad. Very, very bad. My focus was on my career. My career and getting Choo through college without seeing our parents again. Never seeing our parents again. I didn't have time to listen to a girl or tell her about my childhood heartaches.

A girl like Lane Channing didn't fit into my life right now, except for reading. I needed her reading and reviewing scripts. I sighed and flipped a page. Dorothy was here to read, and I wouldn't be banging that reader for sure, because she'd already proven in one day that she had an uncanny ability to climb inside my head.

I focused on the script that was open on the table in front of me. Hunter had mentioned this was the pivotal scene for my character. I didn't want to blow it, especially after the offer he'd just given me for his next film, *The Legend Returns*. I already felt like I was kind of in the shitter with Hunter since I hadn't given him an answer on the Steve Legend film.

"Hot damn," Ryan said. He bent forward and peered out the window. "Who is that?"

I didn't have time to reach over and pull up the shade to check out whatever hot body had Ryan salivating before Dorothy burst through the trailer door.

"Read it!" she called. She bounded up the trailer steps with that brilliant smile plastered to her face. The same brilliant smile I'd seen at Runyon Canyon earlier that day, the smile that made me run a second circuit, give her my car, and hit a cold shower once I got home.

Ryan turned to me and behind Lane mouthed, "Wow!" I squirmed out of my seat. I couldn't blame him. She wore this hot little sundress—a pale color with tiny little flowers all over it. The dress showed off the golden skin of her shoulders and neck. Her hair was piled on her head, but some curls dangled loose and danced around her neck. That dress was short, mid-thigh, and showed off her legs. She wore cowboy boots. In L.A. Brown with blue insets. That dress was obscene, and a part of me wanted to order Ryan to get out, then walk to the top of the steps, grab her, and bend her over the table in my trailer. Slide my hand up that golden thigh to a place I didn't suspect she'd been touched before.

She turned toward Ryan and then back to me. Those damn blue eyes ripped through me. Every time she looked at me, her gaze hit me hard in the chest.

"Hey," Ryan said in that throaty voice. He shot her that hot actor smile. The same type of smile I dropped at every club, every scene, on every girl I wanted to get into bed.

My pulse sped up. I didn't want Lane to want Ryan. I shoved my hands into my back pockets. I shot Ryan my best keep-your-hands-off glare.

"Hi," she said.

A small, cautious smile shimmered across her lips. Her eyes darted to me, then to the floor, then back to Ryan as she pulled a strand of that damn long hair, which was dancing along her collarbone, behind her ear.

"I'm Lane." She took two steps forward and reached out her hand. I didn't even want him to touch her hand.

"Ryan." He moved in close to her. Too close. I didn't like it.

"Nice to meet you." Her tongue traced over her lips, chasing her words. Those pouty sex-pot lips.

"You read it?" I barked out louder than I intended. Harsher than I wanted, but I need to bust up this little lovefest that had started. I knew who Ryan was, what type of guy, and Dorothy wasn't ready for his kind. She was straight-up just in town and wouldn't stand a chance when Ryan put on the heat.

She turned her face to me and her smile dropped from her lips. Her brows furrowed with an unasked question. She looked more tentative, more cautious—if I admitted it, I loved it. I didn't want that smile to be for anyone but me.

"What?" I said and turned my palm upward. "Dude she's my *reader*." I looked at Ryan like he was nuts to consider her. I turned to Lane. "You're here to see me, right? Not flirt with him." I jerked my head toward Ryan.

She flushed red, and a hard look entered her eyes.

"Guy," Ryan said. "Chill. We were just introducing ourselves."

"She isn't here to make friends or find a date. She's here to read my scripts and walk my dogs."

Both Ryan and Lane stared at me. "Even you know how big of an ass you're being, right?" Ryan asked.

A sharp feeling sliced through me. I couldn't stop my need to make certain that Ryan understood that Lane was a no-touch proposition. Lane's eyes raked over me.

"I gotta bounce," Ryan said. "Lane, it was nice to meet you. Maybe I'll see you again if this asshole doesn't scare you off."

Lane's mouth turned to a shallow smile of thanks. I guessed for Ryan acknowledging me acting like a giant prick. The trailer door slammed shut. When Lane turned to me, I got the cold stare. She walked to me and slapped the script on the table.

"It's a shitty action script with franchise potential all over it." Her frigid, clipped tone matched her eyes. "You'll make a gazillion dollars. Enjoy." She hiked her purse over her shoulder and walked back toward the trailer door. The door slammed shut behind her—hard.

She was pissed and actually, I couldn't blame her. What the hell was wrong with me? I lifted the script from the table. Why the hell did I care who Lane dated? I didn't. Did I?

I bounded down the steps and burst through the door. "Lane!" I called. "Lane, stop!"

Her tight little ass stopped moving beneath her flirty skirt and she turned toward me. She crossed her arms over her chest—what a way to ruin a good view. I walked up to her, picking my way over the gravel under my trailer as I'd run out without shoes. I hated wearing shoes.

"Look," I said and slid my eyes from side to side. "I know Ryan. I know who he is and I know what he does and I know how he treats women and—"

"You mean he's just like you?" She pulled her head back and a smug, pursed-lip look settled onto her face. Great, she was going to bust my balls for being a dick. Just what I didn't want to deal with.

"Not exactly," I said. "He's not your type."

"Like you would know?" She turned to walk away.

I grasped her arm and stopped her. Her skin was soft and warm. Lane's eyes landed on my hand. Did she feel it too? The electricity that pulsed between us with even the slightest touch, the electricity that was hot and dangerous

73

and made me want to do some seriously bad things to this little girl from Kansas, no matter her untouchability.

I pulled in close to her. She smelled fresh, like flowers and mint. I got close enough to see the tremble of her pulse in her neck, to know that I was causing her heart rate to jump. I liked being the cause of her fluttering heart.

"Maybe, I don't know," I whispered. I didn't have to work hard to make my voice low. Lane, this close to me, the heat coming off her body, those pretty little nipples pressed tight to the fabric of her dress, that short skirt that was an inch from my fingertips—all of it worked me, worked me in a way that made me want to work her. "You're not the right girl for Ryan."

She was turned on, but she kept her gaze locked on mine. Her pulse hammered, but she played it cool. Cooler than I would have expected.

"You don't get to decide who or what I do. I'm just your *reader*, remember?" She slipped her arm from my grasp and my hand felt cold with its absence. She turned and her boots crunched gravel.

I barely knew this girl, but my belly clenched with the idea that I might have to watch her be with someone else. The idea made me want to slam my hand into the metal side of the trailer.

"What about the other scripts!" I yelled at her retreating ass. I didn't want her to leave, but I wouldn't tell her that.

She stopped walking and turned back toward me. "I finished reading two of the scripts and am working on the third." Her tone was still cool.

"You bring them with you?" I asked.

She took a step back toward the trailer. "They're in my bag," she said and pointed to her purse, which was slung over her shoulder.

"Finish them here," I said. I pulled open my trailer door. "I'm headed to makeup, but we can discuss them when I finish filming my next scene." My words were a command. A command that Lane wouldn't refuse.

LANE

I HAD TEN MORE PAGES OF AN AWFUL THRILLER to read. The pacing was slow and the dialog was stilted. The third act on this project was a colossal mess. My recommendation to Dillon on this project was a big pass.

The door banged open. A ping of excitement pulsed in my belly. I sat straighter. What the hell? I didn't want to be attracted to Dillon. He'd pissed me off grandly earlier that day, but it would seem by the adrenaline rushing through my system that I, like every other female who came into contact with Dillon MacAvoy, lusted after Mr. Chiseled Perfection. The difference? I could lust after him, physically, but I wouldn't act on my attraction. I wouldn't throw myself at Dillon, clutch his arm, mold myself to his side, press my boobs into his chest.

"Yo, yo, yo!"

I crinkled my eyebrows. Unfamiliar voice. Definitely not Dillon. A guy bounded up the steps. He looked like a J. Crew ad in a three-piece suit. Seriously, he wore a three-thousand-dollar suit, shiny, thousand-dollar shoes, and I was pretty certain it was a Rolex that decorated his wrist.

I couldn't see the eyes under the aviator shades. This guy was slick. He oozed car salesman. His blond hair was cropped right at the edge of his suit-jacket collar. His skin was a warm gold. Ease rolled off him as thick as the roll of bills I felt certain was shoved into his pocket.

"You aren't Dillon," he said. He pulled his sunglasses from his face. His eyes traveled over me in a more secretive fashion than most. He stepped toward me. "I'm Webber Conner, Dillon's agent." He clasped my hand in his. His whole being screamed confidence.

My heart sped up because Webber Conner was a big deal in entertainment. A big deal at CTA, and potentially a big deal in my career.

"Lane Channing," I said. I locked my gaze with his. I needed to make an impression. "Dillon's new reader."

A low whistle came from his mouth. "You're the girl Choo wanted."

I tilted my head.

His smile remained fixed on his face, but something in his eyes hardened. "Kansas, right?"

My spine stiffened, but I smiled and nodded.

"Well, if you make it through the summer with Dillon, there's a job at CTA waiting on the other side."

My stomach churned. I'd looked Webber up and his client list was massive. He repped Ryan Sinclair, Jackson Nichols... a huge number of male action stars.

"I'm going to give you a tip." Webber tapped the arm of his sunglasses against his jaw. "Because Nancy likes you and so does Choo, and I like them."

I nodded and waited for his words. Words I was hopeful could steer me to a solid summer and a great career at CTA.

"Don't sleep with Dillon."

The color drained from my face. A slimy, sick feeling soured my stomach.

"Oh shit," Webber said. "You didn't sleep with him already, did you?"

My jaw dropped open and the sick feeling climbed up the back of my throat. "No! I mean, why would you... who do you think..." My feelings jetted from absolute horror to rage.

"Hey, Lane." Webber held out both hands, palms forward in an I-surrender stance. "Babe, I'm not making any judgments about you. It's about him." Webber jerked his thumb over his shoulder, toward the trailer door. "I mean, come on! Every girl in the 310 and 323 would drop their panties for him, and he's not even a *star* yet." He pointed his glasses toward me. "You look like a girl with more on her mind than sex. I'm just saying if you want to stick out the reader gig and land the CTA job next spring after you graduate, don't sleep with Dillon."

This guy really thought he was giving me a piece of valuable advice. "Okay," I said, still mortified. "Got it."

"Great!" A car-dealer smile spread over Webber's face. He shoved on his aviators. "I'm gonna head over to set and watch some takes." He pointed two fingers at me like they were pistols and he was Quick Draw McGraw. "You keep reading."

I was glad to see Webber bounce down the steps of Dillon's trailer and slam shut the door.

DILLON

THE DAY RAN LONG ON SET. THE SUN HAD GONE down. I still had two more scenes to shoot before end of day. The hot, cherry-red ends of cigarettes decorated the darkness and lined the path to my trailer. Both the cast and crew were feeding their nicotine habit on this last break. I'd discovered on my first film that caffeine and nicotine were as necessary to the making of films as cameras. I pulled open my trailer door just as my phone rang. I yanked it from my pocket.

"Hello," I said.

"Dillon?"

A feeling like ice slid down my spine. A chill that spread outward through my limbs. I shut the trailer door but stood, stuck at the bottom of the steps.

"How did you get this number?" I asked.

"I just want to... We need to talk." She sighed and I heard a tremor in her voice. "We want to see you."

"Me?" My tone bittered around my words. I knew the kind of heartbreak a meeting like that would cause, what my mother's words meant. "What about my brother? What about Choo?"

Her silence was her answer. I pictured her lips pressed into a thin line and her jaw set firm and proud as though she had some sort of righteousness. "I... we... your father and I can't see Charles as long as he chooses to live that kind of lifestyle."

My ribs clamped around my chest and the ice-cold feeling shifted to hot rage. I fought to control my words, I fought to hold my temper out of my voice, I fought to keep my emotions stuffed deep down inside. "Choo didn't make a choice," I said. "He was born that way."

"No, Dillon, he was not," she said. "He is a very sick

young man. He refuses our help and we refuse to watch him kill himself and his redemption with his choice of lifestyle."

I fought for breath. I'd listened to her denial my entire life. I'd watched as she'd first tortured him, then sent my brother away to try to "cure" him of his gayness. Until finally, now, because of me and my success, he didn't have to fear our parents anymore and he could be who he was.

"Choo is gay," I said. "He isn't sick." My grip on my temper was slipping. I wasn't able to hold on to myself and my feelings. How could a parent, how could a father, how could our own mother, turn her back on her child because he was gay? My heart hurt, and anger surged through me.

"When Charles decides to face this choice and make a different one, then we will embrace him into our lives again, but until then..." Her words drifted into silence. I didn't need to hear her say it, I knew what she wanted to say, that until my brother chose to "fix" his gayness and be straight, she and my father wanted nothing to do with him. But they still wanted to see me. The son they approved of, the one who had made the right choice and slept with a slew of women. If they only knew that Choo was much sweeter, much kinder, a much better person in his heart than I would ever be, but they couldn't. They would never see the goodness of their son, of my brother, as long as he embraced who he was as a person, because as long as he was honest with the world and was himself, our parents wanted nothing to do with him.

I shook my head. I would never see my parents as long as they rejected my brother. I could never do that to him. I'd watched our parents pray for him, try to forcefully change him, and then cast him out. I'd witnessed the pain and torture in his eyes. I never wanted him to think for a moment that I chose them and their beliefs over what I knew to be true. I had a gay brother, a gay brother whom I loved and would protect like I always had when we were kids.

"Mom, until you face reality, I will never see you."

"Dill—"

I pressed Off on my phone before she could say anything more. I grasped my hair with both hands. I walked up the steps and turned toward the back of my trailer.

I caught her eyes. Sympathy, surprise, shock—all kinds of emotions trailed across her face.

My heart jackknifed in my chest. I pushed a hard breath from my lungs. She hadn't said a word while I'd raged with my mother. I'd forgotten she was still there. This wasn't a part of my life I wanted to share. I didn't want her to see me raw and vulnerable and completely unhinged. This wasn't who I wanted to be in front of any person. I jerked myself around and slammed down the stairs and out the trailer door.

CHAPTER 8

LANE

THE NEXT WEEK I FELL INTO A ROUTINE. WAKE up at six a.m. Take the pups to Runyon Canyon. Come back to the house. Grab a shower. Get some coffee and eat whatever fabulous breakfast Mathilde had fixed while we tried to hold a conversation and understand each other. Read three scripts. Take the dogs for another walk. Read three scripts. Swim. Have dinner and drinks with Choo. Watch a fabulous movie and fall into bed. This was a good gig. Dillon was away on location somewhere in the world, and I prayed that he stayed there for the rest of the summer. This I could handle with him away—I would definitely stick out the whole summer and get my full-time job from CTA.

"It's Friday night, baby," Choo said as he danced in the door from the garage. "Tonight we get our boogie on!"

A thrill chased up my spine. I hadn't yet been out in

L.A. Choo had to be in the mailroom at CTA every morning by seven thirty a.m., and since overhearing Dillon's conversation with his mom, I never saw him.

Choo grabbed my hand and spun me around the kitchen. Kong danced at my feet and yapped. Bernie lay sprawled out on his side, sleeping beside the kitchen table. He jerked his head upward to check out the commotion, but when he saw it was simply Choo wheeling me around like I was a dance diva, he plopped his head back down and sighed.

"Choo, what you do to Miss Lane," Mathilde said as she walked from the kitchen pantry carrying a box of pasta and fresh tomatoes.

"Getting her ready for our big night," Choo said and dipped me at the waist.

I giggled. It felt good to be silly.

"She is going to rock it tonight!" Choo pulled me back up to standing and then bounced his hip against mine. "Go on, girl, go get yourself even more beautiful!"

※

I DIDN'T OWN MUCH WHEN IT CAME TO CLOTHES and shoes and purses, but I tried to make what I did own be exactly what I wanted. I pulled a cream-colored baby-doll dress with gold threads woven through the fabric over my head and pulled on my strappy gold high-heel sandals. I turned to the mirror. I'd amped up the makeup tonight. The smudged, smoky eye shadow made my eyes pop. I'd chosen a light, blush-colored lip gloss and a shimmering rose for my cheeks. I tossed my hair over my shoulder and turned from one side to the other.

My palms were sweaty and my stomach churned. What was I so nervous about? Maybe because I'd never gone out in a city even half the size of Los Angeles? Maybe because my L.A. adventure so far had been completely different in every way from what I'd imagined? Maybe because I was living in the house of the hottest guy I'd ever seen on the planet? A guy who seemed to loathe my existence. I pushed thoughts of Dillon out of my mind. Tonight was meant to be fun. Tonight I was going to hang out with Choo and have a bangin' time. I scooped up my purse and headed to meet him.

&

"DAMN, GIRL, YOU CLEAN UP GOOD!"

I glanced to the bottom of the staircase where Choo was standing. He wore another one of those uber-expensive graphic tees and some skinny jeans. I held the rail as I walked down the staircase. I was nearly to the bottom when Dillon rounded the corner.

My heart jumped in my chest. I hadn't known he'd returned to L.A. tonight. This was the first time I'd seen him since he'd banged out of his trailer on set, furious that I'd heard his conversation with his mom.

He stopped at the bottom of the stairs. His eyes traveled up over my feet and legs, the bottom of my skirt, my chest and neck. A tiny curl of heat licked over my skin. When his gaze hit mine, my face flushed. Heat pulsed through me and between my legs.

I tried to push a smile onto my face. I tried to breathe, to walk, to not stare at Dillon's complete and utter physical perfection, but it was so hard. His lips pursed and the emotion in his eyes didn't look happy—in fact, he looked angry. He folded his arms over his chest. I forced my gaze away from the muscles in his arms.

"Where are you two going?" Dillon didn't look at his brother but kept his eyes glued to me.

"Area," Choo said.

Dillon's eyes roamed my body one more time and then he turned toward the back of the house and walked away.

I stepped into the wooden foyer and looked at Choo. "What was that about?"

Choo shook his head. "With him? Who knows? He gets so moody sometimes. Come on, let's go get our party on." Choo pulled my hand and we hurried out the door.

❧

THE LINE THAT SNAKED FROM THE FRONT DOOR of Area went for a block and a half.

"You look discouraged," Choo said. A huge grin decorated his face. "Don't be. While my brother can be a jerk there are perks to being related." Choo skirted the crowd and made his way to the front door where a guy stood with two giant, beefy bouncers. He had shocks of white hair tipped in blue.

"Choo, man, how are you!" He grasped Choo's hand and pulled him in for a hug, then turned from Choo to me. His eyes widened as he looked me over. "Damn Choo," he said and shook his head. "Who is this beautiful creature?" A giant smile broke over his face. "Choo, my man, if I didn't know you, I'd say you'd been holding out on me."

"Lane," I said and held out my hand. "Lane Channing."

"Lane, this is Viggo. He's the guy you need to know to get in."

"Well, Lane Channing, you may be the hottest-looking girl in this club tonight." He leaned forward and heat flushed through my body with his compliment. "You need anything at all tonight, just drop *my* name." He tapped his chest. "Got it?"

I nodded and Viggo winked. The bouncer behind him unhooked the rope and we were in.

The club was dark but had a light, airy feel. The walls were cream-colored stone and blond wood. We followed a hostess in boy-toy shorts and lace-up high-heel boots to a giant, camel-colored couch beside the dance floor. On the table, in front of the couches reserved for us, the bottle service was already set up.

"I called ahead," Choo said.

While I wanted a drink, I couldn't. I might be from Kansas, but I knew what bottle service cost.

"Choo special?" Choo leaned forward and poured vodka into two glasses. I shook my head no.

I'd been at clubs before without enough cash to drink. I knew I could use the tricks my friends did—especially the ones that absolutely didn't need to use tricks—but I didn't. Something about smiling and flirting just to get a free drink made me feel cheap.

"Come on," Choo said.

Embarrassment raced through me. Choo knew where I was financially, but I didn't want to discuss it, not here. Tonight it was enough just to be in the club and out in L.A. I could dance for free. I suspected Choo thought he'd pay for my drinks tonight, but I just didn't feel right. I was already getting room and board as part of my job. I couldn't expect him to pay for my drinks too. I leaned over to Choo and bit my bottom lip.

He crinkled his brow. "What is it?"

"I can't..." I looked out at the throbbing mass of bodies on the dance floor, then back to Choo. "I just can't pay for this right now," I said softly. Heat flushed at my neck.

Choo threw back his head and a giant laugh burst from his mouth. My chest burned. I furrowed my brow. I didn't think that me being broke was really that funny.

"Oh, Laney, I love you," Choo said. "I am so sorry. I'm not laughing at you. Lane, baby, nobody is paying for this tonight."

"What?"

"Lane, they want me here because they want my brother here, because he is about to pop into a big star. The crowd goes where the celebrities goes. So this"—he waved his hand over the bottle service and the couch that we inhabited—"is free."

"Free?" I whispered.

Of course I knew that celebrities got special treatment, but I hadn't thought about how much special treatment.

"So I ask again." Choo held up the now completed drink. "Choo special?"

I smiled and nodded. How could I possibly say no? I gulped down the first drink and held out my glass toward Choo for another.

"Damn, girl! You do know how to drink."

"Not much else to do where I'm from," I said and dotted my fingertips to the corners of my mouth. The liquor made my limbs feel loose. My foot bounced to the beat that pumped out from the speakers. Choo handed me my drink.

"Jackson!" he called. A giant smile swept over his face. I turned my head to see a gorgeous man walking toward us. He wasn't as tall as Choo, but he was thicker. His skin was a beautiful shade of brown, his eyes big and black. He had to be a dancer or an athlete. The man moved with some solid grace.

"Lane, this is my guy," Choo said and wrapped an arm around Jackson. He planted a giant kiss upon his lips. "Jackson, baby, meet Lane. She reads for my brother."

Jackson turned his eyes to me. "Glad somebody does." He laughed around his words. "Nice to meet you, Lane." He shook my hand. "Dillon needs to capitalize on his opportunities," he said and squeezed his arm around Choo, "and give you more free time with me."

Choo leaned toward me. "Is he hot or what?" he whispered in my ear. We both turned and checked out Jackson's ass as he chatted with a couple of people he knew.

"Way hot," I said. A tiny little burp escaped over my lips.

"Lane!" Choo said and pressed his hand to his heart as though he was shocked and appalled. He slipped my empty glass from my hand. "Darlin', it sounds and looks as though you need another Choo special."

Two Choo specials later I was in the center of the dance floor with Choo, Jackson, and a half dozen of Choo's friends. I wasn't sure if they were truly friends or just gadflies that wanted free drinks. But I absolutely didn't care because it felt so fantastic just to dance. The DJ bounced beats that throbbed heavy.

The guy beside me was blond and tall and could dance. He stepped behind me and pressed his body into mine. I leaned back and surrendered to the music, to the beat, to the hot sweat that dripped down my neck, to this guy's hands that roamed up the sides of my dress as we danced. I threw my head back and smiled. My hair stuck to my neck; I'd twisted it up on top of my head a half dozen times, but it kept falling to my shoulders. I didn't care. I didn't care that his hands were all over my body. I didn't care that Dillon looked at me like I was nothing. I didn't care that the last seven nights I'd fallen asleep thinking about what it would feel like to press my body against his chest, to run my fingers across his broad back. I didn't care that when I thought of Dillon and his hands and his lips and his eyes that hard hot tingles pulsed through me. All I cared about was this moment. In this moment, I cared about dancing and feeling so incredibly free.

DILLON

Webber and Ryan were already at the club when I pulled up in my Rover. They were just ahead of me at the valet. Two girls chatted up Ryan while Webber, still in his suit from being at the agency, scrolled on his phone. That guy was always working. Even with two hotties clinging to Ryan and four more looking to score, Webber couldn't pull away from work mode.

"Hey man," Ryan said. He slapped my hand. The hot smell of whiskey was on his breath and his voice was already thick with booze. Two girls molded to his side. One was a redhead in a pink dress and the other a dark-skinned, dark-haired beauty in black leather pants. Both of them could have been models. The hottest women on the planet lived in L.A. Most nights, I'd peel one off Ryan or let one of the other four checking me out cling to me, but tonight I wasn't feeling it. I hadn't been feeling it for nearly a week. I needed to get back into my groove, to find a girl to relieve some of the tension that threaded through me, because the girl I kept seeing when I closed my eyes wasn't an option.

"Hey," I said.

Ryan leaned forward. "The action is smokin' tonight."

I knew what he meant. The girls were hot and willing. I ran my eyes over a blonde.

She sauntered toward me and pressed to my side.

"Hey, Dillon," she cooed.

Her big baby blues gazed up at me through her eyelashes. I put my arm around her. This was a start. This fit my image. This was a way to keep Lane out of my head.

⁂

I SAID HI TO VIGGO AND WALKED INTO THE CLUB. Two seconds later, I had a girl under each arm. On my left was the blonde and on my right a black-haired beauty who claimed to have worked on my first film, *Mission Ranger*, with me. I wouldn't argue. She wore one of those bandage dresses in jet black. Her hair was long and luscious and danced over my wrist as I clasped my arm around her. Her lips were lush and cherry red. I grew hard thinking about what I would put between those lips later tonight.

I skirted the dance floor and made my way to my table. The couch was clear, but I knew Choo'd been there because there were raspberries in a bowl beside the vodka.

The Choo special. I didn't want a Choo special. I wanted whiskey neat.

The brunette poured me a drink and settled under my arm and onto the couch. Webber stood beside Ryan, both of them sucking on whiskey and scoping the scene. I glanced out at the dance floor. I had two girls to take care of me tonight. I didn't need to worry about acting on any of those dirty little thoughts about Lane that climbed through my mind. I didn't need to shove any feelings away. I didn't have feelings—not for women. Feelings were a luxury I couldn't afford.

I glanced at the floor and saw my brother. He was pressed up against Jackson. The guy had become semi-regular for Choo. He was a sports agent and repped athletes. They were on the dance floor with a bunch of Choo's friends.

No Dorothy.

I scanned the club without being obvious. Gold high heels flashed, long lean legs, a twirl of caramel-colored hair. A big hand groped up the side of that tiny thing she called a dress.

Adrenaline burst through me. The muscles in my jaw tensed. I fisted my hands but held them tight to my thighs. I could play this cool. I leaned back. My stomach clenched as my eyes locked on Dorothy. I nodded at something Webber said and pretended to listen to his words. I tossed a smile toward Ryan and put an arm around each girl to my side. My eyes returned to Dorothy.

The blond-haired guy she was dancing with pushed in tight behind her. His hand skirted up her thigh. He pulled her against him hard and fast. My heart jolted and I shot to my feet.

Webber jerked his head up from reading an e-mail. His gaze bounced toward me. "What's up, man?" He followed my gaze toward the dance floor. "Oh right, the hot piece of ass with your brother? She is totally wasted on Choo, you know what I mean?"

Ryan edged closer and followed Webber's gaze. Lane pressed her ass against the guy behind her. What was she trying to do?

"Dude, that chick is killin' me." Ryan pressed his hand against his heart. "You know that's Dillon's new reader." He pointed toward the dance floor and nudged his elbow into my arm. "There is no way you're not tappin' that."

I fought the urge to slam my fist through Ryan's drunk face.

"I met her last week," Webber said. "Shit man, I'm sorry. Guess another reader will bite the dust. I'll keep looking for a guy, because I don't know how you'll ever be able not to hit that."

Lane pressed against the guy's chest and his hands ran over her bare back. This was not cool. Anger surged through me and thumped in my chest. Choo shrugged his shoulder as though Dorothy and her dirty dancing was not his problem. This was *so* his problem. Choo created this mess. Ryan and Webber watched like two hounds in heat. I didn't need this shit. I didn't need the entire club thinking that Lane was either a whore or an easy piece.

※

"EXCUSE ME," I SAID AND GRABBED LANE ABOVE the elbow. The douche she'd been dirty dancing with scowled, then he locked eyes with me. "You got a problem?" I pushed into his face while I kept hold of Lane.

He backed away with both hands held high like I was robbing him.

"What... what?" Lane's eyes widened and her perfect pout of a mouth turned into an O as I steered her toward the far side of the dance floor. Away from Webber and Ryan, away from Choo, away from anyone I knew and into a corner of the club.

Blood thundered in my head. Why would she dance that way? How could she dance that way?

I backed her against the wall and placed one hand on either side of her head. She wouldn't leave until I was done, until I finished telling her exactly how it was going to be.

She turned her face to me. Surprise shot through her eyes and then anger. Her gaze was sharp and her lips were pursed. She was a tiny bit wobbly on those too-high heels.

"What was that?" I asked. I pushed my face close to hers. "Some kind of show you want to put on?"

She flipped her hair over her shoulder. Her neck, damn that pretty little neck, was an inch from my lips. My eyes slipped over her collarbone and toward those pretty tits that were crushed against the front of her dress. This corner of the club was dark, but I still saw the tiniest red flush come up over her golden skin.

"I was dancing." Her tone was an attempt at tough. "We dance in Kansas." She tilted her smart mouth toward mine.

The image of that guy's hands all over that pretty little body pumped through my mind. I leaned closer. My lips were near hers. I saw the flutter of her pulse and felt the shortness of her breath. I hadn't touched her and yet my cock throbbed. I pressed my lips close to her ear, so close that a tiny gasp of air sucked over her lips. The heat from her flicked over my skin. Her tongue licked her bottom lip and she shifted her body. Energy, want, pure desire burned through me.

"I think you're a little out of your league," I whispered into her ear. I took the pad of my thumb and pressed it to the corner of her raspberry-stained lips. I leaned in. With her fast breath her breasts pressed into me, I whispered the words. I let the air of each one caress her ear. "Maybe you shouldn't try so hard, Dorothy."

The color dropped from her face. "Get away from me." She pushed at my chest and her bottom lip quivered. She stomped toward the door of the club. I'd hurt her with that comment, but I wouldn't have to watch every guy in this club ogle her for the rest of the night.

CHAPTER 9

<u>LANE</u>

TEARS FLOODED MY EYES. I COULDN'T SEE. I couldn't catch my breath. I pushed past the crowd edging the dance floor. I pressed through the bodies. Why did Dillon hate me so much? Why would he embarrass me like that? Why did I care so much what he thought? I bit my bottom lip. This wouldn't work. It would never work. I couldn't—

"Hey." Choo grabbed me. "What's wrong?" Confusion swept across his face and worry inhabited his gaze. "You were there and then you were gone."

I couldn't tell him. I couldn't speak poorly about his brother. Dillon was Choo's only family. Still, I felt like an idiot. According to Dillon, not only could I not drive but I couldn't dance right either.

"Nothing," I sputtered out. "I just... I just—" My eyes darted past Choo where Dillon stood between his agent and his costar. His gaze locked on mine. Four girls that looked like models lounged on the couch behind them. Four girls that seemed to be the type of girl Dillon wanted and needed for his image. Beautiful girls with the right hair and the right clothes—girls who looked like they belonged in L.A. in a club with one of the hottest guys in town. Girls that didn't look like they were from some fly-over state that no one from California could probably locate if given a map.

His stare was hard and cold. There was no emotion. Nothing. Just an empty gaze. That emptiness hurt worse than the anger I'd seen a few minutes before. At least with the anger, I knew Dillon felt something, but that hard cold look seemed to say I meant less than nothing.

A deep breath shuddered through me. I pulled my gaze away from Dillon. My eyes locked with Choo's. I loved Choo; he was my friend. He'd saved me, but right now I couldn't talk to him. I couldn't tell him why these emotions were churning through me.

"I just don't feel very good," I said.

Choo bit his bottom lip. He was worried, but I didn't want to ruin his night out. He and Jackson didn't get to spend much time together with Choo's job at the agency, and they were having such a good time.

"I think…" My gaze darted from Choo toward Dillon, then back to Choo. "I think I'm going to go home, okay?"

"Are you sure?" Choo asked. "I'll come with you."

I shook my head no. "Please stay. I'm seriously going to take an ibuprofen and go to bed. I know it's just because I'm tired."

"Are you sure?"

I nodded. I was sure. I was sure I needed to get away

from Dillon and I was sure that I wanted Choo to stay with Jackson and have a great time. I was very, very sure.

"Okay." Choo walked me toward the door. He'd texted Bob, and within a minute, the car was waiting on the other side of the glass. Choo leaned down gave me a tight squeeze and a peck on each cheek. "Call me if you need anything."

I smiled, nodded, and shook my head yes, knowing that no matter what, I wouldn't call.

❧

MY EYES FLUTTERED OPEN. I KICKED MY FOOT out from under the comforter on my bed. I'd had trouble falling asleep when I got back to the house. I flipped over my cell phone and glanced at the time—it was 2:07 a.m. and I was wide-awake.

Kong lay curled up on the pillow beside me while Scorsese and Spielberg slept at the foot of my bed. Bernie lay lengthwise beside me like a human. I ran my hand across Bernie's thick fur. My heart hurt. Last week I'd felt bad for Dillon. I'd felt bad that he was trapped in a horrible place between his parents and his brother. Parents who, from what it sounded like, wouldn't accept Choo for who he was, but yet still wanted to be a part of Dillon's life.

But tonight?

Tonight I didn't feel bad for Dillon. I felt angry and hurt and shocked at how intense all my feelings were. There were two Dillons and I kept ping-ponging between them. There was the guy who'd humiliated me when I was lost and then made me feel embarrassed again tonight.

Frustration spiked through my chest as the feeling of embarrassment flooded through me with the two memories.

Then there was the other Dillon. The guy who'd rescued four dogs. The guy who smiled and gave me the keys to his car. The guy who was sexy as hell and seemed interested in what I had to say. That was the Dillon my heart hurt for. That was the Dillon I wanted to know and be around. That Dillon seemed to pop out, be wildly nice, and then immediately disappear. Maybe I was lucky that the sweet version of Dillon wasn't around more. The jerky version I could work for and ignore.

He wasn't someone who wanted a relationship. Already, I'd seen him with a multitude of different women. Dillon MacAvoy wanted me to walk his dogs and read his scripts. I brushed a stray hair back from my forehead. Something about Dillon pressed hard against my heart. I was drawn to him. When he'd grabbed my arm tonight, heat had jolted through me. When he'd whispered in my ear, even with the awful words he said, I still couldn't catch my breath with him so near. I wanted to kiss him. I wanted to feel those giant hands on my body, stroking over me where no one had stroked before.

"Oh, yessss."

A moan drifted up from the yard. When I'd gotten home, I'd taken two ibuprofen and pulled open my balcony doors before I'd gone to bed. I'd hoped the fresh air would cool my body and my mind.

"Please, yesss."

My heart clenched and I scrunched my eyes closed. A hard, sick feeling lodged in my belly. The voice was female. There was only one man in this house who could cause a woman to moan like that.

"Yes, please, Dillon. Please."

I didn't want to hear this. I couldn't stand to hear this. I slid my foot to the floor beneath my bed. I wouldn't look. Looking would be so bad. I pressed forward across the floor to the balcony doors. I would pull the doors closed and then please, hopefully, I wouldn't have to hear the things I definitely didn't want to hear.

I placed my hand on the knob of the door, but instead of pulling the door closed, my body moved forward. My heart accelerated as though it would burst through my ribs. What would I see? My foot stepped out on to the balcony. Every good part of me screamed don't do it, don't look down, but every part that was curious had to peer over the balcony. I had to see.

I looked over the edge. The pool lights were on and an aqua glow lit the yard. The girl with the long black hair was bent over the outdoor lounger. Her eyes were closed and her mouth was open. Her tongue flicked over her lips as soft, deep moans flowed from her mouth. Pleasure rushed across her face. She was naked. Barebacked. Her breasts rocked rhythmically and her ink-black hair fell to the side of her face.

Behind her was Dillon. His hands clasped her naked waist with a tight grip. My fingertips covered my mouth. His face was clenched and his head rolled from side to side as he pumped his body into her. The muscles of his chest glistened. His biceps tightened. He threw his head back and opened his eyes.

Our gazes locked. His blue eyes seared through me—I was frozen. I couldn't move. Heat surged through me while my eyes were anchored to him. Heat that pooled in my belly and between my legs. My heart pounded. The world tilted with the thought that burst into my brain.

I wanted to be that girl.

A growl coursed over his lips as he pumped into her and stared at me. Tingles cascaded over my skin. I wanted Dillon to strain and growl and be inside me. I'd never been any of that to any man, but I wanted to be that for Dillon.

I watched as she moaned and pressed backward. I watched as he thrust hard into her.

"Yes, yes!" the girl yelled.

The sound of her voice broke my trance. I jumped backward into the darkness of my room. I shouldn't have watched. I shouldn't want this.

DILLON

THE GIRL DIDN'T SPEND THE NIGHT. I DIDN'T want her to. I didn't know her name, hadn't even asked. I wouldn't remember her face—didn't care to. I'd used her to forget. I'd thought if I shoved my cock into her, that I wouldn't see those turquoise eyes flecked with green. Those eyes had been laced with pain. Those eyes had been tear-filled and hurt. Those same eyes that had watched me with the girl. Instead of erasing those eyes, those lips, that face, while I'd been with the girl, there'd been only one face, only one smile, only one set of eyes, only one scent that pulsed through me while I pumped in and out of her—Lane.

I scrubbed my hand through my hair and let the hot jets of water wash over me. I was sick. I was depraved. Don't get me wrong—sex felt good, it felt damn good—and that girl, I knew she'd been hot, but she wasn't Lane. I tilted my head back under the water and scrubbed my hand through my hair. Hot water and soap couldn't clean away who I was, what I was, what I was becoming. I was an actor; I would be a star. I was every girl's fantasy and every girl's dream. I didn't have the type of life that a girl like Lane deserved. I couldn't commit, didn't want to. I wanted to make movies, make money, and make certain my parents never bothered my brother again. No, I wasn't right for Lane and never would be. Lane Channing deserved more than I could give her.

I turned off the jets of water and wrapped a towel around my waist, then stepped out of the shower and turned toward the steamed mirror. I wiped it clean and looked into that face of mine. The hard, cold eyes of a man who would never get the chance to love a good girl like Lane Channing stared back. Sometimes I hated that guy.

CHAPTER 10

LANE

No matter what time I fell asleep, the fellas had me up by six a.m. They were better than an alarm clock. They needed their walks. Bernie nudged my elbow. I didn't want to open my eyes. I didn't want to drag myself out of bed. The image of Dillon's eyes drunk on lust flitted through my brain. I pictured the girl naked and slamming her body against his. Jealousy stabbed my chest.

What if that girl had been me?

My body tingled with the idea of Dillon's hands grasping my waist, the idea of Dillon's hard body pressed into me, the idea of him moaning my name, of me being the reason that his face contorted and his body crushed forward with desperate need.

Kong licked my cheek. "Okay, okay," I mumbled. I pressed my fingertips to my eyes and scrubbed the images from my brain. Scorsese and Spielberg were already prancing around the bedroom door when I finally sat up.

I plodded into the kitchen, thankful that Mathilde always set the coffee pot for the morning. I grabbed a to-go cup and poured coffee into my mug. Choo wasn't home. I'd gotten a text from him late last night that he was staying at Jackson's, which meant I was home alone with Dillon and possibly his overnight guest. I grabbed the four leashes. The fellas and I would walk to Runyon today. Hopefully we'd be away long enough for Dillon to get that girl gone.

I walked out of the garage door and stopped. Bernie rolled his head toward me as if to ask "What's up?"

"My Jeep!" I said and darted toward the bucket of bolts that was worth next to nothing, but was the most precious thing I owned. The value was not in the money but in the mobility it provided and the sentimentality of my mom and me picking it out together. I ran my hand along the side of the hood. My Jeep was cleaner. And the tires were . . . *newer*? I opened the driver's side door and popped the hood. I peeked over the engine.

There was a new air filter, new plugs, and a new timing belt. I guessed that the oil had been changed too. I slammed shut the hood of my vehicle. I wasn't keen on taking any type of handout. I already felt like a mooch living in Dillon and Choo's house and eating their food. Choo assured me this was the most convenient setup for Dillon since he was filming back-to-back all summer.

I chewed the inside corner of my mouth. This... this was exactly the type of thing that created so much confusion in me about Dillon. Last night he slept with some random girl outside my bedroom window, and today not only has he found my Jeep, but he'd also had it detailed, delivered, and overhauled. I glanced toward the house and the upstairs window I knew was Dillon's. I couldn't figure him out.

Why try?

Our interactions seemed random. It wasn't necessary for me to decipher his mercurial moods. I pulled open the driver's door and before I could pull the seat forward, Scorsese and Spielberg jumped up, climbed over the console, and settled in the back seat. Bernie flashed me a look that seemed to say "I need some help with this."

"Okay, buddy, no problem. But you have to work with me." Bernie weighed a ton. I'd never lifted him, but I knew how heavy he was because he slept beside me and was a bed hog. I often had to try to scoot this big boy over in the middle of the night. I walked around to the passenger side and opened the door. Bernie put his front paws on the seat and I wrapped my arms around his middle. "Okay, boy, we got this." I lifted and Kong barked. Bernie scrabbled his paws forward across the seat. "Bernie, you've got to cut back on the food," I huffed.

"I got it."

The deep voice was like soft sandpaper on wood. My skin prickled. His bare shoulder brushed by me as he leaned in, picked up Bernie, and set him on the seat.

He turned to me. He didn't have on a shirt. We were inches apart. He was as close as he'd been the night before, but anger wasn't rolling off him. The heat was still there, the chemistry that curled between us. His face didn't move, he didn't smile, but his eyes studied my face.

They held something—something like a little boy who expected to be scolded. There was pain, and sadness, and want, and something so... so... broken.

I fought my urge to lean into him, to place my hands on his chest and rest my head under his chin. I had a compelling, indescribable want for him. Even with last night still fresh in my mind, I wasn't angry. We weren't together, had never been together. The Dorothy comment at Area hurt me much more than seeing him with that girl.

"Thank you for my car," I whispered.

"You're welcome." His gaze dropped to my mouth.

"I'll"—my eyes darted past him—"I'll pay you back." My chin jutted forward. I felt wobbly standing so near him. The scent of him washed over me. His body—I needed to feel stronger, not so lost, when I was next to him.

"Don't," he said. "Please." He reached out and his fingertips brushed against the back of my hand. I shut my eyes and my tongue licked over my lip. How could such a tiny touch cause such a powerful response?

Kong hopped up on the seat. He twirled and whined.

"I have to go." I stepped back away from his magnetism. "Kong won't wait." I pretended that his touch didn't matter. I pretended that I didn't feel the surge of energy between us. I pretended that—God help me—I just didn't care.

❧

RUNYON, ON A SATURDAY AT SEVEN A.M., WAS

full of hard-core fitness people—not my peeps. I liked a good run, maybe a hike or a swim, but I definitely wasn't a sporty girl. In fact, being a reader was a perfect gig for me, but today I wanted the exercise. I wanted to clear my mind of all that had happened over the last twenty-four hours. I didn't want to think of the club, or the girl, or my Jeep, or the tingling sensation flicking over my skin when Dillon pressed close to me. I needed to sweat and exercise and suck in clean air and sunshine, because those things I knew would clear my head.

I unsnapped Kong and Bernie's leashes and let them sniff. Scorsese and Spielberg whined.

"Guys, you got to run free yesterday," I said and patted them each on the head. "It's their turn."

They seemed to understand my words and fell into step beside me and behind Bernie and Kong. We made quite a quintet, me with the pups. After taking the dogs to Runyon every morning around this time for over a week, I was starting to see some familiar faces and even getting some smiles and nods. I turned the first bend and kept pumping my arms, fighting hard to keep up with Kong's pace. Bernie didn't need to work too hard—he had four long legs to Kong's short ones. Scorsese and Spielberg were holding back. They were so filled with energy that if I let them off their leashes, they'd bound up to the top of Runyon Canyon in minutes.

I made another turn. I spotted Bernie, but no Kong. I crinkled my eyebrows. Bernie stood just to the side of the trail next to a giant bush that grew out of some flat rocks with ledges. His big brown-and-white tail wagged when he saw me.

Adrenaline surged and my stomach bottomed out. I didn't like seeing Bernie without Kong. Kong was little. If Bernie, Scorsese, or Spielberg got bit by a rattler, they had a fifty-fifty shot, but Kong? His body was too little to survive a snakebite.

"Kong?" I called. Panic laced my voice. I stepped carefully through the bush toward the rocks. "Kong!" I yelled louder.

"You call *this* guy Kong?"

I whipped around. A tall guy with sun-kissed hair held Kong in his arms. His smile was huge and a girl could fall into his dimples. He scrunched his eyebrows together and scratched Kong's belly.

"You must have an awesome sense of humor." He looked around at my dog pack. "And a deep-seated affection for dogs."

A smile spread across my face. "My boss has the love of dogs, not sure about his sense of humor."

He settled Kong onto the ground. He was lithe and lean with the hint of a well-built body beneath his T-shirt and shorts. His arms were well muscled and his skin a light bronze.

"Taylor." He held out his hand. "I think I've seen you here before."

"My name's Lane. And maybe," I said and was, like always when speaking to a member of the opposite sex, thankful for my sunglasses. "We come here every morning about this time."

"Then it is you. The gorgeous girl with the dog pack."

A blush burst across my face. I didn't think I was gorgeous, but it was certainly nice to hear a guy say it. Especially a guy with a smile like Taylor's. Kong pranced, weaving a figure eight around my legs. Finally he looked up at us and let out a little bark.

"Sorry," I said and glanced at Taylor. "He doesn't like it when we stop."

"*Now* I see who's in charge." Taylor leaned down and petted Kong. Kong walked right into his hand. The other three circled, looking for their piece of the attention that Taylor was doling out.

"Affectionate bunch," he said from his squatting position. Spielberg jumped up and planted his front paws on Taylor's chest. Taylor fell back and Spielberg gave him a jumbo lick. "Very affectionate." Taylor rubbed Spielberg's head and jumped to his feet. He dusted off the back of his shorts with his hands. "Mind if I walk with you to the top?"

I tilted my head and checked him out. He seemed nice and all the dogs liked him. "Sure."

I could use the company. After the last week, it would be nice to spend time with a guy who smiled and seemed to think I was good-looking and funny. As we walked, he laughed at my jokes. I didn't feel tense around him. I just enjoyed walking with him and the dogs.

"Great view, isn't it?" Taylor said when we got to the top of Runyon.

"Amazing." The beautiful blue sky was always cloudless and perfect.

"Listen," Taylor said, his hands on his hips. "I know this is kind of out the blue and you don't know me, but my roommate and I are having a party tonight." The sun shone on his blond hair. His smile was charming and his voice was hesitant but hopeful. "Would you like to come?"

"Maybe." I was a little anxious at the idea of going to

a party at a guy's house I'd never met, but I was living in a house with two guys I barely knew. "Sure, why not."

"Awesome. Bring a friend if you want." He pulled out his phone, then looked up at me. "Not that you have to bring a friend. I mean, it's totally cool if you want to come alone. It's great, but if you want to bring a friend or more than one friend, that's okay too."

He scrunched his eyebrows together and tapped his fingers to his forehead. "Okay, I am just totally rambling. Lane, please come to my party tonight and bring whoever you want."

"Okay." I smiled. "I don't have a lot of friends in L.A., I just moved here, but I might bring my friend Choo and his boyfriend."

"Awesome!" Michael said. "Give me your digits." He pulled out his phone and I rattled off my number to him.

"That number isn't from here," he said as he typed in the last digit.

"Nope," I said and mentally prepared myself for the bit of teasing I would get about being from a fly-over state. "I just moved from Kansas."

"Great state. I grew up in Missouri."

I scrunched my eyebrows together. "Seriously?" My eyes roamed from the top of Taylor's bleach-blond hair to the tips of his toes. He looked like a serious L.A. kind of guy.

"We moved here when I was in high school," Taylor said. "Been here ever since."

My heart did a little flip. I wasn't sure why; maybe because it was nice to meet someone that knew where I was from and understood the Midwest. I liked the idea that Taylor could at least point out the state of Kansas on a map.

Taylor walked the downhill part of the Runyon with me and the boys. When they stopped for their water break, Taylor gave each of them a final pat on the head.

"Okay, I'll text you the address," Taylor said. "And I'll see you tonight."

He put on a burst of speed and headed back up the hill from where we'd just come. I watched him run. He turned toward me and waved. A giant smile curled over my face.

I was happy that I'd met somebody that didn't make fun of me or where I was from or give me strange looks or confront me or run hot and then cold. He didn't seem to like me and then loathe me. Taylor didn't confuse me. I was happy that Taylor just seemed normal.

DILLON

BOOM BOOM'S ASSISTANT SCURRIED AROUND Boom Boom's all-white living room. The girl set down a tray of fresh fruit, a carafe of fresh coffee, even scones. She had a wild-eyed look of terror. Of course she did. Even I was afraid of Boom Boom, and I employed her. My eyes flitted across the room to where Boom Boom stood muttering into her headset. She stared out at her view. She wasn't a good-looking woman. But from what I knew of fashion, she dressed well. Her hair was jet-black and right at her shoulders. She was Asian, so her features had all that went with her nationality, and she was sharp. When Webber signed me as a client, he'd insisted that I hire Boom Boom as a publicist. I hadn't wanted the added expense, but after checking around, everyone said yes. Hire her. So far, I was more than glad that I had. She turned toward Webber and me. He lounged on a chair and looked to be nursing a bad hangover—his skin was a little green.

"Boom Boom, it's Saturday," Webber whined.

"Darling, a publicist never takes a break. My work requires me twenty-four seven." She settled on the chair next to Webber. "Unlike you lazy-ass agents." She snapped and pointed to her coffee cup. Her assistant jumped forward and filled it.

"So here's the deal, my beautiful Dillon." Boom Boom pointed her sharp black eyes at me. "Pictures of you with one Miss Lola Rodriguez will hit the rags at the same time as pictures of you last night with Ashley Weston." Boom Boom's wicked smile crawled over her face.

I remembered Lola. She'd been the girl decorating my bike one night. The same night Choo had shown up with Lane. But Ashley? Even though she was from last night, I wouldn't be able to pick her out if Boom Boom hadn't slapped a photo of the two of us leaving Area together onto the table. The only face I'd seen was the one I couldn't have. My jaw clenched tight and I rolled my head to the side, trying to loosen my neck. The face I'd seen while I'd been with Ashley was Lane's.

Webber bent forward and lifted the pic of the hot model off the table. "You, dude, you bagged that last night?"

I didn't answer. Two weeks ago, a sneaky grin would have climbed across my face at Webber's words. Today, I wasn't proud of last night.

"Webber, wipe the drool off your chin," Boom Boom ordered. She smiled, but there was no joy in her eyes. She was calculating. Every move she made was planned, and she focused that same crazy attention on her clients. Right now she was focusing that crazy-ass attention onto me.

"So it's working, darling," Boom Boom said. She leaned back in her chair and raised her coffee cup to her lips. "Not that it's a stretch, darling, with your looks, your womanizing, and your"—her eyes roamed over me and I felt like a slab of meat on a hook—"assets."

I shifted in my seat. That wicked smile again played about her face. My gaze bounced from Boom Boom to Webber.

"When's his meeting with Steve Legend?" Boom Boom asked Webber without pulling her gaze away from me.

Webber was still ogling the picture of the girl from last night. "Next week. Hey, B," Webber asked, "you think she'd be interest in an agent?" Webber's gaze shifted from the picture he held to Boom Boom.

"Ashley has an agent darling," Boom Boom said. "And a publicist." She tapped the giant gold pendant that hung from her neck and mouthed the word "me."

"Right," Webber said. "I don't want to rep her, I want to fu—"

Boom Boom tossed her hand into the air to halt Webber's words. "I *know* what your disgusting little mind wants."

"Why isn't it disgusting when he does it?" Webber whined and nodded his head my direction.

"Because *he* is my client. Because he doesn't look over photos as though shopping for a woman at a supermarket." She turned the full force of her gaze on Webber.

"Because he is creating a brand, which will in turn make him a star and all of us an obscene amount of money!" A smile crept across her face. "Right, my darling?"

I suddenly felt a little cheap and a little dirty. I'd been down with this plan, this building an image and building a brand since the first time Webber and Boom Boom had told me what they wanted, what they needed, and why they wanted me.

I was the whole package.

Young. Hot. Talented. Single.

Me they could sell. Sell me to the highest bidder like a piece of overpriced beef. And they had been. I was on movie number three, but nothing had opened yet. *Mission Ranger*, my first film, my first role, would open next month and that was why Boom Boom wanted me in the mags. She wanted to build awareness of me and my name in the public so when the movie opened and did well, the fans would start to know me. Then the *big* money offers would roll in.

"You'll get the role in the Steve Legend film," Boom Boom said. "I have no doubt. The meeting is a formality."

"She's right," Webber said. "Fabian wants you, Legend wants you—"

"Kiley Kepner wants you too," Boom Boom said.

Webber screwed up his face. "Did she get it?"

Boom Boom nodded. "Ten minutes before you walked into the room."

"How do you—" Webber's phone beeped and interrupted his words. He pulled it from his pocket. "She sure did. Boom Boom, you're better than *Deadline Hollywood*."

"She's a client," Boom Boom said and shrugged.

Those three words explained everything.

She nodded toward me. "Go meet Steve." She pointed a finger toward Webber. "You, negotiate the hell out of the deal." Her gaze returned to me. "And you"—a sharp black eyebrow pulled upward and she pointed a long red fingernail my way—"you keep banging every hot actress and model you can find."

CHAPTER 11

LANE

By the time I got back to the house, Taylor had texted me the details for his party. I spent most of the day avoiding Dillon and reading scripts on my balcony. Choo finally got home around two. He looked tired but happy. He flopped on the lounger on my balcony.

"How's your tummy?" he asked.

"What?" I'd totally forgotten the excuse I'd used the night before at Area to get out of the club and get home. "Oh... right. So much better when I got up today. I am so glad I went home when I did."

Choo's eyes looked past me and toward the view, then his brilliant blue eyes locked on to me. The brilliant blue eyes that looked so much like Dillon's. My heart leapt with the memory of last night—of Dillon pinning me to the wall at the club, his breath so close, his body pressed against mine, and then the flush of embarrassment that had coursed through me with the things he said. I wasn't trying too hard; I wasn't trying for anything other than having a good time. Memories of him with the girl. The rush, the thrill that had pulsed through me while I watched him have sex with her. Then the other Dillon. The one from this morning. The "good guy" who'd found my Jeep and fixed it. That guy had pinned me this morning with his looks and his face and the attraction I felt for him.

"Is something going on with you and my brother?"

A short gasp broke over my lips. I dropped the script I'd been reading to my thighs.

"I thought so." A sad little smile crept across his face. He looked up at the sky. "That man-whore."

"No." I shook my head. "Nothing. It's not like that." I searched the sky with my eyes and let out a heavy sigh. "Nothing has happened between us. Nothing can happen between us. He doesn't even want me in the same room with him. I can't figure him out. Sometimes he seems okay with me working for him and sometimes it seems like…" My words drifted away into silence.

"Like what?"

"Like he can't stand me."

"Oh, he can stand you. That's the problem." A smile curved over Choo's lips. "It's complicated," Choo said. "The last two years have been a roller coaster. Our parents toss me out. I'm homeless. Dillon tries to work three jobs, I try to work two jobs all to pay for my college and his college plus a place for us to live. Out of nowhere he gets plucked for that Armani ad. And now this?" Choo held up his hands at our surroundings. "The whole thing is surreal."

I nodded. My gaze latched onto the script on my lap while a picture of my mother played in my mind. I understood how life could change in a second. One phone call. One diagnosis. One moment and your entire existence, your entire reality upended.

"Now Webber and Boom Boom—"

"Boom Boom?" I couldn't hold back my skeptical grin.

"I know, right? Sounds like a stripper." Choo sniffed. "She's not. She's Dillon's publicist. So now Webber and Boom Boom have this whole plan to brand Dillon. To sell him to the public like he's some packaged product. Like diapers or deodorant." Choo leaned his head onto his hand. He crooked his lips to the left and shook his head, but his voice held the sound of surrender. "His first movie comes out in July and they are selling him as this unattainable bad boy. Ungettable, but sexy as hell."

Heat curled up my thighs with Choo's words. "I see it," I said.

Choo raised his palms to the sky and shrugged. "I mean, I get it, but it's my brother. To me he's always going to be the disgusting, pudgy twelve-year-old who lights his farts on fire."

"Oooo." I scrunched up my face. "That is disgusting." The thought of a goofball preadolescent Dillon with a lighter and bad gas made me laugh.

"But it is true as far as never committing," Choo said. "He never really has. I mean, there are girls—there have always been girls—but just no girlfriends."

A tiny bit of joy pulsed through me, some weird sense of pleasure that Dillon had never given his heart away. "We don't have to worry about that."

"Right," Choo added. A question hung in the air

around his word. Something unsaid that Choo was thinking but didn't say.

"What?" I blushed. "It's nothing like that… I mean, we haven't been… I've never been…" I couldn't bring myself to say it, even to Choo.

He leaned toward me and put both his hands on his knees as if he was being told a most outrageous secret. "Wait, Lane . . . Are you telling me you're a…" He slid his eyes to the left and to the right as if he couldn't quite get his mind wrapped around the idea. "Are you telling me you're a… virgin?" He whispered the word as though it was too dirty to cross over his lips.

My entire chest, neck, and face flamed red. I bit down on my bottom lip and closed my eyes, then gave one silent nod.

"Oh my God!" Choo shrieked. He jumped to his feet and covered his mouth with both hands.

"Stop!" I was completely embarrassed by his reaction.

Choo pressed his lips tight together widened his eyes and sat down on the lounger again. "A virgin," he whispered between his cupped hands. "I don't think I've known one since eighth grade."

"Come on," I said. "It's not that unusual."

"Oh yeah, it is. In L.A. You're starting your fourth year of college and you haven't had sex with a guy? You're like a two-headed pink unicorn out here."

I sighed. This reaction was exactly why I didn't share this tidbit of information with many people. "Look. I had a boyfriend in high school, and he was great but… we were more friends than anything. Then I started college and I have to keep a three point five for my scholarship and I have to work and there just wasn't time, and then there was the thing with my mom last year."

I closed my eyes. I forgot because it felt like I'd known Choo for forever that I actually hadn't, and he didn't know all the details of my life. So much had happened in so little time.

"When she was sick." I didn't want to get into the details. "Before she…" I wasn't sure I could share all of it. "She just…" Not yet. "She just…" I shook my head. I felt so empty when I talked about what had happened. "I spent most of last year trying to juggle all that. There wasn't time for anything else."

"So you and Dillon haven't?" He ran his pointer finger through a circle he made with his other hand.

"Please," I said, "don't be disgusting. I've known him two minutes and I am obviously not his type."

"Most girls that's how long it takes." He leaned forward and picked up Kong. "No, you're not his usual type." Choo petted Kong on his belly.

My teeth ground with Choo's comment. I got that I wasn't as hot as the type of girls Dillon usually was with, but I didn't want my only friend in L.A. confirming what I already knew.

"That was part of why I hired you." Choo's eyes raked over me. "You're not Dillon's type right now. For later, when he's done with his branding opportunity, you're exactly the type of girl I could see with my brother."

My toes curled with Choo's comment. He could see Dillon with me? He could picture it?

"Look, he's just…" Choo's eyes gazed out over the view again. "He's complicated. His relationship with our mom and dad"—he shook his head and rubbed his fingers over his eyes—"we don't really have much of a relationship with them."

I bit my bottom lip. "I overheard him one day on the phone with your mom."

Choo whipped his eyes toward me. "Overheard Dillon? Talking to our parents?"

His surprise alarmed me. I hoped I hadn't completely stepped into a mess. "I think it was your mom."

Choo leaned back and rolled his eyes toward the sky. "Yeah, they still call him. He's not contaminated. He can still be saved."

I took a deep breath. "You're an amazing person with an amazing heart." I grabbed his shoulder with my hand. "I'm sorry your parents don't see that." I squeezed and he placed his hand over mine. "Maybe someday…"

Choo shook his head. "No. Not ever." He pulled his lips tight and I saw a deep sadness in his eyes. "They sent me to be deprogrammed twice. The last time I nearly died." He pulled his bottom lip into his mouth and closed his eyes. "I'm the reason Dillon works so hard." He scrubbed his hand over Kong's belly. "Lost puppies aren't the only thing my big brother saves." He looked into my eyes and I saw the slick tears.

They were so lucky they had each other. What I wouldn't give to have someone… anyone… some family for me. I didn't have anyone anymore. Not a soul. Sometimes I felt so alone. I couldn't imagine what it felt like to have parents who hated who you were so much that they would intentionally hurt you.

"You guys are really lucky you have each other," I said.

"Yeah, we are," Choo said. "And now you're here too. At home on our island of misfit toys."

"I *love* that movie."

Choo nodded and smiled. "The best. Girl, we have so many movies to get through this summer. What's on the agenda for tonight?"

I grabbed my computer. "I pulled up the AFI lists earlier. I thought we'd do drama first and then comedy."

Choo shook his head no. "We do a comedy and then a drama. I need to intersperse the funny with the tears."

I pointed at him. "Good call."

"So what's first?"

"We already went through the first fourteen, so tonight it's *The Philadelphia Story*."

"Oh, but she's so yar," Choo said, doing his best Katherine Hepburn impersonation. He placed the back of his hand on his forehead as though he might swoon. He wiggled his eyebrows at me and I clapped at his performance. Choo popped back up. "Can I ask Jackson to come over?"

"But of course."

My phone beeped and I pulled it from my jean shorts pocket. I read the text and a smile broke across my face.

"What is it?" Choo asked, curiosity in his voice.

"Just this guy I met," I said and shrugged my shoulders. I looked through my eyelashes at Choo. "He's having a party and wants to know if I'll go."

"Hell yeah!" Choo said and nodded. "Hot guy? Party? Katherine, Jimmy Stewart, and Cary Grant will just have to wait."

I bit my bottom lip. "Here's the thing, I don't want to go alone and—"

"Girl, say no more. I am all over this." Choo pulled his phone from his pocket. "Can Jackson go?"

I nodded. Choo's fingers danced across his phone. "What time," he asked without looking up.

"Ten?"

"Perfect."

I texted Taylor that I would be at his party with two friends.

CHAPTER 12

LANE

BOB DEPOSITED CHOO, JACKSON, AND ME AT THE address for Taylor's party. The house was high in the hills off Laurel Canyon. Light shone out from the sleek glass windows and music trickled toward us as we climbed the stairs to the front door.

Excitement churned through me. I was excited to go to a party, meet more people, talk to a cute guy who smiled at me and made me laugh. I knocked and the door swung open. Music blasted from the house.

"You left the pups at home?" Taylor said. A so-happy-to-see-you smile spread across his face. He held the door open for us. He looked past me and reached out his hand to Choo and Jackson.

"This is Choo and his boyfriend, Jackson," I said.

"I'm Taylor," he said and shook both their hands. "Thanks for coming." He stepped away from the door to let us in. Choo looked over his shoulder at me and mouthed, "So hot."

I smiled and nodded. We followed Taylor into the house. The place was modern and minimalist. If not for the crowd, I would see straight through to the backyard.

"This is huge!" I yelled over the music. "You have a lot of friends."

He skirted around a group that contained two CW stars and a guy from the last Christopher Nolan movie. "I just have a few. My cousins grew up in L.A. Most of these people are their friends."

Taylor nodded toward a leggy, raven-haired girl who looked too beautiful not to be on the cover of *Vogue*. Her hair draped to the middle of her bare back. Her skin was fair, and she had high cheekbones and a swan-neck. She turned and looked toward us and her blue eyes nearly pierced me.

"That's my cousin, Amanda," Taylor said.

She glanced from Taylor to me and the corners of her mouth tilted into a tiny smile.

"She's so beautiful," I said. "She doesn't even look real."

"Tell me about it," Taylor said. "But Amanda is very real. A real pain in my ass most the time." He smiled when he said it. I sensed that Amanda was more like a sister than a cousin to him. "And that's her brother." Taylor nodded as a black-haired guy in a T-shirt and jeans walked up beside Amanda. He was taller, but their skin tone was the same and their hair was an inky-black color and loosely curled.

"Are they twins?" I asked. They were both so beautiful —nearly unreal.

"No." Taylor tilted his beer to his lips. "But they get asked that a lot. "Sterling is three years older than Amanda."

We stopped at the bar and Taylor got me a vodka and tonic. "Sterling's out of school and works for their dad, but Amanda is at USC."

"And you live here with them?"

Taylor nodded. "When I'm not touring."

"Touring?" I asked. "What? Are you a musician?"

A sly smiled spread on his face. "Nah," Taylor said. "I ride a bike." He took a swig of his beer.

"As in it's your job?"

Taylor nodded.

"I've never met a professional athlete before."

"It's part of the reason my mom moved us to Cali. I can train year-round and, well..." He tipped his bottle toward Amanda, who now wove through the crowd toward us. "We have family here."

"You must be the girl with the dog pack?" Amanda said. She slid her eyes from her cousin to me. There was a sharpness to her, an edge as though you had to earn the right to get close to her. "I've heard a lot about you."

"Really?"

Taylor shifted from one foot to another. "Not a lot," he said and took another sip of beer.

"Okay," Amanda said. "If that's how you want to play it, cousin." She leaned forward and cupped her hand over her mouth. "A lot," she whispered to me and smiled.

I'd only noticed Taylor today, but he must have been checking me out for a while.

"Taylor said you just moved to L.A.," Amanda said.

I nodded. I realized that aside from some hurried

phone conversations with Emma, I hadn't spoken with a girl in what seemed like forever. "I had an internship at CTA," I said. "Or I *thought* I had an internship at CTA, but that didn't work out."

Amanda bit her bottom lip and we all sat on the couch.

"But they found me something else. I'm reading scripts for one of their clients," I said.

"Which one," Amanda asked. She combed her fingers through her long hair.

"Dillon MacAvoy."

Amanda's eyes flashed from me to Taylor. "You're Dillon MacAvoy's reader?"

A wave of panic crested through me. Choo had said Dillon was a complete man-whore. I hoped that didn't mean that he'd slept with Amanda. I mean, she was completely his type—put together, beautiful, so completely L.A.

"Do you know him?"

Amanda shook her head. "Not personally," she said. "But he may be working in my father's next film."

This moment was so L.A. Amanda's father was probably some outrageously famous movie star. I had to ask the question. I wanted to know. Oh. My. God. I'd become just as bad as Nancy's assistant in HR at CTA.

"Who's your dad?" My insides cringed with the words.

"Steve Legend," Amanda said. "King of the action film."

"And the highest grossing producer of all time," I added.

Amanda tilted her head and sipped her drink. She pulled her lips together into a pucker, then rattled the ice in her glass. She sighed. "If you're reading for Dillon, you'll want to meet my brother." She nodded toward Sterling, who stood on the far side of the room with two other guys and a girl. "He and my dad want Dillon for their next film. Hunter—"

"Fabian is directing." I finished Amanda's sentence. "I read that script this week. I liked it. I told Dillon I liked it."

"Sterling will be happy to hear it," Amanda said. "The entertainment community…" Amanda rolled her gaze toward the ceiling. "Once you're in it, you can't ever get away from it. It's like a small town in a huge city."

"I have a hard time believing that anything about Los Angeles is small-town. I know what a small-town is. I grew up in a small town."

"You don't believe me?" The corners of Amanda's lips raised in a puckish smile. "There are only ten thousand professionals in the entertainment community. *That* is a small town." She gazed across the room. "See the guy with the baseball cap?"

I nodded.

"His dad won the Academy Award last year for best actor. And the girl he's got his arm around?"

Again I nodded.

"Her mom runs Galaxy Pictures." She leaned forward and waved her hands toward the room. "Everyone in here has some sort of industry connection. Most of us went to school together, same summer camps, same parties, our parents worked together. It's like a specialized business in a big city. A small town." She shrugged her shoulders. "And for us"—she placed her hand in the center of her chest—"it's a family business."

Taylor wore an amused grin. "Don't look at me, I'm just the stupid jock in the family."

"The stupid jock with a degree from Stanford," Amanda said. "Not very stupid at all. Plus a shot at the next Olympics if you play it right."

"Really?" My eyes widened. "That's amazing."

"There are about a million miles between me and the next Olympics," Taylor said. "Good thing I like to ride my bike."

Amanda stood up. "Sorry. I have to go help a girlfriend of mine, she's being accosted by this guy who loves her but she can barely stand."

My eyes followed Amanda's gaze. Her friend, the one she was saving, just happened to be Zoey Collin, the female lead in the number one film in theaters right now. I worked hard to pretend not to notice.

"Maybe we could go out this week," Amanda said. "Grab some dinner?"

"Uh… sure." I was surprised by the invite. "I'd love that." I missed palling around with good girlfriends, and while Amanda seemed in a completely different league than me as far as beauty and class, and well, just everything, she also seemed to genuinely like me and I thought she seemed nice.

"Have fun tonight," she said and drifted off toward her superstar friend Zoey.

"I know, right," Taylor said. "It all seems a little unreal."

"It does." My eyes glanced around the room, taking in all the famous faces that I recognized from film and TV. I now knew that even the faces I didn't recognize at this party worked in entertainment too.

"I mean, my entire world is so different. Who would ever believe I would be living with Dillon MacAvoy and going to a party with Zoey Collin?"

Taylor coughed on his beer. He shoved his fisted hand in front of his mouth and cleared his throat. "You *live* with Dillon?" He tilted his head like he wanted to be certain of what I said.

Of course that sounded weird and strange. "Not like live with, I just... I didn't have a place to stay and when the gig at CTA fell through, well, Choo"—I nodded to where Choo and Jackson stood across the room, speaking to a cute-looking couple—"offered me the job and I took it. They wanted me in the house because Dillon is getting so many offers."

"Any possibility that Choo's brother Dillon is gay too?"

"Hardly." I rolled my gaze toward the ceiling and shook my head.

The memory from last night of Dillon having sex with that girl in the backyard flashed in my mind. I glanced at Taylor, thankful he couldn't read the thoughts in my mind.

"You two aren't..." Taylor let his words trail off like he didn't want to have to ask.

"Me and Dillon?" I wasn't something that Dillon wanted. He tolerated my presence because he needed a reader. I was disposable. "We're nothing," I said. "Choo's my friend and I read for Dillon. That's all."

"I like that," Taylor said.

Even with this really gorgeous guy smiling at me, I still couldn't get Dillon MacAvoy out of my mind. Taylor's fingers ran over the edge of my wrist. The touch was soft and felt... nice.

"Let me get you another drink," he said.

I handed him my empty glass. Taylor walked to the bar. He was so good-looking, tall, and muscular. He had golden hair and his skin was a golden-tan color. Girls looked at him when he went by; he was definitely that kind of guy. His smile was megawatt with ultra-white teeth and bright blue eyes. His whole face lit up when he smiled. And he was nice. I sighed. But it wasn't a good sign when I didn't feel anything when his fingertips touched my wrist.

Taylor shot that brilliant smile at me and I returned his smile. Maybe I could learn to like Taylor as more than a friend? I didn't have much experience with dating. That could happen? Right? Maybe I could build some sort of fire between us. I thought was Taylor nice and cute. Nice and cute was good, it was safe, it was so very different than what I felt when I was with Dillon. The fire I felt around Dillon was only something that could hurt me and burn me and wouldn't give me the gentle warmth I needed.

Choo was suddenly beside me. "He is so hot." Choo nodded over his glass toward Taylor. "And nice."

I nodded. "He is."

"Did you know his uncle—"

"Is Steve Legend."

Taylor chatted with his cousin Sterling on the far side of the room.

"He races bikes," Choo said. "So sexy. He hasn't had a serious girlfriend in like a year and—"

"Where did you get all this information?" I turned to Choo.

"Girl, I dig," Choo said and tilted his chin. "If I'm

going to be an agent, I have got to know how to collect the dirt."

Choo would make a great agent.

"So what are we thinking about Mr. Biker Boy," Choo asked. He leaned his head toward mine and we both checked out Taylor.

"We'll have to see," I said. A sinking sensation dropped through my chest. Taylor was nice and I liked him, but not in the way he wanted. I could tell already. There was no pounding in my chest, no fiery ache between my legs—no need—no want. Maybe I was just too internally messed up to actually fall for a good guy. Maybe I had deep-seated abandonment issues or a lack of self-confidence—who knew?—but whatever the hell it was, something made me want a guy I shouldn't have, a guy who the night before had sex with a girl other than me under my bedroom balcony. I shivered. Dillon wasn't good for me, he wasn't good for my future, but I wanted him.

Taylor and I might become friends, but I didn't think that this would become more. There was just no spark, no thrill, when he looked at me. My heart already knew. Taylor was a good guy, but he wasn't Dillon MacAvoy.

CHAPTER 13

DILLON

"Man, Steve Legend is in love with your ass." Webber practically yelled into my ear. "I just got off the phone with Steve's agent. The guy *loves* you. What the hell did you do?"

I yanked open the door to the Pampered Pup and nodded toward the owner, Allison. She smiled and waved and then turned down the dog-food aisle. I walked past the chew toys—Allison would have already put a couple of bones in the care package. I stopped in front of a rack of leashes.

"Nothin' man, we just totally hit it off. Shot the shit, talked about his movies and making movies. It was pretty awesome."

"He's approved you. Now all we got to get is Kiley."

"I hear she can be tough," I said and grabbed a bright blue leash from the rack.

"Tough?" Webber's tone indicated the word was an understatement. "She's a crazy-ass bitch. But you have to meet with her. Aside from Legend, she's the biggest actor on the project. I mean, it's his and Fabian's decision. She doesn't *have* to like you, but it would help."

I pulled a matching blue collar off the rack. It was the right size for a lab.

"I hear she's banging Legend," Webber said.

"Man, that can't be right," I said. "He's like sixty and she's what? Twenty? Twenty-two?"

"He's still got the goods." Webber chuckled. "I should be so lucky at his age. Hell, at *my* age!"

"Legend is *married*," I said. "I met his wife."

"Who you might have noticed is *about* the same age as Kiley, or at least she was five years ago when she and Legend got hitched."

I shook my head. Why bother? Why get married if it wasn't for forever and you were just going to sleep around? What was the point? I walked to the counter and set the leash and collar down.

"Mr. Legend does, in fact, like his ladies young. I hear Kiley actually went to high school with Legend's daughter."

"Ouch," I said.

"Okay, enough gossip. You want the good stuff, call Boom Boom. She knows *everything* about *everyone*. She even knows some shit about me that I don't know."

I laughed out loud at that comment.

"Negotiations start today. Good job with Legend."

"Go get 'em, my man," I said and pressed the Off button on my phone. I slipped it into my jeans and tapped my knuckle on the counter. I hoped to get Allison's attention. Where was she? I turned and walked toward the pet-food aisle where I'd noticed Allison disappear. I turned the corner.

The breath whooshed from my lungs and a hot thrill chased up my spine.

I'd know that ass anywhere.

The golden-colored legs. The caramel-colored hair that fell beside her face. The pug nose that tipped out. The pout of a mouth. The obscene denim short shorts that made me hard by showing off the under-curve of her tight ass. I hadn't seen Lane in nearly a week. We e-mailed. We texted. Always about scripts. Only about scripts. I hadn't seen her since the morning she found her Jeep. The morning after the night before, when Lane had watched me, when she'd watched me have sex with another girl. A girl I didn't want. A girl I'd been with only because I couldn't have Lane.

"Hey, Dillon," Allison said in her breezy voice. She tucked a strand of her short gray hair behind her ear. Lane turned away from the giant bag of dog food she was trying to lift. She caught me in her blue gaze.

"Allison," I said.

"I didn't know you were coming by," Lane said. Her gaze drifted over me. "Mathilde said the guys needed food and—"

"And Lane didn't know that we deliver to your place when you call us." Allison dropped her gaze to the blue leash that I held in my hand. "Oh," she said and pressed her hand to her heart, "you got another one today?"

I nodded.

"Give me the address for the care package and it'll be waiting for them at the house."

I fished a scrap of paper out of my jeans pocked and handed it to Allison. Lane's head tiled with a curious look in her face.

"I'll take care of it," Allison said.

"Thank you," I said.

"You're taking the leash and collar with you?"

"Yeah." I reached out and handed them to Allison so she could add them to my bill. She took both and scurried toward the counter, and I turned my gaze back to Lane. She twisted a lock of that caramel-colored hair between two fingers and shifted her weight from one foot to the other.

"Guess I'll go," Lane said. "Allison said they'll have this bag delivered to the house."

I nodded and hitched my thumbs in the loops of my jeans. I didn't know what to say to her or how to say it. I was just an actor—people wrote my words for me. I couldn't begin to explain to Lane how this desire for her wrapped in my gut like barbed wire and tugged, or how try as I might, I couldn't get rid of her face or the scent of her hair or those damn blue eyes. I couldn't find the words in my throat to say it.

"Okay," Lane said. "Maybe I'll see you back at the house."

She walked toward me and her shoulder brushed past me. I reached out my hand and grabbed her arm. We both locked our gazes to each other.

"Go with me," I said. My voice was soft and thick like the words were almost painful to get out of my mouth. There was a reflection of all the emotions I felt in Lane's eyes. "Please come with me."

She nodded. Silent. But aware of my need.

LANE

WE EXITED PAMPERED PUP AND DILLON HELD the door for me.

"Where's your Jeep?" he asked.

"I walked."

"What it is it with you and the walking?" He slipped his aviator sunglasses over his eyes. "We'll take my bike." He nodded toward a sleek creation of chrome and black steel. I wasn't a motorcycle fan. In fact, I had managed to avoid riding one until just this minute.

The wicked smile that seemed to permanently inhabit Dillon's face whenever he discovered something new about me was once again there, reflecting back to me my naiveté, my innocence, my very Kansas-type quality.

"Don't worry, Dorothy," he said, all slow words and sexy tones. "I'll take care of you."

The want that slid through me when I was with Dillon shivered up my spine. The very idea of Dillon MacAvoy taking care of me and all that might entail was enough for desire to thrum over every inch of my skin.

He walked to the rocket on wheels and pulled a helmet from the back of the bike. "See, already protecting you."

I grabbed the helmet. Dillon straddled the bike. The outline of his thighs, thick with muscle, pressed through his jeans. I couldn't tear my eyes away from watching him handle the bike. How he mounted it and pulled hard on the handlebars and made this machine be a part of him. He turned to me and just that—him astride a giant engine with wheels—almost turned me to a puddle on the sidewalk.

"Get on," he growled.

I pulled the helmet over my head and threw my leg over the bike. There was only one place to hold on. My heart hammered hard in my chest with the realization that I would need to grasp Dillon. Not only grasp, but hold on to him as though my life depended on it, which it did. I pulled tight to him and slid into him. The tenderest parts of my body pressed up against his smooth wall of a back. Through the flimsy material of his T-shirt and my T-shirt, my breasts felt the very pressure of his skin, the heat radiating from his body, the curve of his broad, muscled back. A hot tingle rolled through my body with this machine beneath me and Dillon in front of me and between my legs. He kicked the bike and it roared to life.

"Where are we going," I yelled over the wind. He either didn't hear me or chose to ignore me because instead of an answer, he pulled on the throttle, accelerated around a curve, and blew past a Prius and an Audi. He zipped around a city bus and I clasped him tighter around the chest.

I felt a low laugh rumble through him. He slowed for a red light and turned his head over his shoulder toward me. "Not an adrenaline junkie, I see."

"No, I like adrenaline," I said. "I just don't want to die on the streets of L.A."

Again that low laugh. The laugh that made heat spiral through my belly.

"Not much farther," he said. He pulled past the Beverly Center and into the parking garage across the street. He grabbed a spot near the door to Cedars-Sinai.

"Is someone sick?" I asked.

He slid from the bike and my body missed his near-ness. The warmth of him pressed to my chest. I slipped the helmet from my head.

His face looked harder, nearly sad, as though he didn't want to do whatever waited for him inside this hospital but a solid have-to-do attitude sealed around his entire frame.

"Someone is always sick," Dillon said. He waited for me beside the automatic hospital doors. We went inside and walked toward the elevator. When we got to the pedi-atric floor, a woman in a blue nurse's uniform stood beside the elevators.

"Dillon!" she said. She hugged him and a smile deep with gratitude broke over her face. "Thanks for coming by."

"No problem." He slid his eyes toward me. "This is my friend, Lane."

"I'm Sheryl." She reached out and shook my hand. A yellow lab sat obediently by her side. He wore a blue service vest around his chest. "And this is Brokaw," she said and patted his head.

"May I?" I asked before reaching down to give Brokaw pat. Even I knew that you weren't supposed to pat a service dog that was on duty without asking its master. Sheryl nodded and I gave him some pats on the head. His tail wagged back and forth across the linoleum floor, but he kept his body still.

"You're a good boy," I whispered to him.

I followed Sheryl and Dillon down the hall, past room after room after room. I hated hospitals. Every hospital smelled the same. With a whiff of the antiseptic, the memories of last fall clattered into my mind. I'd spent a giant chunk of time with my hand clasped into my mother's while there was test after test and procedure after procedure. I bit my bottom lip and forced the memories out of my mind. Instead, I focused on following Brokaw and Sheryl and Dillon down the long hall with pink-and-yellow polka-dotted elephants painted on the walls.

"This is it," Sheryl said. She handed the leash to Dillon.

I watched him pull a giant smile from out of nowhere —this wasn't a place where smiles were easy. He walked into the room with Brokaw. Sheryl and I followed a few steps behind.

In the bed was the cutest kid. His mom sat beside him while his dad stood between the bed and the wall with his arms crossed over his chest. His mom looked up and her eyes were just filled with sadness. Dark circles hung beneath her eyes. His father's shoulders sagged, and his cheeks looked sunken with defeat.

"Hey, Matty, I'm Dillon." He reached out his hand to the kid, who couldn't be much older than nine.

Matty's skin was yellowish and he didn't have any hair. He was so sick. I could see it. I could feel it. The whole room just held this unshakeable sadness.

"And this is Brokaw," Dillon said, and as if on cue, Brokaw jumped up onto Matty's bed.

"A dog!" Matty said and his whole face lit up, just exploded with joy.

I clenched my jaw because it took everything inside me not to cry. I mean, here was this little kid that to me looked like he might die, and he was suddenly so happy over having a visit from a dog. I looked at his mom and her eyes were just wet, like she could barely hold it together, but she fought hard and there was a smile on her face. His dad actually turned away and I saw him squeeze his fingertips to his eyes.

"He's a great dog," Dillon said and sat on the corner of the bed. Brokaw was up near Matty and settled right beside him, and he was careful of the tubes coming out of Matty's arms, almost like he knew.

"So listen, Matty, I was wondering if you could take care of Brokaw for me?"

Matty's face lit even brighter. He looked to his mom and his dad and they both nodded yes. Matty beamed at Dillon and started to speak, but then his smile froze, his lips turned down. His eyes filled with a deep worry, a worry that no kid at nine should know. He looked at Brokaw and gently stroked him, then Matty looked at his bed.

Dillon leaned toward him. "Matty, man? What's wrong?"

Matty peered up at Dillon, his mouth fixed like a little man with a big responsibility. "I want to take care of Brokaw," he whispered, "I really do, but... I'm sick." He took a long, hard breath. "And, well, I can't promise you how long I can take care of him."

I pressed my lips together. I couldn't—I could barely breathe.

Dillon's smile stayed fixed on Matty's face, but I could see him fighting, his eyes looked red-rimmed, and he was doing everything he could not to lose it. He reached his hand to Brokaw and patted him too.

"Matty, don't you worry about it. I am always here for you and for Brokaw. If you need to, you can call me or your mom or dad can call me and I'll help take care of him. But for now, I think being with you is the best place for him."

Matty's smile burst out again. "I love him already."

Dillon smiled and stood from the bed. "I know you do." He hugged Matty and then, while Dillon shook hands with Matty's parents, I waved good-bye to them and scooted from the room. Sheryl dug a tissue from her pocket and handed it to me as I exited. I held it together until I got into the hall.

"I know," Sheryl said. "It's never easy."

"It's sad and amazing, and—" I looked up from wiping my eyes and met Dillon's gaze. He stared at me. His face contained this shadow of vulnerability and pain, but with this inner light like he totally realized he'd just gotten to do the most amazing thing for a little boy.

"Thank you, Sheryl," Dillon said and stuck out his hand.

"Of course. I'll call you again sometime next week."

Dillon nodded and we both walked back toward the elevator bank. We got onto the elevator without a word. I started to think about Matty and Brokaw and his mom and his dad and what Dillon had just done, and my bottom lip started to tremble with the thought of Matty's life and how it might be short, but Dillon had just impacted it in this amazing and huge way and he—

"Dillon, I… I mean, that was amazing to watch and—"

He spun on his heels and his eyes met mine and they were wet and desperate and filled with this bottomless pain—our gazes locked and then in an instant he grabbed my arms and his lips were on mine.

DILLON

I COULDN'T STOP MYSELF. I WANTED TO. I DIDN'T want to hurt Lane. I didn't want to draw her into my insane world. I wanted her to read for me this summer and then go back to Kansas where she could meet someone good for her, someone who would take care of her, but when I looked in her eyes and saw that she understood, I wanted to keep her for myself. She understood how hard it was to go into that room and pretend to be happy, but how it was also an honor, and of course I couldn't cry in there. It was tragic and sad, but it would be selfish to cry—that family was experiencing that pain and it would only add to it if I'd started crying.

It was my job to do the very best I could to bring some light and joy into that room. If they only got to have their son for six days or six months, I was meant to lighten their load. I wasn't the star of that show, it was always the dog.

And Lane got it.

Her lip was trembling and her voice was shaking and her eyes, those damn turquoise eyes with specks of green, were wet and wide and she was just so there and so alive and so beautiful—there was nothing else I could do. She touched a piece of me, deep in my heart, that I tried my damnedest to lock away from the world, to pretend didn't exist. A piece that Lane seemed able, with one look of those eyes, to connect with and know that goodness existed within me. She made me feel and even though it scared the hell out of me, I wanted her. I'd wanted her from the moment I met her.

In that moment I needed to kiss her. It wasn't a choice. I reached out and I grabbed her by both arms and pulled her to me. I pressed my lips to hers and they were soft and at first surprised, but her lips yielded to mine. I pressed her against the elevator wall. My mouth was so greedy for her. I wanted her. I needed her.

My hand skimmed over her bare thigh and along the edges of her shorts. Damn, that amazing, beautiful thigh. My hand pressed up over the top of her shirt, against her waist and to the edge of the roundness of her breast. A soft moan came from deep in her throat. I was so hard. So hot for her. She pressed her hips forward against mine, and as I touched the edge of her breast another soft little moan escaped her throat. A moan that nearly undid me. I pressed harder against her.

Then the elevator dinged. I looked at her and the heat in my body stunned me. What was I thinking? We were in an elevator in a hospital. I wasn't... I couldn't think, that was obvious—I couldn't even think when Lane was around. I burst off the elevator and toward the doors we'd entered through. I needed air. This... I hadn't meant to, didn't... shouldn't have. What had I done? I looked over my shoulder once before I slammed through the automatic doors. The look on Lane's face—the look that said she was shocked and surprised and stunned. Her fingers lingered on her lips where minutes before my own lips had been.

CHAPTER 14

DILLON

I HAD TO STAY AWAY FROM LANE. I HAD TO. THAT kiss had been too close and too much. I wanted so much more from her. I wanted everything. The way she tasted. The way her body had melted into mine. The soft sounds that had come from her throat. Just thinking about it made me hard. She was sweet and kind and innocent. That tough-girl act didn't fool me. I suspected it didn't fool anyone.

Beyond my bedroom window, she turned a lap in the pool. She usually swam late in the evening. Her beautiful body with her long, golden legs and full hips slipped through the water. I wanted to grab that body with both my hands and pull her against me.

I wanted Lane. I wanted to keep her for my own. I wanted to lock her up in this house and keep her for me.

She popped up at the shallow end and ran her hand

over her long, caramel-colored hair, now dark with water. The pool lights shimmered around her. She looked like something from a dream. I could pretend I was looking at the view, but I wasn't, I was watching Lane. I loved watching her. I couldn't have her. I couldn't keep her. She couldn't be mine, not with the life I led. Not with the image I needed to maintain. Not with the decisions I had made and my responsibilities.

My bedroom door opened behind me. I glanced over my shoulder. My brother stepped into my room.

"I saw some of your dailies," Choo said.

I nodded. Webber must have gotten some from the director. "Any good?"

"The camera loves you," he said. "I hate to say it because I think your ego has already inflated past an acceptable size, but Webber, me, and every agent at CTA is pretty sure you're the next big thing."

I'd been hearing I was "the next big thing" for the last six months while I waited for my first film to hit screens. The reviews for *Mission Ranger* had started coming in and the comments were solid. The studio and Webber were banking on the film breaking records. If that happened, my life, which had already changed, would change even more. I could kiss good-bye any remaining anonymity in my life or privacy. I turned back toward the window. Lane pulled herself from the pool. Water, silvery in the pool light, slipped down her body. The body I wanted to clasp and hold. The body I wanted to bury myself in. The body that, for her future and for mine, I had to make sure I would never touch again.

LANE

DILLON HAD DISAPPEARED. HE'D KISSED ME AND then he was gone. I wasn't even certain the kiss had happened. The memory of his lips, the taste of him, the smell of him, the heat of his body, his hardness throbbing against the ache between my legs, was the only proof I had that he'd pressed me against the elevator wall.

Yes, the kiss did happen.

I kept up my daily routine while questions simmered in my mind. I got up, walked the dogs in Runyon Canyon, came back to the house. I showered and got ready for the day. I'd spend the morning reading scripts. Some really bad scripts and some really great scripts. There was a never-ending stream of stories. Just as I thought I'd gotten to the end of the pile, there'd be a delivery from CTA with four more or Mathilde would have printed out another and dropped it on my desk.

After I read each morning, I'd have lunch with Mathilde. We struggled through our language barrier and she was becoming my friend. She'd been with Choo and Dillon since they'd moved to L.A. She told fun little stories about them. She obviously adored them and liked taking care of their home. After lunch, I'd go for another walk with the dogs. Then I'd come home and read some more and wait for Choo.

My heart hurt. I couldn't keep the memory of Dillon's kiss from traipsing through my mind. I wasn't a complete innocent—I'd kissed a boy before. I'd had a boyfriend my last year of high school who'd been more a date to certain dances than anything else.

I'd never kissed a guy with that much heat and passion and feeling. I thought Dillon had liked it as much as I had, but he'd pulled his body away from me. I wanted to understand why he'd stopped kissing me. Why he'd bolted from me. Why, even though he lived in the same house, I hadn't seen or talked to him in what felt like forever.

No one could kiss with that much heat, that much passion, and not feel it, could they? But Dillon was an actor. He pretended for a living. He got paid to kiss people. He kissed some of the most beautiful women in the world, and if he could kiss them and not fall in love, then I guessed he could definitely kiss me and feel nothing.

&.

I TURNED INTO THE DRIVE AND PULLED THE parking brake. I opened my door, slipped out, wandered around to the other side of my Jeep, and pulled open the door. Three dogs bounded out: first Kong, then Spielberg, then Scorsese. Finally Bernie lumbered out from the back seat. He stopped on the passenger seat and looked me in the eye.

"Love you, buddy," I said and scrubbed both sides of his head. Aside from Choo, Bernie was quickly becoming my best friend. This was my glamorous Hollywood life. According to Choo, I seemed to be killing it. He'd mentioned just this morning that I'd managed to last longer than his brother's last four readers. Hooray for me. Now if I could just stop the fantasies that raced through my mind when I thought of Dillon.

My phone beeped. "Hey, buddy, I have to get this," I said to Bernie.

He seemed to understand and slowly lumbered out of the Jeep and onto the drive.

I didn't recognized the 310 number that flashed across my screen, and I pressed the green button. "Hello?" I said, curious as to who was calling me.

"Lane?"

The voice sounded vaguely familiar, but I wasn't sure who it was.

"It's Amanda," she said. "Amanda Legend. I'm cousins with Taylor? We met at his party?"

Excitement laced with guilt traipsed through my gut. Taylor had texted three times since his party. Each time I'd found some vague and pretty lame excuse for not getting together with him. None of the excuses were lies, but all of them were barely legitimate reasons. I couldn't admit it to Taylor; I could barely admit it to myself. The reason I was avoiding him was Dillon. All Dillon. I couldn't chase him from my mind. Seeing Taylor while thoughts of Dillon hammered away in my brain just didn't seem right. I liked Taylor as a person, as a friend, and I was certain he liked me as more than just that.

"Hi, Amanda," I said, my voice a little tentative. I wondered if she was calling to see if I wanted to go out with her cousin.

Amanda Legend was way out of my friend league but just exactly the kind of girl I could become friends with. She was funny and smart and sharp and she was calling me. I slammed shut my Jeep door.

"Listen," she said, "I wondered if you wanted to grab some dinner tonight? Maybe sushi?"

I looked down at my clothes. I was covered with sweat and a thin film of grit from hiking Runyon Canyon a second time today. "Uh... what time?"

"Around eight?"

I paused. This was a great way to get my mind off Dillon. "I can do that." I hustled into the kitchen and waved to Mathilde.

"Great, how about Sushi Roku?"

"See you then," I said and pressed off on my phone. My stomach tipped over the edge. I was having dinner with Amanda Legend. I was a little excited and a whole lot nervous.

❧

I STOOD IN FRONT OF MY CLOSET WITH A PLUSH white bath towel around my body and another around my head.

"What do I wear?" I whined into my phone.

"What about that little dress with the flowers," Choo said.

"No, it's all wrong." I pulled the dress from my closet and examined it just to be certain. That dress was completely not right for dinner with Amanda. "It's not what I want to wear to this."

"Girl, I have gone through your entire wardrobe over this phone."

I sighed and slumped onto my bed. "I just want to look good."

"It's like you have a girl crush," Choo said.

"I kind of do. I mean, she's funny, she's smart—"

"She's drop-dead gorgeous."

"Her dad has been in a gazillion great movies."

"And he produces too," Choo said.

"Don't remind me. She's kind of one of those people that I should meet if I want to work in this industry." I pulled the towel from my head. "It's an added benny that I like her too."

"Fo' shore," Choo said. His fingers tippity-tapped over a keyboard. He wasn't pushing the mail cart today but instead subbing for a sick assistant on the president of the agency's desk.

"Hey!" Choo said. "What about that graphic T-shirt from Fred Segal?"

"That's your shirt," I said.

"And that's exactly why that shirt and that little denim skirt with those ass-kicking boots of yours would look adorbs!"

I sat up and ran my fingers through my damp hair. "You know, you could be right."

"Lane, how many times do I have to tell you," Choo said. "I am never wrong."

❧

"LOVE THE SHIRT," AMANDA SAID AND AIR-kissed both my cheeks.

"Thanks." A wave of relief splashed through my belly.

I did have a girl crush. Part of it was I simply wanted a friend. A friend who was a girl. Choo was great, but he had Jackson and work and really, except for a couple of nights a week, was never around. The last week I'd had the pups and my scripts to keep me company, nothing else. I was lonely. I needed something to keep my mind off Dillon. Maybe Amanda would be that friend.

"Best sushi in L.A.," Amanda said.

My stomach tightened and the back of my throat got thick with the idea of putting raw fish into my mouth. I pretended to look at my menu. I had tried sushi before and I just couldn't get my mind around the idea of a raw fish tasting good. All I tasted was yuck.

"What?" Amanda tilted her head to the side. She studied me with her sharp gaze, and her brows pulled together in a quizzical expression as though I were a puzzle to solve. "Wait…" She leaned forward. "You don't eat sushi?"

I closed my menu and tilted my chin down. I shook my head no.

A giant smile spread across Amanda's face. "Then why are we here?"

Why were we here?

"Because you suggested it and I couldn't think fast enough to say I don't like sushi."

Amanda folded her menu and set it on the table. "Let's go get cheeseburgers instead," she whispered as though she'd just asked me to rob a bank.

Twenty minutes later, we sat in my Jeep in the parking lot of an In-N-Out, eating fries and sucking down milk-shakes. We watched the crowd of people walk back and forth across the street when the lights changed.

"I love sushi, but I love cheeseburgers even more," Amanda said and shoved a fry into her mouth. "No one will eat cheeseburgers with me. None of my friends, unless they're incredibly stoned." She turned to me. "*You* are my new cheeseburger buddy."

I slurped on my chocolate milkshake. This was a girl I could definitely hang with. She might be dressed in thousand-dollar shoes and carrying a thousand-dollar bag, but any girl who could sit in my broken-down Jeep and gobble down a double cheeseburger and an order of fries was my kind of girl.

"We've officially bonded over cheeseburgers and fries," Amanda said. She slurped on her shake. She'd ordered a vanilla shake, but I was willing to forgive her for that one indiscretion.

"Do you like L.A.?" Amanda leaned back into the headrest and turned to me.

I pulled in a long, deep breath and watched the crowd amble past when the light turned green. "Yeah, I do. I like it a lot."

"It's hard for me to know if I'll like anywhere else," Amanda said. "I mean, we've traveled. My dad used to always take us when he was shooting a film, but that isn't like living somewhere."

"Where do you want to go?" I asked.

"New York," Amanda said. "Maybe Paris." A smiled pulled on her cheeks. "Anywhere. Most of all I want to get out of Los Angeles."

I could understand wanting to experience something new, something different, something other than what you'd grown up with—those were some of the very same reasons why I'd come to L.A. for the summer.

"People here are so casual. I go by the agency to pick up scripts and everyone calls everyone by their first name." I shook my head. "Even the president of the agency. That would never happen in the Midwest." I pressed a napkin over my lips. "What are you going to do after USC?"

"Anything that doesn't involve actors or movies." She flipped her thick black hair over her shoulder.

I couldn't imagine ever being bored with making films, but I hadn't been visiting film sets since I was three months old.

"My major is art history, so I'd probably work in a gallery, at least for a while."

I knew nothing of art and I wouldn't be going anywhere in Europe anytime soon. Amanda's life was so different than mine, and yet I liked her.

"And what about you?" she asked.

"I want everything you don't," I said. "I want to work in movies, make films, be there while they shoot them."

I sounded like a starry-eyed, silly girl from Kansas. But this was my dream, and I'd promised my mom I would try to make my big dreams come true.

"I think it's fantastic you've found something you love," Amanda said. "I wish I had. I just don't know what I want to do for the rest of my life. My brother has always known, and Taylor has always known. My dad knew from when he was a little kid that he wanted to act and make films. I guess that's kind of like you? Right? Aside from the acting part." She settled her chin onto the back of her hand. "I'm just not sure. Nothing has grabbed me yet."

She sounded like my best friend, Emma. She too wasn't certain what she wanted to do once we graduated from school.

"One more year, right?"

Amanda nodded. "Then the big, bad real world." She opened her bag and plucked her lip gloss from her purse.

Amanda pulled down the visor on the passenger side and opened the mirror. "Was it hard leaving your family for the summer?"

My heart plucked and the tiny knot that seemed to always be somewhere in my belly tightened. The most innocent of questions could cause this black box of pain I seemed to always carry to tilt over and spill its usually hidden contents. I was always unsure how much to tell or what to tell. I didn't want to make light of the fact that I had no family—none—because that broke my heart. There were moments when the sheer enormity of my aloneness terrified me and seared through me with a blinding pain.

"I don't really..." My words drifted into the night air. Was it too soon to tell my newfound friend about my mom? "My mom died last year." I twisted the sapphire ring that she'd always worn and had given to me. My gaze slid toward Amanda, who paused, her hand in midair. "And it was just the two of us, so it wasn't hard to leave."

Amanda blinked. Her glossed lips softened and her eyes held a pain, a pain that seemed familiar to me. "My mom died when I was fourteen." Her lips pressed into a thin line and the corners of her mouth turned down. "It's so hard," she whispered. "I'm sorry."

The heat behind my eyes spiked and big, bold tears filled them. I pressed my lips tight, willing back into submission the pain that threatened to swamp me and send me reeling into the abyss of gut-wrenching, rib-thrashing sobs and tears.

I pressed my fingertips to the corners of my eyes. Amanda threw her arm around my shoulders. She tilted her head so the side of hers rested against the side of mine.

"It sucks" was all she said.

We sat for a couple of minutes, both of us lost in the memories of the women we loved and would spend the rest of our lives without. Tears dripped down my face.

"Here." She passed me an In-N-Out napkin.

I wiped my eyes and blew my nose.

"Now we've bonded over cheeseburgers and moms."

"Sorry," I said and swiped under my nose again.

"Don't be," Amanda said. "I still cry about my mom. I always will."

My heart ached with the idea that I knew what Amanda said was true. I had loved my mom so deeply and we had always been together—just the two of us—her and me against the world. I knew that this loss would never heal, that the grief, the slicing sadness, the aloneness, might fade but that the feeling of loss would be lifelong.

"How do you like working for Dillon?" Amanda asked, changing the subject.

I glanced at her and I could see it was a purposeful attempt to pull us back, away from the moments of pain.

I looked down at my half-empty order of fries. "He has good taste. He listens to what I have to say about scripts." My gaze met Amanda's.

"You're not his typical type."

Typical type? Was there a type of reader that Dillon always chose? "Choo took pity on me."

"Pity?" She cocked her eyebrows.

"I was jobless, homeless, and completely broke." I told her the story of how CTA had given away my summer job as well as my confusion over it being an unpaid internship versus a paid summer gig. "So actually I ended up winning. I get paid, I have a place to live, and if I make it through the whole summer, I'll have a job after I graduate next spring."

"Plus the other perks," Amanda said.

I wasn't sure exactly what she meant. Maybe she liked dogs?

"You should come to the premiere of *Mission Range* with me," Amanda said.

"I've never been to a premiere, but I've always wanted to go."

"Premieres are kind of strange," Amanda said, "but then again nearly everything in this town is incredibly weird."

CHAPTER 15

DILLON

LANE WAS OUT AND I DIDN'T KNOW WHERE. CHOO
had mentioned Amanda Legend. Even with that tidbit of
information, I was close to losing my mind. Since I'd
cornered her in the elevator, I'd avoided Lane, but I always
knew where she was. I had to know where she was and
who she was with. I wanted her with me, but I couldn't
let myself have her. My life wouldn't be fair to her,
wouldn't be good for her.

I lay on the leather couch in the rec room and tried to
lose myself and these thoughts in the Dodgers game. Her
voice tugged at my soul. Her lips, her eyes, they were
right there in front of me, in my mind, and I wanted them.
I wanted her. That kiss had seared its way into me and I
couldn't seem to break free. My phone beeped—it was
Webber.

"Dude, what's up?" Webber said. His voice sounded

half happy and half not.

"Watching the game."

"If you want, the agency has box seats—next game we go."

"Yeah, sure," I said and muted the sound. Not even the idea of box seats behind home plate could yank my mind away from wondering about Lane.

"I got some news," Webber said. His tone sounded cautious, as though he didn't want to have to tell me whatever the news was. "I got a letter from your dad."

I pulled myself up from lying on the couch. My shoulders tensed. "Why are you getting letters from my dad?"

"Maybe because you took out a restraining order on him?"

"He threatened to have my brother abducted and deprogrammed again." My chest tightened and my heart started to pound. "Like being gay is some sort of disease."

"Look, man, I get it. He's a whack job. All I'm asking is do you want the letter or should I forward it to your attorney to deal with?"

I rubbed the hard knot of muscle now pulled tight in my neck. My dad was a zealot, a nut, a threat to both Choo and my sanity. He'd flipped a biscuit when I dropped out of college to model. He'd completely gone off the rails when Choo came out—like that was a surprise? It just proved how deep into denial about my little brother my dad had been. Choo had been playing with Barbies since he was five. My dad treated my kid brother like Choo was some sort of diseased creature. He'd shipped him off to some religious camp in the middle of Utah to teach Choo how to be straight. I would never let that happen again. I wouldn't let my dad close to my little brother. He wasn't going to hurt him or me again.

"Forward me the letter," I said.

I didn't want to read the letter and I didn't want my dad to have contact with my brother, but I wanted to know what was on the nutball's mind. I might better be able to protect Choo if I knew what kind of hate my dad was spewing right now.

"You got it," Webber said. "So, dude, I found you another reader."

"Another reader? I'm not looking for another reader." I stood and walked toward the stairs.

"After last week at Area, when you nearly flipped? With that chick Lois, Lala—"

"Lane." I climbed the staircase to the second floor.

"Whatevs. You can't keep her as a reader if you're banging her. You've tried that before—"

I turned the corner into Lane's room. All four dogs were piled on her bed. They were always with her. The dogs always wanted her. Smart dogs. The room smelled like her, fresh and warm, with hints of flowers.

"I'm not sleeping with her," I said. "Don't talk about her like that."

"Seriously?"

Webber was more surprised that I told him not to talk about Lane than he was about me not sleeping with her.

"Yeah, seriously." I sat on Lane's bed beside Kong. "She's not like that."

"Well, whatever she's like, you nearly lost it and I don't need you losing it in front of a camera, right? Seriously, you are about to get hit with some heavy shit.

Already you're scheduled for an interview and photo spread for next week. Did Boom Boom get a hold of you?"

"Yeah."

I wasn't looking forward to the photo shoot or the interview. I didn't like people digging into my life. I wanted some sort of privacy, but I was pretty sure that any privacy I had was about to evaporate. "She did."

Scorsese rolled over onto his back and put his head on my thigh. I loved these guys. And they loved me. I'd saved them all. But now they loved Lane more.

"No new reader," Webber said. He sounded pissed.

Too bad. I couldn't date Lane because of the image that Webber and Boom Boom and even I had spent a ton of time developing, but I could have her here for the summer. I could keep her close for a while. Keep her as my reader.

"Nope," I replied.

"Not even an ugly-ass guy?"

"Not even an ugly-ass guy."

"Dude, watch yourself. I see something coming for you. You don't usually get attached to anything in a skirt."

"Later."

No, I didn't usually get attached to anything in a skirt, but there was nothing in a skirt that had looked like or acted like Lane, nobody I wanted like Lane. I flopped back onto Lane's bed. Bernie stood up and resettled closer beside me with his head on my neck. Spielberg snuggled in beside me and Kong actually curled up on my chest. They were like a giant dog snuggly.

❦

"WHAT ARE YOU DOING ON MY BED?"

My eyes fluttered open. Her voice brought me out of a dream. Darkness seeped through the windows. Kong was still on my chest but now he stood and wagged his tail at Lane.

I slowly sat up on her bed, making certain that the dogs weren't on my body. "Nothing, uh, I just…" I looked around at the pack. Traitors. They'd all abandoned me and now stood beside Lane. They wore the same look on their faces as Lane. A look that seemed to yell "what the hell are you doing on her bed?"

"I was lonely downstairs and came to find these guys, and well, I started petting them and I must have fallen asleep." I hadn't spoken to Lane since last week. "How was your night?"

"Good." Her lips were tight and she had crossed her arms over her chest.

She didn't look at me. I guessed that she didn't want to look at me. Her gaze darted past me and then back to Kong. I can't say that I blamed her. I mean, I had humiliated her, and then kissed her, and then ignored her, and then… I looked into her turquoise eyes. There were so many questions, questions that I wanted to answer but couldn't. A hard tightness squeezed through my chest with her look, that uncertain look filled with questions and self-doubt. She was too beautiful to look that way, too good, too kind. I had put that look on her face.

I closed my eyes. I wanted to tell her, I wanted her to know why and how and that it wasn't her, it was me and my messed-up life. That I couldn't be with her, not now, and it wouldn't be fair not to her and I knew… a voice, a feeling, something deep inside me knew that if I was with

Lane—actually with her—I wouldn't want to pull away. Lane would ruin me for anyone else. She needed someone better, someone who could give her a life that she deserved.

"Lane." The need scraped over my throat and out of my mouth. Her name was like a prayer on my lips. I reached out to her arm.

She turned to me, her face so soft, so open, so beautiful. My fingertips smoothed over her cheekbone. She was so close, so near, and suddenly... suddenly her lips were on mine.

LANE

I WANTED THIS. I WANTED DILLON TO KISS ME. I wanted the low moan that came from his throat. I stepped closer to him and wrapped my arms around his neck. My fingertips wove through his hair.

His lips pressed against mine, at first soft, almost like he was surprised that we were standing in the middle of my room with his lips on mine. I pressed forward. I wanted more; I needed more. I could no longer fight the heat that coursed through me when I was near Dillon. I couldn't deny this deep ache. Heat swept through me. He grasped the back of my head and his lips grew impatient as he pressed harder and his tongue slipped past my lips and entangled with mine.

His hand rushed up over my body and touched the underside of my breast through the fabric of my shirt and a moan escaped over my lips. His body tightened with the sound. And he pressed harder. He lifted me and turned me to the bed. I lay back and he lay beside me. His fingertips were on my jaw and then my thigh, at the edge of my skirt, and a hot thrill raced through me. I could feel the clutching in my belly, the tingling between my thighs, the spot that begged to be touched, that had never been touched by any man. His lips descended to my neck and heat seared through me. Then to my chest. His hand slipped under my shirt and his hot fingertips traced up over my ribs and paused beneath my breast. Then his fingertips danced over the lace of my bra, slipping over my tight, pert nipple. My hips arched upward into him.

"Lane," he growled.

My hips rocked against his hardness. The sound of my name on his lips ignited a deep heat. I pressed harder against him, the throbbing between my legs needing the hard pressure from him.

"Lane, you're going to drive me over the edge." He pulled at my shirt and pulled it off my body. He unsnapped my bra and my breasts sprang free.

I gasped. I'd never been so exposed to any man.

Dillon stopped. The heat in his eyes was laced with worry. "Lane," he said, his voice ragged and his breathing shallow, "are you okay with this?"

I nodded. I wanted to feel his body rocking against mine. I wanted his touch, his kiss, all of him. His eyes locked with mine—that bright spellbinding blue—and then he ducked his head. He slipped a taut nipple into his mouth, and his tongue laved around it. A white-hot heat seared through me. A whimper I couldn't contain pressed over my lips. I watched his mouth suckle me. I pressed upward into him and sought the hardness between his legs. I sought the pleasure of him pressing into the spot that throbbed between my legs. I watched his mouth and tongue lick over me. My hips wouldn't stop moving.

He pulled his mouth from my nipple and his eyes looked into mine. "God," he whispered out, his voice ragged and deep. "You're beautiful, Lane." His hands caressed my bare skin and his eyes swept over my body as though he were eating me with his eyes. "You're the most beautiful person I know."

My heart exploded and with it a deep, hot need. His lips pressed to mine. I grappled with his T-shirt and he arched forward and ripped it over his head. I wanted his skin, I needed to touch his body, which I'd seen and dreamed about—his muscled abs, his tattoo that whispered around his arm and down his back. My hands found his chest and I clutched his shoulders as his lips pressed between my breasts. Hot, lingering kisses moved slowly across my skin. My hips arched forward, aching, aching for more from him. His fingertips traced up my thigh and under the edge of my skirt. They slid along the edge of the lace of my panties. My breath clutched in my chest. I couldn't breathe. All I could feel was the hot trails along my skin. Explosion upon explosion of want, of need. One finger slipped under the fabric. He pressed between my folds, which were hot and swollen and aching for his touch.

"Lane, you're so hot. Baby, you're so wet."

His fingertip paused at the entrance of me. I pushed forward. I wanted him to fill me, to be inside me. His fingers danced upward and pushed against that hot spot that ached between my legs. My whole body convulsed with the tiniest touch and his name rushed over my lips.

"Oh my God, Lane. I can't, baby, you're driving me over the edge."

His lips were on me and I felt the stroke of his fingers on my swollen nub. I pressed into him, grabbing for that wave of feeling that I wanted to climb into, that heat.

"Lane, come for me," Dillon whispered.

My eyes fluttered open with his words. Embarrassment would have pulsed through me if I wasn't abandoned to the desire that throbbed through my body. Dillon watched my face and he brushed his finger over my nub again with a harder, more insistent pressure. A wave of pleasure crashed over me again and grasped the edges of me.

"Dillon," I yelled in a raspy voice I'd never heard come from me. "Oh, Dillon!"

The pressure clutched me and my entire body shook with pleasure. I grabbed his shoulders. My nails dug into his tattoo. I held onto him and reached for that feeling. His fingers slipped inside me as he continued to pulse on my nub.

"Oh, Dillon," I moaned out around the pleasure.

"Come for me, baby. Come for me, Lane."

I clutched tight around him and my hips bucked upward into his fingers, and pleasure pulled me over into the edge where I shattered again, and again, and again.

DILLON

SHE WAS A VIRGIN. I'D KNOWN IT FROM THE first kiss. The soft moan. The response to my touch. The open wonder in her eyes. I probably knew of her innocence since the first time I saw her.

Lane lay limp in my arms with her face nestled into my neck. I didn't deserve her. I would never deserve her, but I'd had to have her, and now that I had, she was mine. My chest filled with a dark need. A possession. No one would touch her but me. No one could ever touch her but me. No one could see the grip of passion on her face, watch her hips roll upward and hear the tremble of pleasure in her voice. Those pleasures were mine now. I pulled my arm tighter around her. Pulled her closer to my side. I was still hard. A deep, throbbing uncomfortableness that wouldn't release. I'd watched her face as she came and nearly unloaded, but I hadn't and I ached.

"Lane, you okay?" I put my hand under her chin and tilted her head upward to me.

She nodded but wouldn't meet my eyes.

"Lane, baby, what's wrong?"

She shook her head no and then those beautiful blue eyes, the ones I would give my soul to spend a lifetime looking into, met my gaze. She was embarrassed and scared. I watched her emotions glide through her eyes. I pressed my arm tighter around her and pulled her in closer to me. She molded to my side and I could feel the heat and press of her body against mine.

"I'm..." Her words drifted off and her gaze left mine and again she looked down, away from me. "I've just never done anything like that before."

A thick heat coiled deep in my belly. It circled tight around a need to protect, a need to possess. I throbbed with the idea of pushing into a hot and wet Lane, still tight with innocence. A feeling of power coursed through me. A feeling I didn't deserve Lane, but alongside the power was the deep possession that Lane was now mine.

"But you liked it." I couldn't prevent the wicked smile that curled over my lips.

A blush crept up over her bare breasts with their pretty little pink nipples that tasted like sugar and flooded her neck and finally her cheeks. She smiled and nodded her head. She buried her face deep into my arm. This was a shy, innocent part of Lane She could be tough, all lip, all heat, and sometimes anger, but with a definite attitude that said she would stand her ground. Here, in my arms, in this moment, with a light pink blush on her cheeks and her mussed hair, her face buried in my arm, there was a soft shyness about her that I already loved.

"I did." She bit her bottom lip and the hardness ached in my pants. "I didn't want to stop."

"Baby, you're killing me." I took a deep breath. I ran the pad of my thumb over her bottom lip and saw a flash of want in her eyes. I leaned forward and kissed those beautiful plump lips. Lips I wanted to bite and suck.

"I didn't want to stop either, but I want you to be sure… I want us to be sure—"

Her eyes clouded over and that wall of toughness flashed up around her. She started to roll away from me.

"Hey, what? No, don't pull away."

She tucked her chin even as I pulled her closer to me. She felt suddenly distant.

"What, Lane? Please, don't pull away from me."

Her lips flattened and the corners turned down. "It's just"—she shook her head I felt her hair brush over my arm—"I'm not the right type of girl for you."

"Right type? What the hell does that mean?"

"I mean…" She pressed her eyes closed as if she didn't want to say it, but struggled to say it. "I'm not pretty enough, I'm not L.A. enough, I'm not—"

I pushed my lips onto hers. I couldn't think fast enough to say the right words to make her stop. I wanted her to feel the heat coursing through me, the desire she caused, the want, the ache. Finally I pulled my lips from hers and looked into her eyes. A smile curled around her lips.

"You're everything I could ever want," I said, "and definitely more than I will ever deserve."

Her smile turned into a blush.

"I've wanted this since the first time I saw you," I said.

"Maybe not the first time," Lane countered. A smile curved the edges of her lips. "You were kind of too busy being an asshole."

I smiled. Yeah, I deserved that. "You scared the crap out of me," I said. "You don't know this, but one of the reasons I was so pissed is that I'm supposed to die before I'm twenty-five."

"What?" Lane lifted her eyebrows and the little furrow between her them was too cute for words, so I planted my lips there.

She pulled her head back and looked at me, really looked at me, and there was worry there. "Are you sick? Why do you think you're supposed to die before you're twenty-five?"

"I had my palm read and this woman said I wouldn't make it to my twenty-sixth birthday."

"And you believed her?" Lane said. The look of incredulousness on her face like I was somehow nuts to base my fear on this woman got to me. "Some stranger telling you

you're going to die for no reason other than the lines on your palm and you believed her?"

I rolled my gaze upward. How could I explain it so she'd understand? "It's just this feeling, I have. This feeling I got when she said it, like it's true. Completely true. Then look around you. This? This life that came out of nowhere. This life is like a rocket. One day I'm walking around campus, the next I'm lying on my back shooting an underwear ad? Then I'm above Sunset Boulevard and every agent in town is after me? That shit doesn't happen, Lane." I brushed my fingertips across her cheekbone. She was too damn beautiful for words. "That shit doesn't happen to a guy like me."

She settled her chin onto my chest and peeked up at me, my arm draped over her back. I could lie like this for the rest of my life.

"I think," Lane said and her fingertips played across my chest, "that you got lucky. You got a chance and you ran with it. Now you're taking advantage of that luck for you and for your brother and you're turning that luck into a career."

Her words didn't completely quell the fear lodged in my brain that this life was too good for me, but they helped.

"I know one thing," I said and let my hands skim over her back. "No matter how much time I get, I want to spend as much as I can getting to know you."

CHAPTER 16

LANE

THE MORNING AFTER I WAS WITH DILLON, HE left for seven days. They were shooting action scenes in the desert. He'd made me feel things physically that I'd never experienced with another person, and then he'd gotten up at five a.m., kissed me good-bye, and left. He'd been gone for nearly a week and was meant to get back tonight. My stomach flipped with the idea that soon I would see him. Soon he would kiss me again, touch me again, make me feel so many amazing things in my body. His touch—I shivered with the thought of his fingertips over my skin. I licked my lips and the anticipation of being in his arms caused desire to curl between my legs.

I'd spent the last seven days trying to keep thoughts of Dillon from taking up every minute of every day. We texted. We Skyped. We talked on the phone. But I still felt an uncertain shyness with him.

I parked my Jeep at the bottom of Runyon Canyon and climbed out with the boys. The best way not to miss Dillon and to try to forget his absence was for me to stay busy. I set a fast pace as the five of us passed through the gates and started the ascent to the top of Runyon. Scorsese and Spielberg bounded around me, seeming excited by my energy. Bernie looked at me like "are you serious?" I smiled. Bernie would do Runyon, but he liked a leisurely pace that included pauses to sniff and pee and breathe. Today I didn't want pauses, I didn't want breaks, I didn't want to think too much. I wanted to sweat and suck in oxygen. I wanted to think of nothing but trying to conquer this hill. There were so many thoughts crashing through my mind. The main thought was Dillon, and where I fit in Dillon's future?

In a very short time Dillon would have everything. He would be the hottest celebrity in the world, and I knew enough to know what that level of fame would mean for him. *Mission Ranger* was tracking huge and the studio anticipated the film to be the biggest of the summer. Soon Dillon wouldn't be just a gorgeous face attached to a gorgeous chest with a giant package decorating a billboard above Chateau Marmont. Dillon would be the hottest commodity in Hollywood. Women would be throwing themselves at him, and I just couldn't believe that he would want to be with someone like me.

"Hey Lane!"

I recognized the voice. I turned back but kept my pace. Taylor sped up his run until he was beside me and the boys.

"Hi Taylor," I gasped out. I stopped and turned to him. I sucked in giant lungfuls of air.

"Trying to work up a sweat today," Taylor said.

Kong hopped up on his back legs and placed his front paws on Taylor's shins.

"Hey buddy," Taylor said and bent over to give Kong a pat.

Bernie ambled over and licked Taylor on the side of his face as a sign of thanks, I was certain on Bernie's part, for forcing me to stop my wicked pace. Scorsese and Spielberg sniffed the bushes beside the path. Taylor had a great smile. My heart crumpled. I didn't want to make him feel bad.

"You must be really busy with those scripts," he said. "I haven't heard from you in a while. Did you have fun the other night with Amanda?"

"I did. We ate cheeseburgers." I added some emphasis on the word cheeseburger.

Taylor's eyebrows tightened. "Amanda ate a cheeseburger?"

I nodded and began to walk again and Taylor kept pace beside me.

"Wow," Taylor said. "I don't think I've ever seen Amanda eat anything but vegetables or fish."

"We bonded over grease," I said.

"I know she thought you were great when you guys met at the party. But cheeseburgers? Looks like you two may end up best buddies." His beautiful, playful smile curved around his lips.

Some girl deserved that smile. Some girl would swoon over that smile. But that girl wasn't me.

"Amanda has great taste," Taylor said.

I was flattered. I didn't know what to say and I blushed.

"You're gorgeous and completely down to earth."

"I'm not so sure about either," I said. "I feel like a hot mess most the time."

"You don't look it," Taylor said. "Well not the mess part anyway."

I sighed. Yeah. I had to tell him. I had to be honest. I stopped walking.

"Taylor, I..."

He nodded, his eyes flitted to the distance as he settled his hands onto his hips. His gaze came back and landed upon me. "He got to you, didn't he? Dillon?"

Got to me? My stomach clutched. My eyebrows perked upward. Taylor spoke about Dillon as though I was a prize to be won or a possession to be owned. Kong wrapped his leash around my legs.

"After your party... we... I... there was nothing before. I wouldn't want you to think—"

Kong barked.

"Hey, I believe you," Taylor said.

He turned back up the path, and I unwrapped Kong's leash. We started to walk again. Taylor's face was hard, pensive, like he was fighting with something he wanted to say.

"What is it?" I finally asked. What weighed on Taylor's mind?

He pulled up short and again settled his hands on his hips. His face emanated disdain, almost disgust. "Here's the thing. I don't want this to sound like sour grapes because it's not, but you know about Dillon right?"

"What do you mean *know* about Dillon?"

"Look the only reason I know any of this is because Sterling and my uncle hear everything about everyone in town. He's a great actor with a big future, and Sterling says he's a good guy to hang out with, but... if you're a girl... he's not that great of a guy to be involved with."

My stomach knotted and my heart dropped. I understood what Taylor was saying. The first time I'd met Dillon, a California bimbette had been wrapped around his arm, and then there was the night at Area—which when I did the math really wasn't that long ago—when he'd been having sex with the girl in the backyard... while looking at me. I shook the memories from my mind and forced the fear and clutching doubt deeper into my belly.

"I know he's been involved," I said with a quiet in my voice.

"Involved?" Surprise with hints of irritation inhabited Taylor's voice. "Is that what you want to call it? More like a new girl every twenty-four hours. That's the thing, Lane, Dillon doesn't become involved. He uses girls like most people use trash bags. He changes them out every couple of days."

I froze with Taylor's words. I chewed on the inside of my cheek. I definitely wasn't a trash bag and I didn't like the implication.

"You know about what he does with his readers, right?" Taylor continued.

My stomach pitched forward with his words. A tilting sensation gripped my head.

"Webber, his agent, was supposed to find him a guy."

"His readers?" I whispered. Nausea careened through my belly and the left side of my neck tightened. Bernie crowded next to my leg, bumped my hand with his nose, and whined. I put my fingertips on his head to reassure him I was okay.

Taylor leaned forward and his voice was low as though he didn't want to say it, didn't want to tell me, didn't want me to feel like he knew I was going to feel.

"He sleeps with his script readers and then fires them," Taylor said. "That's Dillon's thing."

Dillon's thing?

A shaky breath rattled through my chest. I was so thankful for my sunglasses. I didn't want Taylor to witness the hot tears in my eyes, the tears that were about to drop onto my cheeks and roll down my face.

"You're an amazing girl, Lane. I don't want Dillon to do that to you."

I nodded. I didn't think it was sour grapes on Taylor's part. He seemed sincere, as though he really was trying to tell me something he thought I needed to know. We were back at the gate for Runyon Canyon.

I called to Scorsese and Spielberg and clipped their leashes to their collar, then forced a fake smile to my face. I wouldn't let anyone see me cry. I wouldn't tell anyone that Dillon had started to mean something to me. That I'd believed, that I meant something to him. That I was different. That I was somehow special. That Dillon connected with me the same way I connected with him. That we were meant to be together.

"Lane, I'm sorry," Taylor said.

"No worries. Thank you for telling me. I'd rather know now than later."

"I hope it's different this time," Taylor said. "You're a special enough girl that it definitely should be." He ducked his head. "I know it would be for me."

A sad little smile decorated my face with Taylor's words. He would be such an amazing catch for the right girl. "I've gotta go. These guys have an appointment with the vet."

"I'll see you soon," Taylor said. He turned and ran up the path.

I turned back to my pack, tucked my head down, and walked toward my Jeep. I wasn't sure I wanted to see anyone at all.

DILLON

THE DESERT WAS HOT. I WAS DIRTY AND exhausted. Bob pulled the black Escalade to a stop in front of the house and I slid out with my duffel bag. We'd done four days of night shoots and two days of day shoots and all I wanted was a shower and a bed. Preferably a bed that had Lane snuggled in it.

"Thanks," I said to Bob. Lane's Jeep wasn't parked in the drive and my heart dropped a little in my chest. I hadn't been able to stop thinking about her face, her neck, her nipples in my mouth, and the hard shaking orgasms that she had experienced at my touch.

Heat surged through me. I wanted to kiss her this instant, needed to kiss her, but I was a wreck. They'd shot my last scene and I'd headed out. My shirt was filthy with sweat and dirt. I should have showered, but all I'd wanted was to get home. Cool air slammed into me when I walked into the house. The scent of something meaty roasting in the kitchen hit my nose. There was no click-clack of claws on hardwood, so that explained the absence of Lane's Jeep. She must have taken the pack for a run. I'd hoped that Lane would be with them wearing a cute sundress filled out by her amazing curves.

I ambled toward the stairs and up to my room, dropping my duffel bag and then heading into the bathroom. I turned on the shower jets to let the water heat up and then slid off my shirt and my jeans. My phone rang and for a split second I didn't want to answer, but I knew it was Choo by the ringtone.

"What's up," I said.

"She's leaving." His voice was panicked.

"Who's leaving?" I asked. I settled my hand on my hip. I was too tired for guessing games.

"Lane is leaving," Choo said. "What the hell did you do?"

I was stunned. Shocked. Surprised. "What the hell are you talking about?"

"I like her," Choo said. "I handpicked her. She's my friend. You're never home and now she's leaving, too?"

What the hell had happened? I'd just texted her last night and everything had been fine. "This is a mistake, Lane isn't—"

"Dude, she just called Webber and told him he needed to find another reader. I'd say it isn't a mistake."

My heart slammed in my chest and a solid, cold tingle slithered up my spine. "Where was she? Where is she?"

"I have no idea brother, but you'd better find her." Choo clicked off his phone.

The steam from the shower fogged the mirror. I heard the clamor of clickety-clackety dog claws. I walked into the hall holding my towel at my waist. Lane stopped.

"Lane?" I held out my hand while I held the towel with my other.

Her eyes roamed up my body and back down. She flushed. With her eyes all over me, I grew hard. I wanted her hands on my skin, not her eyes. I wanted her body pressed to mine. I wanted her. "What's going on? I just got a call from Choo and he said you're leaving?"

"I... I can't talk about it," she said and started to walk past me.

She brushed my arm with her shoulder and I grabbed her. A jolt coursed through me. It took all my resolve not to yank her close and plant my lips on hers. I'd missed her. I wanted her. I'd never had these feelings for a girl before.

"You're leaving me?" I asked.

The pain in my chest with the thought of it caused my voice to deepen. It nearly shook. I couldn't imagine coming home without Lane here. The realization hit me. My head pulled back with the thought, the idea, that in such a short time Lane had become a need. How had this happened? Why had this happened? Her eyes. Her mouth. The smile. Just everything that was her made me want to keep her and protect her and be only with her.

Lane's eyes widened with my question. She looked startled.

"I'm just your reader," she said. Her jaw jutted forward and she yanked her arm from my grasp. "I *know* what you do with your readers."

My heart thudded and my throat thickened. I closed my eyes and licked my lips. I was an asshole. I was a man-whore. I was a guy that used girls and kicked them to the curb and now finally, when I met a girl I couldn't get out of my system, a girl I wanted to stay, a girl I cared about, I was going to pay for my past sins.

"You're not like that," I said.

"I know I'm disposable to you." Her gaze locked onto mine.

There was loads of pain in her eyes. Pain that I had caused by my past. This was one of the reasons I hadn't wanted to involve Lane in my life. I wasn't worthy of her. I would only hurt her with my past or my future—something I did would break her apart. But I was also selfish. I wanted her. I wanted her for now and I wanted her for later. I wanted her to be mine and only mine. My fingertips brushed across her cheekbone.

"*You* will never be disposable."

I stepped closer. The pad of my thumb brushed over her bottom lip. With my possessive touch a breath hissed from her mouth. Her tongue flicked out and she bit down on her bottom lip. I wanted that lip. I wanted the body that was now inches from me. Her pulse fluttered. Heat licked out from her. My fingertip trailed from her lip down over her throat, over her top, between her breasts, down her belly, to the edge of her shorts. My hand flattened and skimmed across her belly and slid under the elastic of her shorts.

"All I do is think about you," I said. My voice was rough.

I wanted to yank her to me and bury myself in her. Bury myself and never come out. Carry her to my room and lock the door forever so that no one but me ever saw her, no one but me could touch her, no one but me could be near her. Lane made me feel barbaric and possessive. My fingertips found the edge of her panties and I slipped my fingers down and felt the soft fuzz of her. I pulled her forward. Our lips nearly touched. I let my finger press onto her clit.

"I want you, Lane," I said.

Her hard nipples pressed against the fabric of her tank top and against my bare chest. I wanted her naked against my body.

"I don't want anyone else," I said.

I smelled the sweetness of her breath, which was rapid against my skin. She gave little gasps of pleasure as I pushed my finger onto her clit. Her eyelids fluttered and her head tilted to the side. I pressed again, more insistent. Her gaze latched onto mine, hot and fierce, as though something inside her, something she'd only recently been introduced to, awakened within her.

"Do you understand me," I whispered in her ear. My fingertip pressed and rolled against her hot wet spot. I could barely take standing here. "This," I said and pressed harder, "is mine."

A low moan came from her throat. I couldn't take anymore. Forget the towel. I grabbed her and scooped her up and carried her to my room. I placed her on my bed and my lips were on hers. I wanted her. I needed her. I wanted to consume her. I pressed my lips to her mouth and with a gasp her lips opened to me and our tongues entangled. I explored her mouth. My hands pressed up over her body.

"Take it off," she whispered. I pulled her tank top over her head and unclasped her bra. Her pretty breasts with the tight pink nipples begged to be sucked. I'd thought of these breasts for days. Dreamed of licking them, sucking them, letting her nipple slide in and out of the heat of my mouth. I buried my lips against her breasts. I suckled one nipple while my hand cupped her other breast. I nipped her and then comforted the spot with my tongue. She moaned and her hips rocked upward into my hard cock.

"Baby, slow it down."

My lips pressed against her belly as my hand continued to knead her breast. Again her hips rolled beneath me. I slid my hand under her shorts and cupped that perfect ass. I pulled her shorts down over her hips. Her pretty lace panties barely covered the spot I wanted. I spread her legs with my hand.

I pressed my lips to the fabric of her panties. "Damn, baby, you are so wet."

"Please Dillon, please," she gasped out.

My poor precious girl, she wasn't even sure yet what she wanted but I wanted to give it to her. I peeled the panties from her skin and a gasp came from her. I spread her legs and placed one knee over each of my shoulders. Her body tensed. I knew no one had ever been this close to her pussy before, this was so intimate. I looked up at her—she had to see the want in my eyes, the desire, the fact that I loved being the only man who'd had his face between her legs. I wanted to always be the only man who touched her here.

"Baby, it's beautiful," I said. I flicked my tongue along the edges of her lips. She gasped and her hips pressed upward. I pressed them back down and gently opened the folds of her. I kissed along the edge, so wet. "Baby, you taste so good."

Her breath was so short, so shallow, and I was rock hard. I fought the voice in my head that screamed for me to roll upward and shove my cock into her hard and fast. I wanted so much more for her; I wanted to make her come with my hands, my mouth, my lips, my tongue. I wanted to taste her and tantalize her and make her feel so safe and secure that when I finally did plant myself into her, she would never want anyone but me. I would wait for that release. I would wait as long as it took to get that release.

I licked along the edge of her folds. I licked along the circular opening that I wanted to fill.

"Dillon, please, Dillon."

Her hands grabbed my hair and her hips rolled beneath me, which only made me want her more. I wanted to please her. I pressed my lips onto her clit and kissed the hot nub and sucked it, rolling my tongue over her.

"Ohhhh," she yelled.

I pressed two fingers into her hot wet pussy. "Baby, come for me, please baby, I want to feel you come," I said, then let my mouth suck her pussy.

Her hips rolled and her nails dug into my shoulders. Her tight pussy clenched around my fingers as she bucked and rolled and trembled. I watched her face from between her legs. Her beautiful face contorted and twisted with deep pleasure. My tongue slipped over her clit, dancing with it. Her body lost all control at the mere touch of my tongue. I was sure I would never in my life see anything as sexy again.

LANE

MY BODY EXPLODED INTO A THOUSAND fragmented shards. Tiny bits of sparkling pleasure as his tongue rolled between my legs. He sucked and the heat slid through me while his fingers deep inside me throbbed up and back. My hips rolled. I felt each touch, each bit of heat, and I shattered again and again and again. My body trembled as my muscles shook.

"Dillon, oh my God, Dillon," I called in a voice barely recognizable as my own. I came over and over again.

He pulled his mouth away from me and was over me, his lips on mine. For the first time I tasted myself on his lips. He was so big, so hard, between us. I knew what he wanted, I knew what he needed. I clutched him with both hands. My grasp was automatic, instinctual. So long and so hard, the flesh along his penis was springy and soft. His head fell forward with pleasure.

"Oh baby, I…" His belly tightened and he bit his lip. "I can't take it."

He trembled. This big beautiful man trembled with my touch.

"I want you inside me," I whimpered.

I'd never asked anyone to have sex with me. I'd only just had my second orgasm, given to me by another person, and I wanted to feel Dillon inside me. I had a deep need to feel him push against me, to have his hard shaft penetrate me deep and let me ride him.

"Not yet, baby," Dillon said. His voice was a hoarse whisper as though he could barely get the words out of his mouth.

I stroked him. He was so hard, so big. I'd never touched a man's penis before.

"Baby, you're killing me."

He pulled himself to the side of me, and I watched his face as my hands stroked up and down. He opened his eyes and watched me. I grasped from the base of his cock to the tip.

"Like that?" I asked. I didn't know if I was doing it right. I didn't want to hurt him, but it seemed so hard, so strong, so male.

"God yes, baby," he said.

His breath shortened with my touch. I stroked faster. I pulled harder. A moan came over his lips and his hips arched upward. I licked my lips. I knew what I wanted to do but it was so big. Fear trickled through my body. I bent forward and kissed the rounded head. A tiny speck of liquid came from the tip of him.

"Baby, oh, baby, you're going to make me come!"

A thrill raced through my body. A feeling of power and beauty. I wanted to make him come. I wanted to see this gorgeous man weak with desire, desire for me.

I pressed another kiss to his shaft. I opened my mouth. My lips surrounded the end and sucked along the head of him. He tensed and I looked up as his eyes widened. He watched me. His hand was on my shoulder and his mouth was open. His face was ravaged and shadowed. He wanted me. Only me.

I pressed my mouth farther down along his shaft, inserting him into my mouth. I watched him. His gaze never left mine, I felt him holding himself back, holding tight, holding himself from shoving his shaft deep into my throat. Instead, I slid my mouth up and back, and with each slick motion, I got farther down, closer to the base. I reached around and grasped his balls. I pressed and he jolted.

"Baby, I'm gonna come," he said as if warning me.

"Now, baby, I'm gonna come, oh my God, Lane, yes baby, yes baby now."

I pressed deeper and held his cock in my mouth. I wanted to take him, I wanted to swallow. I sucked. The hot semen hit the back of my throat and the tip of his penis was in my mouth. I swallowed and sucked and swallowed the salty taste that was warm in my throat. I watched him; I wanted to make him feel as good as he'd made me feel. His whole body jolted and shook. I let my mouth slowly run up his shaft and I released him from my lips. He trembled and reached out his arms to me and I fell onto his chest. Not sure. Feeling uncertain. I didn't know what I was doing. Of course I'd heard my girlfriends talk about giving head, but I'd never done it.

I looked up at him. His arms held me so tight, so close, as though he would never let me go.

"My little Laney," he whispered. He kissed the top of my head.

"Was it..." I didn't know how to ask. I wasn't sure what to ask.

"Was it?" Dillon pulled back and looked down at me. "Lane, it was amazing. You are amazing. I can't... I mean... I would never expect you to do that, ever, but it was... it was the best thing I've ever had."

A small smile curved across my lips. I settled my head onto his chest. "I've never..." Again the blush flushed my neck and cheeks. I shook my head in embarrassment. "I've never done any of it before."

"Baby, I am the luckiest man on the planet and I want to do everything to prove to you that while I know I'm not worthy of you, I will do my damnedest to try to be."

The confusion I'd felt after the conversation with

Taylor resurfaced with Dillon's words. Sex couldn't change the fears I had, could it? He must have felt me tense or seen the fear slide across my face. Dillon lifted my chin with his hand and forced me to meet his gaze.

"Lane, there is no one else. I don't want anyone else, and I am not going to get tired of you."

I bit my bottom lip. I wanted to believe his words. I needed to believe his words because I didn't want to leave Dillon, but so much of my life seemed to now rest in his hands. What Amanda had said was true—the industry was a small town in a big city and people talked. Everyone but me, it would seem, knew what Dillon did with his readers—so of course everyone would assume that Dillon and I were doing the same things—and now we were. I wondered if he'd ever told those girls that he wanted them forever? That he was going to prove to them that they were special? I wanted to believe him—I wanted him. I bit my lip and closed my eyes. Dillon's arms tightened around me. I couldn't solve these questions now, so I surrendered to the warmth of his arms around me.

CHAPTER 17

<u>DILLON</u>

"SHE'S NOT LEAVING," I SAID TO CHOO.

He leaned against the door that led into the kitchen with his arms crossed. I stirred the red sauce.

"Ever."

"What did you do?"

A guilty look flashed across my face. I worried that my little brother wouldn't be pleased with me and Lane being together.

"You slept with her, didn't you?" His brow furrowed and anger simmered in his eyes.

"I'm not going to discuss this relationship—"

"Relationship? Dillon, you've never had a relationship with a woman. You sleep with them and then leave them. I like Lane. I specifically picked her so you wouldn't sleep with her. She's too good, too pure, too kind. I want her as my friend."

A giant block hardened in my belly with each of my brother's words. All that he said was true of my past, but none of his words were true of my future with Lane.

"Okay, you're right." I let my hard gaze halt his words. "I have slept with women and tossed them aside, but those women weren't Lane. She's different. I get it."

My gaze shifted back to the sauce. I'd never let myself get attached, feel for a woman in any sort of way, not before now. I'd been too focused on my career, on protecting Choo, but Lane hadn't given me a choice. She was like some kind of drug that I needed.

Choo walked to the kitchen island and planted his hands, palms down, on the marble top. "Are you telling me that you're in love with Lane?"

"Love? What the hell, Choo?" I turned toward the boiling pasta and grabbed for the oven mitts. "It hasn't been long enough to be love."

Had it?

"You're cooking for her," Choo said and a tiny smile curled around his lips. He swiped his finger in the red sauce. "I've never seen you cook for a woman, much less let one stay anywhere near you once you've slept with her."

"I didn't sleep with her," I said, my voice soft.

"But you're cooking for her."

I dumped the hot pasta into the colander and the steam billowed upward. "Cooking for Lane does not mean I'm in love."

Did I love Lane? Could I love anyone but my little brother? Did I have the time or patience to love someone? And wasn't I too big of an asshole to actually be loved?

"Right," Choo said. He twisted his lips into a pucker

and plucked one eyebrow upward, giving me a knowing look like he could read the future.

I dumped the pasta into a bowl and my phone rang. I swiped my hands over a kitchen towel and then answered. "Hey, Webber."

"I know you just got back from location and you're probably wrecked, but Boom Boom and I have big news," Webber said.

"Darling," Boom Boom cooed, "welcome back from the heat and the sand."

"Hey," I said. I nodded at Choo for him to finish dinner and he waved to me, already working on the salad. I slipped out the back door toward the yard. "So what's up?"

"Listen, darling, I just got a call from Kiley Kepner's people," Boom Boom said, "and they want you to attend the *Mission Ranger* premiere with Kiley."

My heartbeat skipped upward and a ball of anxiety burrowed into my belly. Kiley was a huge star, hot and on the rise. She was also my costar in the Steve Legend film I was scheduled to film after *Offend and Defend*, if and when my deal closed.

"I haven't met her yet."

"Right," Boom Boom said. I could hear her typing on her computer in the background. "Darling, this isn't meant to be a love match. The two of you together at the premiere is meant to be a publicity event. Get everyone talking, speculating, *thinking* that the two of you are a couple. We want the fans to *believe* there is something going on. We want them to need to know more about you because Kiley digs you."

I glanced up toward Lane's balcony door. Shit. How did I explain this to Lane?

"Dude, don't pass this up," Webber said. "This is huge. You'll be seen with the hottest star in town. Your name will be all over every magazine for weeks, and just as your first film premieres? This is a golden opportunity. You can't buy this kind of publicity. Plus if you do this for Kiley, it completely solidifies your position in the Legend film."

My heart hammered in my chest. Success in the film business was what I wanted. I wanted a career. My success would guaranteed my and Choo's freedom and security. Lane would have to understand—I would have to make her understand.

"Sure, why not?" I closed my eyes. I channeled the guy I had always been, the guy that did everything for himself, for his career. The guy that suddenly I wasn't sure I still was.

"Perfect," Boom Boom said. "I'll chat with Kiley's people. I think the best first time for you two to be seen together will be a couple of days before the premiere. Whet the tabs' appetites. Then they'll be all over you two on the red carpet."

"Great." My heart dropped farther down my chest cavity with every one of Boom Boom's words.

"Also, don't forget the photo spread and interview with *ET Insider*," Boom Boom said. "Tomorrow at noon. You got the details?"

"Yep. The e-mail came through while I was in the desert."

"Great, can't wait to see the photos. You always look delicious in photos, darling." Boom Boom made a purring sound as though she wanted to reach through the phone and rub up against me. "Gotta jump. boys, I'll call you with details on the Kepner thing soon." Boom Boom clicked off the line.

"Dude, this is huge!" Webber said.

This *was* huge. I glanced back up toward Lane's balcony, but maybe not in the way I wanted it to be huge.

"Every woman in America is going to know who you are and every man in America is going to want to be you. Action star, dating the hottest woman in the world! Get ready for the rocket ride," Webber said.

Yeah, soon I was definitely going to be riding a rocket.

LANE

DILLON HAD COOKED FOR ME. WHEN I WALKED onto the back patio and saw the table set with flowers and candles and dinner, my heart kathwapped against my ribs. I sat between Dillon and Choo at the table and listened to them tease each other about growing up together and their childhood. There was a lot of love and a lot of laughter between them. I twirled my fork in my pasta. This night, these moments, felt like being a part of a family. A heat burned the back of my eyes, I hadn't felt like I was part of a family since my mom died.

"Baby, what's wrong?" Dillon reached out his hand and placed it on the back of my hand.

My gaze bounced up at him and then I turned toward Choo. His eyes watched his brother's fingers and then his gaze met mine. A slow smile curled around his lips.

"I guess it was inevitable. I couldn't resist you the minute I met you in HR, why would I think he could?" Choo said.

A weight I didn't even know I carried lifted from my mind. I'd been worried, scared that I would lose my closest friend in L.A. when I got involved with Dillon, but I couldn't help getting involved. I couldn't have stopped myself—I'd tried to stop myself, but the attraction, the want to be close to Dillon, no matter the cost, was too strong for me to repel. My attraction to Dillon was so powerful, so intense, that I'd risked my entire Hollywood future to see where this relationship between the two of us would go.

Dillon squeezed my hand. A tentative smile crossed over his face. "Are you okay?"

"I was just thinking about my mom."

He tightened his lips and nodded. Losing my mom was still fresh in my mind, but I didn't really talk to anyone about her.

"I just…" I looked from Choo at one end of the table to Dillon at the other. "I haven't felt like this, since…" The tears flooded my eyes. "Since before she died."

Dillon's gaze leapt from me to Choo. He looked scared, like he wasn't sure what to do with my tears. I pressed my fingertips to my eyes.

"I'm sorry," I said. A hot embarrassment circled my belly and flooded upward into my face. They'd made me this awesome dinner and we were having such a good time and I'd gone and made myself look like an idiot with my emotions and my tears and—

"Hey, baby," Dillon said. He was up and by my side in an instant. He pulled me to stand and pressed his body to mine. He enveloped me with those giant strong arms and pressed my head to his chest. "Baby, it's okay," he whispered into my hair. A long breath rattled through me. "Shh, baby, it's okay. I have you."

My body trembled and shuddered. The sobs broke through. In Dillon's arms I let loose with my tears. Maybe it was because I felt safe. Maybe it was because I felt close to him. Maybe it was because Choo was there too.

Choo stood and walked toward us and grasped my other hand. We all three walked toward the patio couch.

"I'm so sorry," I said and sniffled, and Choo handed me a tissue. I wiped under my eyes. "You make me this fantastic dinner, and we're having this great time, and then I have an emotional breakdown. I'm so sorry."

Dillon wiped his thumb over my cheek and a sad sort of caring smile came over his face. "Baby, it's okay."

"Grief comes in waves," Choo said. He curled his feet under him.

I closed my eyes. I could feel that. I could also feel some of the pain shifting. When I thought of my mom now, a lot of the time, I could actually smile. I could hear her voice, something she said or did, and a tiny little smile would curve over my face. Other times I would just have this lonely ache that wouldn't go away.

"I... I just miss her. I feel so alone sometimes." I searched Dillon's face.

He wrapped his arm tighter around me and pulled me close to his chest. "Baby, you're not going to be alone ever again," he said and kissed the top of my head.

I glanced at Choo. He watched me and his brother with a gentle smile. "He took care of me too," Choo said. His glance went to Kong, who now lay on Choo's lap.

Then he looked at Bernie, Scorsese, and Spielberg sprawled out on the tiles in front of us. "These guys too." Choo stroked Kong. "My big brother likes to give lost things a home."

I turned my wet eyes toward Dillon. He met my gaze and his hand stroked through my hair. His lips met mine and the heat flooded through me. I knew that I was different for Dillon, that this—what was between us—was different for Dillon, and that oddly enough, even with all my fears, I had a home here, with him.

CHAPTER 18

LANE

"COME WITH ME TODAY," DILLON GASPED OUT.

I was bent double, grasping my knees with my hands.
He'd convinced me to run from the top of Runyon Canyon
to the bottom, and even though it was downhill and I had
gravity on my side, my chest still heaved. Bernie slurped
water from the bucket at the bottom of the path, and even
Scorsese and Spielberg, who seemed to have boundless
energy, panted and walked in circles. Only Kong still
bounced about as though he were ready to race up the
path to the top of Runyon again.

"Where are you going?"

Dillon stood and turned to me. His physical beauty
stole the breath I'd nearly caught. He was shirtless and his
skin glimmered with sweat in the L.A. sun. I fought the
urge to reach out and touch him, to run my hands over
that body, to claim it as mine.

"You like what you see?" A wicked smile teased his lips.

"I do," I said. I smiled back, a little coy in my reply.

He took two steps toward me and wrapped his hands around my waist. "You better stop looking at me that way," he said. He bent down and his lips nuzzled my neck. The scent of him, outdoorsy and sweaty, filled my nose and heat swirled between my legs. "Or I'll take you home and make you pay for those looks."

His hand smacked my behind and my eyes widened in surprise. Not just surprise at the spank but at the heat that throbbed through me with his touch. He pressed his lips to mine, and desire spiraled through me. He pulled away before I wanted the kiss to end.

"Will you come with me to the photo shoot today?" he asked.

"I have a gazillion scripts to read for you."

His lips thinned and disappointment at my response pulsed over his face.

"Bring them with you," he said. "Read while they take pictures of me." He nibbled at the corner of my mouth.

How could I possibly say no to him?

"I mean, if you can keep your eyes off me." A teasing smiled cascaded over his face.

I rolled my eyes toward the blue cloudless sky. "You think you're pretty hot, don't you?"

He was hot. Dillon was fabulously hot and sexy, and everything that any woman in the entire world could want. His fingertips teased the top edge of my running shorts and drifted down over my hip. The hot spot between my legs throbbed.

"Don't you?" He pressed forward and his hard desire

dug into me. A hardness that made me want to say yes to him about anything, about everything. Dillon created a physical desire in me, but there was more—I wanted him close, I wanted to know him, to talk to him, to be with him all the time.

"Okay," I breathed out on a whisper. I bit my bottom lip and fought the desire to press against him like a cat in heat. "I'll go with you today."

DILLON

LANE WAS SO HOT. IF THERE'D BEEN BUSHES nearby, I would have picked her up off the trail and taken her behind them and peeled every stitch of clothing off her at the park. Instead, I loaded her and the pack into the Escalade and drove home. My cock was so hard. I needed some relief.

I jetted into the house. My intention was to get Lane into my shower. I wanted to feel her body. I wanted to lather her and wash her hair and let her perfect skin slip under my hands. I wanted to wash every speck of dust and every drop of sweat from her. Her hand in mine, we walked through the kitchen. I waved hello to Mathilde and steered Lane straight to my bathroom. Straight to my shower. The need to see her body, to touch her, to be near her consumed me.

I was worried about the photo shoot today. I didn't mind standing in front of a camera and saying lines—I liked pretending to be someone else—but I wasn't looking forward to today. I felt so exposed, so vulnerable. With still photography, I couldn't hide behind a character. I wasn't meant to be another person today when they shot those photos, I was meant to be me, to be Dillon MacAvoy. Lane made me feel strong. She made me feel right. She made me feel like I was exactly who and what I was supposed to be, no matter the changes taking place what seemed to be every second of my life.

I burst through my bedroom door, turned, saw those big beautiful blue eyes, and got no farther. I pressed my lips to hers. She gasped. I pressed harder. My kiss was rough and filled with need. My kiss held heat and want. Lane surrendered to the demand of my lips and her mouth opened to me.

Her hips pressed into me. I reached down and pulled her sports bra off her body. Her breasts were in front of me, beautiful and perfect. I bent my head and stroked my tongue over a tight nipple. Lane's hands clenched my arms and I sucked her nipple harder, rolling it in the heat of my mouth. Her head fell back. A low moan came from her throat. My hand slid down and over the fabric of her running shorts and my fingers pressed between her legs.

"Dillon," she moaned.

I was nearly undone with the sound of my name on her lips, a sound that contained want and pure pleasure. I made Lane feel like this. I made Lane nearly crumple to the floor with pleasure. I possessed Lane.

I rolled her running shorts over those beautiful hips and she stepped out of them. She wore only a tiny lace thong and I let my fingertips dance along the edge. Her hands fumbled and tore at my shirt and then yanked the fabric up over my head. She pulled her lips from mine and pressed them to my chest. Heat seared in the spots where her lips moved against my flesh. Her hands dug under my shorts and she grasped my cock. For a girl who'd just been awakened, she was ready for more. I pressed my finger between the lips of her pussy. She was hungry and greedy with want.

"Baby, you're so wet."

She clutched me. I circled my finger over her clit.

"Oh, Dillon, yes," she moaned.

I slid two fingers into her and pulled in and out while I kissed her breasts.

"Come for me, baby," I whispered. "Come for me again."

I grasped her ass with one hand and she lifted her leg. My fingers played along her most sensitive spot. I watched her. I loved watching Lane's face when she came. I could feel a deep pressure building in me as I watched her face contort and change. Her hips rolled forward into my hand. She pressed up and back as my fingers massaged her clit and pumped in and out of her slick entrance.

"Come, baby, come for me."

Her eyes opened and her gaze locked on mine. Her face tensed and her body, like a tight string, pulled even tighter. Her pussy clenched around my fingers. I couldn't stand it any longer—I had to taste her, I had to have her in my mouth. I pushed her backward onto my bed and pressed my lips to her pussy, sucking, pulling, teasing.

"Dillon!" Lane yelled. She shattered while she called my name.

LANE

I PRESSED UP FROM DILLON'S BED, BREATHLESS. His lips pleasured me again and again and again. I looked down at him, and his gaze met mine. His lips pressed to the inside of my thigh and then he rose, reached out his hand, and pulled me to stand. He was hard between us.

"I need a shower," he said. His eyes glanced down. "A really cold shower."

I pressed toward him. His penis rubbed against my belly.

"I want you," I whispered. I felt his hardness jerk with my words.

He closed his eyes. Desire sharpened his jaw. "Baby..." He opened his eyes and pulled a piece of my bed-head hair behind my ear. "I want you too." His voice was throaty and thick with lust. "But"—his gaze locked with mine—"I want it to be right."

My hand stroked up his shaft. He tensed.

"Baby, I'm trying to be good here."

I pulled harder. My grip tightened.

"Lane." He clasped his hands to my shoulders. "Baby, you only get one first time, and I want you to be ready. I want it to be special."

I knew he was right. I knew he was fighting the urge to sleep with me. I could see the fight in his eyes, the battle he waged. I let go of him and walked toward the bathroom door. I glanced over my shoulder. "Let's get that shower."

DILLON

SHE LOOKED BETTER WET, IF THAT WAS POSSIBLE.

The rivulets of water danced over her skin. I was so hard that I was uncomfortable, but it was worth the pain to see Lane in the water. She turned to me, her caramel-colored hair slicked back, her breasts wet, the water running over her belly, pussy, and thighs. She clutched the base of my cock with both hands. Her sudden grasp nearly sent me to my knees. I bent forward and pressed the palms of my hands against the wall of the shower.

"Are you okay?" She looked a little frightened with my response.

"Yeah," I whispered. My cock was still in her hand.

"Does it feel okay?"

I closed my eyes with the pleasure of her hand stroking me with the warm water. "Lane, baby, it feels better than okay."

I opened my eyes and her smile told me she was pleased. She was finding her female power. She was stepping into the place a woman owned. Each time we were together, I felt her grow stronger, more alive, more assured. I loved experiencing each moment with her. She wanted to keep moving, to keep exploring, to keep feeling, and that excited me.

Her hand stroked up over my shaft, a slow hard movement and then back down. I leaned into it. She pressed her lips close to my ear. "Do you think about me?" she whispered.

Heat throbbed down my spine. "Yes." I didn't want the pleasure of her touch to end. I leaned into her stroke. "Faster," I gasped out.

Her hand stroked harder and faster, pumping me with more urgency. My breath shortened, coming in quick, hard gasps.

"What do you think about?"

The control in her voice, in my little innocent Laney, unnerved me, almost undid me. I opened my mouth to answer but was consumed with the pleasure her hand was giving me as it pulled on my cock.

"Answer me," she said.

I looked at her and saw a dark twinkle in her eyes. She liked the control. She liked her ability to make me feel, to nearly bring me to my knees.

"I think about putting my cock in your tight pussy," I said.

Her stroke moved faster with my words.

"I think about how there's never been a cock in your pussy and how tight you'll be."

I wrapped my arm around her and pulled her close. She had no idea what she was messing with; she had no idea how hard it was for me not to slam her against the shower wall and ram my cock into her. Fuck the first time. Fuck the sweetness of it. Fuck. All I wanted to do was fuck.

I pressed my lips to her ear. "I think about how my cock will be the only cock that your pussy ever feels."

She gasped. I grabbed for her pretty little tit and my mouth clamped over hers. A dark thrust burst through me and I came. A jet of heat pulsed upward and I came all over Lane's pretty little hand.

LANE

I RODE IN THE BACK OF THE ESCALADE, CURLED

up against Dillon. I felt so lush, so comfortable, so alive. I held an open script in my hand but wasn't really reading.

"So what are photo shoots like?" I asked.

"They're boring as hell," Dillon said. "But I have to do them. It's promo for the film."

I closed the script in my lap and looked at Dillon. I thought of our shower together and hot tingles curled through me and licked at the spot between my legs. He settled his hand on my thigh.

"I have the interview and then the photos. Usually they're separate, but this time the interviewer wanted to do it all at once."

Bob pulled the Escalade to a stop in front of a private home in Malibu. The gate opened and we pulled into the drive. I looked out the window. People scurried along the drive with racks of clothes, giant lights on poles, and a makeup mirror on wheels. A guy with a camera pointed toward the front of the house.

"I told them they had me for three hours," Dillon said. "That's it."

Bob opened the door and Dillon slid from the seat. I followed. I reached for his hand, and he squeezed mine and then dropped it as a woman with thick, shoulder-length black hair approached.

"Dillon!" she cooed and pressed forward to kiss each of his cheeks.

"Hey, Boom Boom," he said and pecked both her cheeks in return.

Her gaze passed Dillon and skimmed over me. She waited for an introduction or explanation of my presence.

"This is Lane," he said. "My new reader."

My heart dropped from my chest and a deep hole

pitted my belly. I felt as though I inhabited the shadow of what was real with Dillon's statement. I'd thought my introduction would be different after how intimate we'd been just hours before. I wasn't sure what I expected, but I didn't think I was *just* Dillon's reader.

"We have a ton of scripts to get through, and I thought Lane and I could talk about them between setups."

Boom Boom nodded and seemed to dismiss me with her eyes. I obviously meant no more to Dillon than my ability to read his scripts. After today in his room, in his shower, the idea that I was still just his reader and the way he said it to Boom Boom, especially, hurt.

"We're doing the setups in the back of the house," Boom Boom said. "She can sit at the table on the deck. But they need you in makeup, my darling."

Dillon and Boom Boom disappeared into the house together. I stood alone and watched the crew for the photo shoot finish their prep. I walked past the solid wooden front door and into the house. The inside was bright white and was open straight through to a brilliant view of the ocean. A gasp shot out over my lips. I hadn't ever been this close to the ocean. I walked toward the wall of windows and looked out at the water crashing upon the shore. I wanted to go and touch the water. To let my toes squish the sand. To feel the waves tickle my toes.

"You're Dillon's reader?" a girl with curly hair asked.

I nodded.

"I'm going to set you up right over there," she said and pointed to a small table in the corner of the deck with an umbrella beside it. "That way you can work and be close enough to talk about his scripts when we change setups."

I nodded and followed her to my spot on the deck.

DILLON

I NEVER MINDED ACTING FOR THE CAMERA, BUT I didn't like posing for one. Not even that giant underwear ad that they trotted out on every entertainment show whenever they mentioned my name.

I let the photographer for today's shoot move me and tell me how to cock my hip and turn my body. There were two setups where I had on unzipped jeans and no shirt. I couldn't even look at Lane while we shot those. I couldn't go near her. I didn't really want to explain why I had a hard-on to the photographer and the entire crew. I mean, it happened, they would get it, but it wasn't like I was working with some outrageous model right now. What could I say to them... "Uh, I'm hard for my reader"?

"Dillon, that was fabulous," Boom Boom purred. She walked over and ran her fingernail over my bicep. A sigh of appreciation passed over her lips.

"So now, Sam"—Boom Boom nodded her head toward a woman with a mane of thick blond hair—"is going to do the interview." Boom Boom lowered her voice. "Remember, be yourself, but we are selling this amazing image that is you. Hot. Young. Single. Dangerous. Unattached." Boom Boom leaned closer to me. "That last one is particularly important." Her eye bounced from me toward the table with the umbrella where Lane sat. "Especially with the coup of Kiley Kepner at the premiere."

My heart jerked in my chest. I glanced toward Lane, who'd patiently sat through two hours of me taking photos. I'd gone by twice to check on her and each time she'd told me about the script she was reading. The idea of being without Lane, with someone else, made my stomach uneasy. I wasn't unattached anymore, but I knew I needed to appear that way for my career.

I walked toward Samantha. Boom Boom hovered in the background. I knew from prior interviews she would remain close so that if the questions got too intimate or the interviewer went too far afield, I could look at Boom Boom and she would come and find a way to get me out of the interview.

Sam wore a low-cut top that showed lots of cleavage and a high-cut skirt that showed lots of thigh. Funny, I would have been all over that with my charm, but with Lane sitting near me, I didn't have any interest. After the "hellos" and "nice to meet yous," Sam got into the interview.

"There isn't anyone special in your life?" she asked with a hinting lilt in her voice. She cocked her eyebrow at me, and just beyond her Boom Boom waited and looked at me. I glanced from Sam to Boom Boom to Lane, who was at the far table. She was bent over the table, her eyes eating up the words on the script she was reading. Her caramel-colored hair hung in a wave over her face and teased against her jaw and neck. *She* was special. Lane was special to me. She wasn't just some toss-away girl.

I focused my gaze back on Sam and turned up my high-watt smile. This was my career, and right now, according to my team, what would sell the most movie tickets was the idea that I was single and available, not yet settled down.

"Sam, not yet, but believe me, I am always on the

lookout for that special girl. The one that will complete me." I looked up and locked onto Sam's eyes. "I haven't met her yet, but I will. I can't wait to meet that one girl who I want to spend my entire life with."

Sam blinked twice. Her pulse pitter-pattered faster. Was she swooning? This hard-core Hollywood interviewer was actually swooning at my words. I jerked the corner of my lip upward. I was good. I was so good. I could even convince Sam that I was still single and hadn't found the right girl for me when I was sure I could no longer convince myself of that fact.

Wow, I *was* an awesome actor. I glanced toward Boom Boom, who nodded and gave me a thumbs-up. Then my gaze glanced toward the right, toward Lane.

My heart jerked in my chest. The corners of my mouth dropped.

Lane was gone.

CHAPTER 19

LANE

I COULDN'T LISTEN TO DILLON'S WORDS. I couldn't look at his self-sure grin. I couldn't listen to Dillon tell the interviewer he hadn't found the girl of his dreams yet, but when he did, he'd be willing to spend his entire life with her. Dillon's words carved a hole in my heart. Each one sliced through the fantasy I'd created about our relationship and let the sharp light of reality blind me.

I slipped down the side steps of the deck, away from Dillon, away from his interview. I walked out onto the sand still warm from the sun that now hovered low on the horizon. I walked toward the dark brown line where the water licked the earth. A breeze blew through my hair. I crossed my arms over my chest, not because I was cold but because of the hurt that wound through my chest and tightened around my heart. I walked toward the water's edge, toward the vast blue sea.

The forever blue and the sun just beyond made me think of my mom. I felt close to her here. Perhaps she had walked on this very beach, in this very spot, when she was my age. When, for that brief moment in her life, she had chased her dream.

I wasn't Dillon's forever type of girl. I wasn't the right girl for him. He needed someone who could help his career. Maybe someone who was an actress, an actress with a name, an actress already a success. His words today made everything clear. I hurt, but I wasn't angry. He hadn't made me any promises, and I hadn't made him any in return. Maybe we were using each other. I was using him for a job, for career advancement, for a way to get my foot in the door of the industry. I'd taken the job as his reader because of the promise of a permanent gig if I stuck out the summer. I closed my eyes to the brilliant breeze and the fresh, salty smell of the sea. It's just... being Dillon's reader had become more than just work for me. Being with Dillon, for me, was more than just physical attraction. I had fallen for him. I had fallen for Dillon. I was a complete fool, but at least I was aware of the kind of fool I was. This would never be permanent, this thing with Dillon and me. I would leave in August and he would remain free.

"Lane!" I turned toward Dillon's voice.

He ran toward me across the sand. I hadn't realized how far from the beach house I'd walked. The setting sun danced on his skin. The wind blew through his black hair. Dillon was pure masculine beauty. How could I, Lane Channing from Kansas, ever expect that this man, this gorgeous-beyond-words man, would ever be only mine? He wouldn't. With that sudden burst of knowledge, with that acceptance, a freedom took hold in my heart. I would be with Dillon this summer. Dillon would be mine, as much as was possible, for the summer, and then I would go. I would leave. Dillon would be free.

"Lane." He halted beside me. His eyes carried confusion. He held out his hand to me. "Laney, I'm sorry, I had to... it's for my career. It's a brand that they want me to be. They need me to appear free and unattached and—"

I pressed my finger to his lips. I looked into those eyes that glowed in the late-day golden sun, those beautiful blue eyes. I didn't need to hear anything more. He took my finger from his lips and tilted his chin down toward me. He wrapped me tight in his arms.

"When you weren't there..." He drew a deep breath. "When you weren't there, it scared me." He glanced toward the ocean and then back to me. "Don't leave me like that again." He grasped my chin with his fingers and tilted my face up to where his gaze met mine. "Please, Lane, don't disappear." He pulled me tighter, and my cheek pressed against that hard chest. "You mean so much to me. I'm sorry I hurt you. I don't want to hurt you."

I bit my bottom lip. I fought back the tears that flooded my eyes. I was falling in love with Dillon MacAvoy. A love that could never be returned. I could have my summer, I could have him for a while, but the girl that would have him for forever—I knew for certain that girl wouldn't be me.

DILLON

I HELD HER TIGHT TO MY SIDE ALL THE WAY home. I knew that my words had hurt her; I could see it in her eyes. I was certain that she understood why I'd said the things I had in the interview. Those words weren't my truth. Those words weren't my reality. Those words I told Sam were about me building a brand. Me being a star. Me creating a career. Once I was solid, once I had enough money to feel safe, for me to feel safe for Choo, then... then I would tell the whole world that Lane was mine.

Mine. I'd never wanted any girl to be mine before Lane. The sun had set by the time we returned to the house. Mathilde had left dinner, but neither of us was hungry. I felt raw from the fear and ache that had hammered through me when I'd looked up and Lane was gone. Gone after she heard the words I said. Choo had left a note saying he'd taken the pack to Jackson's for the night. I walked up the stairs, holding Lane's hand. We got to the door of my room.

"I want you to stay in here," I said. My fingertips were on her chin.

"Okay."

"Not just tonight," I said. "I want you to stay in here, with me, always. I want you to move your things from your room to mine."

Her eyes widened. I knew this was a big step for her. This was a big step for me. I didn't let women sleep in my bed. Traces of confusion and want and sadness inhabited her eyes. I wanted to chase away all those fears. I needed those feelings to be gone. I wanted her to be sure that this was what I wanted, that she was what I wanted.

"Dillon, I don't know if—"

I couldn't hear no. I didn't want to hear no. I pressed my lips to hers. She opened her mouth to me and my tongue slid over her lips. Heat fired through me, but I held back. I couldn't scare her off with my want, with my need. She had to know, I had to let her know that this desire for her in my room wasn't just physical. My desire for her was mental, my desire was emotional. An empty ache had pierced through me when Lane had disappeared. I pulled my lips from hers.

"Lane," I said, my voice low, my forehead pressed against hers, "this isn't about sex. We don't ever have to have sex."

"You... you don't want to sleep with me?" she asked. The confusion in her voice shredded my insides.

"I've wanted to since the first night you were here." I met her eyes. "I need you to know, this is about you and how you make me *feel*." I ran both my hands up and down her arms. "When I'm with you, I feel..." I stopped. These words... all these words... "I feel whole. Like a missing piece of me has finally snapped into place. I want you with me. I want to wake up and see your face. I want to fall asleep and see your face." I pressed my lips to her nose and then her eyes. "I just want to see this face all the time."

A smile slipped across her mouth and I pressed my lips to hers.

"Okay." She slipped her hand from mine and turned down the hall.

"Where are you going?"

"To get my things."

"No, baby, I want you in here now. We'll get your stuff later."

She followed me into my room and I closed the door. I sat on the bed and she stood in front of me. I wanted her. I wanted her with a heat I could barely stand. Tonight I wanted to be near her. To be next to her. To feel her body pressed to mine. My fingers ran up over her arm. Her eyes were locked onto mine. I reached up and unfastened each button of her shirt. I pushed the blue-checked fabric over her shoulders and slid it down her arms. She was perfection. My fingers unsnapped the button of her white shorts and slid them down over her hips. She stood in front of me in a pink lace bra and tiny thong panties. My eyes ate her up from her face to her feet. My breath was short and I could barely stand not pressing every inch of my body against hers. My cock pressed hard against my jeans.

She leaned forward, placed her hands on my thighs, and pressed her lips to mine. My hands roamed up the sides of her body and unsnapped her bra from the back. Then I slid a finger under the tiny little string of her panties. She shivered. A shiver that nearly undid me. I tugged them down over her hips and she stepped out of them. My finger glided up her thigh as I watched her face. She bit her lip as I teased my fingers upward to where her leg met her body. I pressed over her tiny belly to her V.

She gasped and held her breath. My other hand clasped her breast. I pulled on it and then gently drew her forward to me. I watched her as I slipped her pink nipple into my mouth. A sharp inhale came over her pout of a mouth. My fingers slid up over her folds and danced across her clit as I sucked on her nipple. She widened her legs. I pulled my mouth away from her nipple and let my lips brush across her chest.

"Baby, you're wet." I slipped two fingers inside her tight pussy. "Why are you always so wet for me?"

Her hips rocked toward me as my thumb massaged her clit. "Oh, Dillon," she moaned.

She pressed her hands into my shoulders and bent her head to the side in pleasure. Her mane of hair drifted over my face and shoulder. Her neck, her pussy, her body—heat surged through me. I slipped my hand from her and flipped her onto my bed. I couldn't take her, I wouldn't take her, not yet, she was too pure, it was too soon, but I would make her come again and again. I would watch the waves of pleasure wash over her. She lay under me. My lips teased along her breasts and down her belly. Her hand twisted in my shirt and I pulled it over my head. She leaned forward and pulled me into a kiss. Her greedy mouth bit at my bottom lip while her hand fought the button of my jeans. She unsnapped them and slid them off my hips. My cock sprang free, so hard between us. She grasped for it with her hands.

"Baby, no, please, I can't," I gasped out.

With one touch of her pretty little hand on my cock I was going to explode. I knew it. She was naked beneath me. All that skin, those beautiful breasts—I could barely stand not pushing myself into her. I pressed my lips to her belly. Her hands grasped my hair and her hips arched upward and pressed against me. Her body craved my cock; her pussy was searching for me. Lane had a greedy want for me, and it was a want that I needed to quench. But now, tonight, wasn't how I wanted Lane's first time to be.

LANE

I PUSHED HIS JEANS OVER HIS HIPS. HIS PENIS sprang free. It was there in front of me. So big. So thick. I grasped it with my hand. I wasn't as afraid as the first time I'd stroked him. I gripped it and the low aching moan that came from Dillon made the hot slick spot inside me want him more. He dropped his head forward and shut his eyes.

"Baby, please," he gasped out through his teeth. He opened his eyes and peered into mine. "I can't take that. I'm going to explode."

I teased my hand once more down his shaft. I wanted him. I wanted to give all of myself to him. I wanted this memory, the memory of our summer together, to be what I took back with me, what I carried forward. I knew we wouldn't be together forever, I knew he couldn't ever have just one girl, and if he did, it would be a girl much different than me, but I was ready for this moment with Dillon.

"I want you," I whispered.

His eyes widened with my words. His face looked shadowed. I reached my hand up to his cheek. "Please, I want you."

He gave his head a gentle shake. "Lane, baby, it doesn't have to be now, it doesn't have to be ever. We can wait, we can just be together. I don't want—"

I pressed my fingertips to his lips like I'd done earlier this day. I wasn't giving in to Dillon, I was taking control of what I wanted. I wanted this. I wanted him even if it was for this short while.

"Don't make me beg." A small smile curved over my lips.

I reached out and pressed my hands to his hardness and again Dillon shuddered. A tremble raced through his body with my touch. "Please, I want you to make love to me. I want you to be my first."

A serious look took over his face. He stared deep into my eyes as if I was giving him the world, and in a way I was. I was giving him my world, my heart, my love. I wouldn't ever forget this moment. It would be forever seared into my mind. Dillon. His body. His arms. His touch. His kiss. Each time I remembered our summer, this man, I would remember this moment.

"Are you sure?" He settled onto his side beside me and his fingertips traced up my belly and around my breast. He swallowed. "I need you to be sure."

I nodded. I was scared. I was nervous. But this was what I wanted. With all my heart I wanted this. "I'm sure."

His lips were on mine with a soft, sensuous caring. Not hunger, not just possession, but more, as though he understood what I was giving him by making him my first. He pulled back and looked into my eyes.

"I need you to know before we do this. Before..." His eyes traveled over me. "I want you with me whether we do this or not. I've never wanted someone to be mine, but I feel it here." He touched his chest. He looked away from me. "I... I don't deserve you." His gaze landed on me. "But I can try."

I smiled a soft smile at him. A half-lidded smile. His lips grasped mine. His hand pressed down over my mound and slid into the wet of me.

"Baby, you're so hot," he growled. "So wet."

My hips arched upward with his touch and his words. His words made me feel hot and fierce; they made me feel good. Two fingers slid inside me and his thumb brushed over my nub. A fire shot off inside me, a fire that raked across my skin and shattered through my body. His mouth suckled my nipple and his eyes watched me. He watched me as I arched and rolled under his touch, unable to control the movements of my body.

"Dillon, please," I gasped. My voice was hoarse and raspy; I couldn't contain the want that seared between my legs.

"Baby, you don't have to do this, we don't have to do this," he said and continued to make me climb with his fingers deep inside me. He circled my most tender spot with his fingers and pressed into my body.

"I want my first time to be with you," I gasped out. My hips rolled up and back under his touch. "Dillon, please, I want you inside me."

He gasped and a low moan combined with a growl crossed his lips. A sound that caused tingles to shoot through me. A sound of possession that stirred something deep within me. A sound that let me know that with this, with me giving myself to him, with this act I have become his. No matter what happened after this moment, I would be forever his.

I heard the drawer beside the bed slide open and the rip of foil. I watched as he pressed the condom onto his thick shaft and unrolled it over the head and down to the base. A shiver burst through me. A hint of fear. How can that fit inside me? I looked away from Dillon's throbbing penis and into his eyes. He watched me. I saw a gentleness next to the desire and I knew, I knew this moment was right. I knew Dillon would make this first time right for me. I trusted him. I loved him.

He rolled over onto me. His eyes never left mine and he spread my thighs with his knee. He held his body above mine. His strong arms, arms that I wanted to remain lost in for a lifetime, were on either side of me. His tattoo was next to my face. I loved the shape of it; I loved the shape of him. His hard, flat belly pressed against mine and I felt the tip of his penis nudging my thigh. He bent forward and his lips grasped at mine. I clasped the back of his head with my hands and pulled my fingers through his thick black hair.

My hips arched upward, anticipating him, wanting him without really understanding what I wanted but knowing that he, his long shaft, would fill me and complete me in a way that I needed.

He gently let the tip nudge into the entrance of me. "Lane, baby, you are so tight."

I gasped and pressed upward, but he held himself still. He reached between us and found my nub. He pressed his fingers to that spot. My hips bucked upward, but he held himself still. He didn't push into me. I writhed to the edge of shattering. My heart pounded in my chest. He waited. The strain on his face was pain mixed with pleasure. He nudged into me. My entrance stretched. My body was so tight around just the tip of him. The burn seared with the pleasure. His hardness stretched me. The hot burn of his thickness pulled through me.

"Baby, Lane, baby, oh my God, baby, so good," he moaned out.

His eyes were bright blue with deep black pools in the

center. His eyes locked on mine and watched me, and I returned his gaze. I wanted to see each moment. I wanted to sear each second into my brain.

I gasped. He was so huge inside me, and I was so full. I couldn't take it, how would I take all of him? He was still. My body stretched around his. My body settled around him. The desire for all of him, to feel every solid inch, burst within me. I wanted to feel all of him. I wanted him to fill me. His fingers played along my slick nub and caused me to grow wetter, to want him deeper. His mouth suckled my breast and I closed my eyes.

A tsunami of pleasure burst over me. I opened my eyes. He watched me. I knew he wanted my gaze locked with his. I arched my hips the tiniest bit and he pressed forward, still watching my face. Pain sliced through me, pain laced with the deepest pleasure. I gasped and he pushed into me. He filled my want with his hardness.

I was full. My body stretched tight. My nails grasped his arms. He was buried deep in me and I felt the pleasure and the pain. Dillon pulled back. Emptiness engulfed me and his absence from my body was blinding. Almost too much to survive. My eyes sought his and his gaze reassured me. He pressed back into me with a long, slow, solid thrust.

I gasped a sharp, hard gasp. This feeling, this thrust, was unfamiliar and yet something I longed for and needed, not even knowing what I was doing but knowing I wanted this, that I needed this.

"Lane, oh Lane," he said. "I've never... it's never been like this."

With a deep growl, he thrust into me. My hips rolled upward to meet him. The pleasure grew with the slowness of his movement. In his face I saw that he held back, that it took all his strength to hold back. He moved slowly and let my body surrender to him, open to him, envelop him.

He was hard where I was soft. I was empty where he was full. I clasped the back of his head and pulled his lips to meet mine. I needed to taste him, to feel his tongue slip into my mouth. The hunger was deep and thick within me. My greedy lips pressed against his and my body rolled beneath him. I pressed my hands to his shoulders and pulled.

"Faster, Dillon, please, faster."

He jerked his lips from mine and our eyes locked. His maleness slid from me and he pushed into me harder and faster and deeper with a thrust that penetrated me. I gasped with the pleasure of it. Again he withdrew and thrust into me. His eyes watched me. I grasped the back of his arms and held on to him, held on to this.

"Lane, baby, like this? Do you like it, baby?"

The smile that rolled across my face made the possession in his eyes grow deeper. He thrusted deeper and I felt myself dancing along the edge of vast pleasure. The curling heat licked through me, a fire that wanted to explode.

"Oh Dillon. Oh God, Dillon." My sounds were not words. These sounds were moans, loud shrieks. The noise of my own voice sounded foreign to my ears, but with each one, Dillon growled and thrust deeper into me. My nails raked down his back and clenched his tight ass. I pushed him deeper inside me. His entire body went to stone.

"Lane, baby, I'm going to come."

My hips rolled upward. My gaze was latched onto his. I

would come with him, I would shoot over this edge with him.

"Come for me, baby. Lane, come for me hard." He growled in my ear. His eyes met mine.

An erotic moan escaped over my lips. "Dillon…"

I couldn't get close enough, he couldn't get deep enough. He pushed hard into me; I clasped his ass and he thrust deep. My mouth grasped his shoulder and there was the sharp taste of salt on my tongue. His skin muffled my screams as I let myself go. I erupted over the edge and pleasure thundered into me. His movements were fast and uncontrollable now as he thrust and thrust and thrust into me.

"Lane, oh God, Lane." The sound of our skin slapping together was loud and filled with pleasure. "My sweet, sweet Lane." His body shuddered, and there was a tightness in him as he paused on the edge before going over. With one final gasp, Dillon stopped.

He collapsed onto me. His eyes locked with mine, and he gave me a soft gentle look, a look filled with love. He said nothing. I didn't need words—I saw all his feelings for me in his eyes. He pressed his lips to mine.

Our bodies were tangled. He slid to the side and out of me. My body instantly missed the fullness of him inside me. His arms wrapped around me, and I looked into his eyes. I saw him. Who he was. I saw the kindness and there was love, love for me, love for us.

His lips grazed mine. "You're mine now."

My heart was full. I didn't know for how long these feelings would last for him, but for me this moment would last forever. In this moment, bound in Dillon's arms, I felt certain that his words to me were true.

CHAPTER 20

LANE

WE STOOD BESIDE THE FRONT DOOR AND DILLON
held my hands. We'd spent the last three days wrapped in
each other's arms. I'd barely read a script and we'd barely
left his bed. I wanted to go with him while he was on location in Moab.

"Come to set with me," Dillon said.

"Who'll walk these guys?"

I looked at the four faces and sixteen paws seated in a
semicircle around Dillon and me. They all looked up at us.
The pack seemed happy with this new arrangement. They
spent most nights waiting in the hall until Dillon opened
the door to his room and then they piled in and lay at the
foot of Dillon's monstrous bed. It seemed so natural to
Kong, Scorsese, Spielberg, and Bernie that Dillon and I
would now share a room.

"Choo?" Dillon asked.

"Uh, negative, big brother." Choo rounded the corner. He wore skinny jeans, boots, and a T-shirt under a jacket. "I have work and then I have Jackson." He flashed us a smile, winked at me, then teasingly pressed out his lips, and made a big smooching noise.

"I am so good," he called from the staircase. "Look what I managed to do. I found the perfect girl for my big brother to love." Choo disappeared upstairs. I looked back at Dillon. He pressed his forehead to mine.

"I am going to miss you," Dillon said. He wrapped his arms around me. I'd miss him too. Our time together was whooshing by and some time apart, some time alone, would be good for me. I hoped it would prepare me for the ultimate absence that was destined to take place in less than a month. Yes, Dillon cared about me and I cared about him—but an impermanence hovered around this relationship. I knew I'd never feel this safe, this loved, this protected, this happy. I also knew that happiness could slip away in an instant. I knew we hadn't discussed a future together, our future together, or even if there was an "our future."

"I'll be fine," I said. "I'm supposed to see Amanda this week."

Dillon nodded. I seemed to have acquired one female friend in Amanda Legend. I wasn't certain why she wanted to be my friend, but I liked her. She made me laugh. I loved her crazy Hollywood stories. I loved how she wasn't high maintenance or entitled like I had expected her to be.

"I'll call you," Dillon said.

Bob opened the door. The studio's private plane was waiting for Dillon. He was already late. His lips pressed to mine and his arms squeezed me close to his body. I felt his hardness pressed against me.

"See what you do to me," he whispered in my ear. I smiled at his comment and he kissed me again. "Miss you," he whispered.

"Miss you too," I whispered back.

He bent down and patted each pup. "Take good care of her, guys," Dillon said. He looked at me once more, smiled, lifted his hand, and then walked out the door.

My heart plopped to my feet. He was gone now for ten days, and while I had tons of scripts to read and the four dogs to keep me company, I knew Dillon had created a permanent dent in my heart. Just the act of him closing the door to go to work had created a sadness within me. I knew he was coming back. I knew his absence wasn't permanent, and still I could barely stand the idea of him being away from me. Of sleeping in his bed without him. I closed my eyes.

This was bad.

Bernie pressed his nose to my palm. I ran my hand over his head. This time without Dillon would be good for me. It would help me prepare for when I had to leave... to go back to school. I pressed my forehead to the closed front door. Who the hell was I trying to kid? Nothing could ever prepare me for the heartbreak that I was destined to feel.

DILLON

MOAB WAS HOT AND DIRTY. I WANTED TO BE

home, with Lane, in bed. My body ached for her. I knew what this meant, I knew what she meant. She was the girl I had to be with, the girl that was meant for my future, but I wanted her now. Choo had been absolutely right with regards to Lane's utter perfection, but absolutely wrong about her untouchability. I wanted Lane, I wanted her presence, her love, even more than I wanted my career.

"Dillon," Webber's assistant said, "I have Webber on the line and I'm putting Boom Boom on now."

This had to be done. My team had to understand that no matter what being with Lane did to my career, I was unwilling to play pretend where Lane was concerned. She had become a nonnegotiable. A week in the desert without her body, her touch, her smile, had proved that to me that I couldn't live without Lane. I couldn't survive without her. I wouldn't survive without her. Of that I was now certain.

"Hey, big D!" Webber said. He sounded pretty pumped.

"Boom Boom is on," Webber's assistant chirped.

"Hello, boys," Boom Boom soothed into the phone with her deep, dulcet tone. I heard her fingers flying across a computer keyboard as we spoke.

"Listen, guys," I said. "I need to talk to you about the *Mission Ranger* premiere."

"We've got the limo, the stylist," Boom Boom said. "The timing is right—"

"It's about Kiley Kepner."

Boom Boom's fingers stopped tapping on her keyboard. "What about Kiley Kepner?" Her tone colder and deadly serious.

Neither Webber nor Boom Boom would be pleased with my decision. I wasn't a known commodity yet; I hadn't yet opened a film.

"I can't go to the premiere with her," I said. I felt better just letting go of the words.

"Why the hell not?" Webber shot out.

"Ahhh," Boom Boom said. "So the rumors are true."

Rumors? "What rumors?" I peered out the side window of my trailer toward the red rocks that surrounded me.

"Rumors, my love, that there is a relationship between you and your current reader," Boom Boom said.

"What the hell?" I plopped down on the leather couch in my trailer.

"You're sleeping with your reader again?" Webber shot out. "I told you I should have found you a guy or some ugly-ass—"

"Cut it, Webber." My tone was cold.

Silence came from the two other phone lines. I'd never spoken sharply to Webber or to Boom Boom. "She's not just my reader and we're not just…" I couldn't bring myself to say the word where Lane was concerned. She was so much more than just a random girl. She was becoming my everything. I needed her the way I needed light. The way I needed air. "She's important to me. I don't care who found out or how, but she's important and our… relationship is important to me too."

I heard a long, exasperated sigh from Boom Boom, and Webber muttered something I couldn't make out.

"Look, I get it, darling," Boom Boom said. She was a publicist and I knew she could spin fast. "The heart wants what the heart wants. But here's the thing—we've already committed to Kiley's people and the premiere is in less than a week. If we bail now and you arrive with some no-name chica... No offense, my darling, you will seriously piss off one of the planet's biggest female stars. And let me assure you when I tell you that you do not want to piss off Kiley Kepner."

"I don't care who I piss off—"

"Of course you don't *now*, darling," Boom Boom purred into my ear. "But you will. You will care when the studios start pulling those seven-figure offers because Kiley Kepner has told them in no uncertain terms that she will not do a film with you, nor will she do a film at a studio that has recently employed you. You are exception-ally good-looking, my love, and very talented, but truly, you are still nobody, at least until the public knows who you are."

My stomach churned. I closed my eyes. What Boom Boom had said was true. The public would have no idea who I was until *Mission Ranger* came out. There was hope —more than hope—that *Mission Ranger* would make bucket loads of money and that the public would love me, and therefore I would have an incredible career. A career that would keep Choo safe from our parents. A career that would allow me to pay for his college. But none of these great things had happened yet.

"Did you close the deal for the Steve Legend film?" I asked Webber.

"Today," Webber said. "But you know Kiley Kepner is the female lead."

"Darling," Boom Boom interjected, "ever since you said yes we've been teasing everyone in town with the idea that you and Kiley are a thing. There are hints all over, but then again if you've been shacked up and on set,

I don't suppose you know. Kiley's people and I just leaked something today. I'm sending you a link to *TMZ* now. Take a look, darling, when we're done."

"Man, just go to the premiere with her, don't commit career suicide now. Wait to go live with the other girl. Once *Mission Ranger* comes out and makes huge bank, you'll be a free man. Okay?"

"Darling," Boom Boom said, "if this girl… what is this girl's name?"

"Lane," I said.

"If Lane truly loves you, and I am sure she does, then she will understand, will she not? She will understand that this is simply part of the Hollywood game that you have to play. You keep your and Lane's relationship under wraps until a couple of days after the premiere, let's say a week. Kiley's people only wanted this supposed 'relationship' with you and her to last seven to ten days."

I scrubbed my hand through my hair. Lane had to understand, didn't she? I loved her. She loved me. She would understand why I needed to play my part in this fake Hollywood relationship. She knew how important Choo and his safety were to me. Lane understood how the industry worked. I was doing this for Choo and for me and even for her… for our future together.

"Okay," I said and sighed. I closed my eyes. I didn't know how I was going to explain this to Lane. How I was going to endure the look of sadness that I was certain I would see in her eyes when I told her I had to go to the *Mission Ranger* premiere with Kiley Kepner. I would make this up to Lane. I would. No matter what I had to do, I would make this up to her.

LANE

"LANEY, OVER HERE!"

I scanned the pool deck of the W and saw Amanda with a drink in hand standing by a cabana and waving.

"Could her figure get any more perfect?" Choo asked.

No, Amanda was pretty perfect with her raven hair and tiny waist and giant boobs. She wore a bright red swimsuit and heels. She had two cabanas side by side. This was just how Amanda rolled. So different than me and my life, but so fun to experience.

Choo and I walked over and she kissed us both on the cheeks. I settled into a lounge chair beside Amanda. She poured champagne into a glass and handed it to me. I pressed my lips together.

"What? You want something different?"

I shook my head no. I pulled the glass to my lips and sniffed. The bubbles tickled my nose.

"Oh my God, you've never had champagne before?"

The corners of my mouth lifted.

"How is that possible?" she asked.

"Beer and vodka," I said.

She reached out her glass and clinked with mine. "To first times."

I tilted my glass to my lips but my brow furrowed. Did she know? Amanda and Choo were becoming close and they were both related to actors who were famous—or Dillon was meant to soon be famous—plus Dillon was doing Amanda's father's next film. I wondered if Choo had let slip that Dillon was my first. Not that it really mattered... or maybe it did.

Sleeping with Dillon was something that was mine to keep. Something to forever hold close to me even after our time together ended. He would forever be the first man to touch me there, to fill me, to kiss me, to make me come over and over and over again. I closed my eyes. A wave of want began in my cleft and climbed through my body. I pictured Dillon's hard body hovering over me, I felt him pushing into me, I heard his growl and his words.

"So when does Dillon return?" Amanda asked.

Her words jerked me from my fantasy. "Three more days," I said.

"I'm sorry, my love," Amanda said. "You must miss him desperately." She pulled her lips down into a frown. "Perhaps we'll just stay busy shopping and going to dinner for the next three days to keep your mind off his absence."

I doubted spending time with Amanda would keep my mind off Dillon's absence, but it might help with the lonely feelings that surged through my body since he'd left for location.

"What does he say about your return to Kansas?" Amanda asked.

My stomach tightened with Amanda's question. I turned toward her. "Not much," I said. "We haven't really discussed it."

Amanda's lips pulled into a flat line, but the corners curled into a smile. "Not the right time, I'm sure." The look on her face seemed to say that Amanda felt sorry for me. That she, like me, didn't believe that there was any future for me with Dillon.

"Do you want to go to the *Mission Ranger* premiere with me?" Amanda asked.

My gaze bounced from watching the bubbles in my

champagne to Amanda's face. I'd thought I would go to the premiere with Dillon. He hadn't yet asked and we hadn't discussed the premiere, but it was right after Dillon returned from location. "I'm not sure... I thought—"

"Amanda!"

I turned my head toward the semi-familiar voice. A luxurious girl with a half dozen beautiful people tagging along behind her strutted toward us. I forced my jaw not to drop. Kiley Kepner, the former teen queen of TV and the hottest film star in the in world right now, waved at Amanda.

My heart pattered in my chest. She was even more beautiful in real life. Her long, lean legs that seemed to go on forever were capped by a pair of red heels. She wore a white cover-up that barely covered the jet-black teeny-tiny bikini on her body. Her long, golden locks were piled high on her head. She looked as though she'd just stepped off the cover of *Vogue*.

"Kiley!" Amanda jumped up and encapsulated Kiley in a giant hug. "I had no idea you were here."

They air-kissed while I remained on my lounge chair, completely shocked and wide-eyed at the lovefest I was witnessing between two of the most beautiful women in the world.

"I'm not, darling, we're on our way to Malibu. Are you going to Greece in August?" Kiley asked.

Amanda nodded. "On Daddy's boat."

By "Daddy's boat," I knew from Choo that Amanda meant a fully staffed yacht with a helipad.

"Oh! Kiley, this is Lane Channing," Amanda said.

I stood and reached out my hand to her. Kiley tilted

her sunglasses over her nose. Her eyes traveled from my eyes to the tips of my toes and back up.

"So, *this* is Dillon's little reader," she said. While her face held a smile, her voice was sharp like knives and sliced through me.

Shame tunneled through my belly. What did she mean by her comment? How would Kiley Kepner know I read for Dillon? Why would she care? Even though heat bloomed in my belly, I kept a smile on my face.

"It's so nice to meet you," I said.

"You too, darling," she said. "Amanda, I must go. I'm late." Kiley turned back to me and leaned in so that her lips were beside my ear. "No worries, darling," she whispered. "He's all yours once I've finished with him. I don't keep them long."

The air smashed out of my lungs with her words. I managed to keep my smile molded to my face, but my fingertips tingled. A dizzy feeling spun through my head. Her smile held ice. She waved at me and gave Amanda another two kisses. She and her entourage tottered off in their high heels toward the far end of the pool. I stood there, stunned and unable to speak, unable to move, unable to fully process what Kiley had just whispered in my ear about the man I loved. The man I'd given my heart and my body to.

"You okay?" Choo stood beside me. His face held concern.

I shook my head no. I wasn't okay. Nausea clutched my belly. The idea of Dillon with another woman made me feel ill. But yet as I watched her retreat across the pool deck, I knew for certain that Kiley was the type of woman that would be best for Dillon.

I knew how the industry worked. I knew that magazine articles and photographs of big sexy stars together kept them hot in the public. I'd listened to Dillon talk to the reporter in Malibu—I knew what kind of image they wanted for him—at least now at the start of his career—and that image didn't include Dillon being in a committed relationship with a college girl from Kansas.

"Oh honey," Amanda said. She sat beside me on the lounger and Choo was on the other side. "Drink this." She held out a glass of champagne, but I couldn't. The sweet smell now sickened me.

"It's part of the business," Amanda said. "I thought you knew. I assumed Dillon would have told you."

"He knows?" I looked at Choo, who took a long breath. "He already knows that they want to set them up together? For the premiere?"

"Lane," Choo said. He grasped my hand. "You have to talk to him. Okay? I know my brother and he loves you. He's never been this way with anyone else. Ask around, he is—"

"Oh, Dillon's a complete whore," Amanda said. "Or at least that's what I hear." Amanda pressed her hand to her cleavage. "I've never experienced—please, don't think that for a moment. But I know from friends he is completely wham, bam, thank you, ma'am. The boy has never been with a woman more than one night." Her gaze locked onto me. "Except for you."

My heartbeat steadied. I closed my eyes. What did this mean? What did it mean that Dillon hadn't told me about the premiere or Kiley Kepner? The ache inside me hardened into a deep knot. I had picked this. Staring into the ocean after hearing Dillon's words to the reporter, I had picked this moment, this pain. I had decided no matter what his feelings were for me that Dillon would be my first and we would have this summer together and then I would leave. I would leave with the memories. I would come back to L.A. next spring with a job and a future and Dillon MacAvoy in my past. I took a long, deep breath. No matter the pain, I knew where I stood. Dillon wasn't ever going to be my future, he was simply going to be my present, and I would have to accept whatever the present meant.

CHAPTER 21

DILLON

JETS DIDN'T FLY FAST ENOUGH. I HIT THE DOOR
to the house and the dogs all clamored to meet me.

"Hi guys," I whispered and gave them each a quick pat.
My breathing jerked in my chest as though I'd run all the
way from Moab. I had twelve hours before I shot my next
scene, but I had a lifetime of fear hammering my heart.

"Lane!" I yelled.

I bolted to the stairs and took them two at a time. I
rounded the corner and sped down the hall toward my
room. One text from my brother and I'd commandeered a
private plane and gotten the hell out of Moab. Why hadn't
I told Lane first? Why hadn't I called her immediately
after I got off the phone with Boom Boom and Webber? I
was such an idiot. How could I keep forgetting L.A. was a
small town? Everyone heard everything and especially
with Laney running around with Amanda Legend, of

course Lane would find out about Kiley Kepner and the *Mission Ranger* premiere. I'd wanted the whole damn mess to go away. I wanted to tell her in person. I had expected more time before Boom Boom leaked the story, and I definitely hadn't anticipated Lane running into Kiley at the W pool.

"Lane!" I yelled again. I needed to get to her body, peel off her clothes, taste her lips, see her eyes... Please let me see the love in her eyes and know that she was mine.

"In here," she called.

I walked past my empty bedroom and farther down the hall to Lane's old room. My heart beat hard in my chest. She was finished with me. She wouldn't be here... She stood next to the open suitcase that lay on her bed. She folded a shirt and placed it inside. My heart hurt watching her.

"What are you doing?" I asked. I knew that I had hurt her; I knew that I hadn't told her about the premiere or why I had to do it. "Are you... are you leaving me?"

She turned her face to me and smiled a smile that didn't reach her eyes and walked toward her dresser.

"You know I have to go home someday," Lane said. "Classes begin in two weeks. I'm planning on leaving after the premiere."

We hadn't discussed the end of summer. I didn't want to discuss that she would have to leave me soon. My mind acted like a crazy amusement-park ride, twisting and turning facts when it came to Lane. If I could just ignore reality and pretend her leaving wasn't happening—wouldn't happen—then maybe she would stay.

"Lane." I pushed my body into her back.

Her thick, round ass pressed against me. She stood

pinned against the dresser. I took a long, deep breath. The smell of her filled me, the scents of lavender, and soap, and a softer, underlying scent that was simply pure Lane. I ran my hands up her sides and over the top of her clothes. I was so hard from just standing behind her, simply smelling her, simply being this close to her. There was no other girl I'd met who made me this hard simply by standing in front of me. My hands grasped her hips and ran up her sides. I pressed under her shirt and felt her hot skin. She leaned her head to the side and I kissed her bare neck.

"Lane," I whispered around a kiss that I pressed to the warm skin where her neck met her shoulder. "Don't leave me. Please, baby, don't leave."

My hands cupped her breasts. She closed her eyes and my fingertips plucked at her nipples under the lace fabric of her bra. She gasped and I grew thicker, harder, and pressed against her.

"Dillon," she moaned. Her back arched and her ass pressed into my throbbing cock.

"Baby, you can't leave me," I said. I had to convince her not to go, that I was worth the pain, that I would try for the rest of my life to make her happy. I lifted her shirt over her head with her back still to me and unsnapped her bra. Her breasts sprang free and I ran my hand across them. I fought the urge to spin her around and suckle those pretty little pink nipples. Instead, I reached one hand down the front of her shorts to the hot wet spot on her panties.

"Baby, you're wet for me."

With my words she pressed her ass back into me. I let my fingers skim over and press against the fabric of her panties right at her nub, her pleasure button. A low moan erupted over her lips and her head rolled, loose on her neck.

I watched her in the mirror above the dresser. I watched her body respond to my touch. I watched her soak up the pleasures of us together. I loved making Lane feel good, having this control over her body. My fingers skirted upward to the edge of her panties. I slipped my hand along her flat belly, underneath her panties, and paused just at the edge of her cleft. I listened to her breath, which was shortened by desire. My other hand still massaged her nipples while I kissed her bare shoulders and neck. She held her breath as she waited for my touch. She waited for me to slide my fingertips into her cleft; she waited to feel the release of pleasure.

"Dillon, please, please," she whimpered.

I slid my fingers into her and pressed on her hot, swollen clit.

A cry like a moan but softer and more sensuous burst from her lips. I circled her clit with my finger. Her hips went wild. She bucked her ass backward into me. She wanted my hardness. Needed the satisfaction of my cock. She raised her arms up and circled them around my neck and I watched as her tongue came out of her perfect pink pout of a mouth and she licked her lips. Her gaze locked with mine and her eyes were heavy-lidded and filled with pleasure. I was going to explode.

I ripped my hand out of her pants and spun her around. In an instant I ripped her shorts off her. She reached for my jeans and scrambled her fingers over the button and zipper. She shucked them off my body. Her hands clasped my cock and stroked downward. I had to have her. I had to be inside her. I needed to know she was mine. I lifted her and she wrapped her legs around me and I walked backward to the bed. I sat with her still clasped to me.

I reached my fingers down between her legs and stroked her hot, wet place and her head fell back. My mouth clamped onto hers and her lips parted to me. God, her taste, I would never get tired of her taste, those plush lips on my lips, her hot tongue inside my mouth, searching and probing. I slid a finger into her tight pussy.

"Baby, fuck me like this," I said.

She'd never been on top. She pulled her head back and looked at me. Suddenly the girl who was becoming so wild, so uninhibited, looked shy. A tiny blush bloomed on her face. She bit her bottom lip. I pressed my finger to her clit and sucked on her nipple. I rolled her nipple in my mouth, my tongue caressing and sucking until her head fell back.

I pulled my lips from her breast. "Baby, I want you to feel it like this. I want you in control."

She was ready; her body was slick and wet. I cupped her ass and lifted her. She put her knees on the bed on either side of me, then looked down at me. There was excitement and curiosity and the tiniest glimmer of fear as she looked at my cock. So hard. So ready for her. Like a giant spear for her to sit on.

She lowered herself slowly and I held her hips.

"Like this?" she whispered as my tip nudged into the edge of her tight entrance.

"Yeah, baby, just like that."

I used all my restraint not to ram upward into her or slam her down upon my lap. I wanted inside her, inside that white-hot heat that made me feel alive and whole and pure and clean. It was the place, the only place, where I felt real.

She bit her bottom lip and the muscles at her entrance tightened around me. She slipped slowly down over my shaft. My fingers circled her clit, and she tightened and tightened again, and I took her breast and sucked her nipple. She sat on me, not moving just squeezing my throbbing cock with her tight pussy.

"Can I move," she whispered out as her pussy clenched and tightened and clenched again.

"Whatever you want to do, baby," I said and pressed harder on her clit.

She gasped. She pulled upward and her tight muscles slid along my shaft, the heat gliding over me.

I'd never felt anything like this. She was the best. I looked up at her as she hovered above my cock. She smiled at me as though she liked this, this being in control. My hands were on her waist and I waited, God I waited, and just when I could barely stand the waiting, she plunged down onto me and speared her body onto my cock.

"Fuck, baby, fuck," I yelled.

"Oh, Dillon," she said. She grasped my neck and her lips were on mine.

Her body pressed hard upon me. Heat shot up my spine and my cock throbbed. My body tensed as the rupture started to tear through me. Lane was so beautiful and so caught up in pleasure. She was swept away with the feeling of our bodies.

"Dillon, I'm going to come," she wailed.

"Come for me, Lane, come for me now," I said and

pressed my palm to her back. I felt her movements grow wild. I pressed my finger to her clit to give her one gentle push into the wave of pleasure. She shattered. I watched her with her head thrown back and her tit in my mouth. I pumped hard and deep into her and I pulsed with a hard heat that threw me over the edge.

LANE

I LOVED SEX. I SMILED AS I CURLED INTO THE nook of Dillon's arm. I absolutely loved it. I didn't think I could love sex this much with anyone other than Dillon. The idea of letting anyone but him touch me or be inside me made me feel sick. I could never be this exposed, this vulnerable, with anyone but Dillon. I would never trust anyone like this other than Dillon. His eyes were closed and I looked at his face. His perfect face that soon every woman in America would know and want. His eyes fluttered open. The brilliant blue of his eyes grabbed me. That blue with flecks of silver was spectacular. I fought for my breath. He was so close and I was in his arms and right now I was the only girl for him. Or so I had let myself believe, if only for a while.

"I'm sorry," Dillon said. He pushed a lock of my hair back behind my ear. He took a long breath. "Kiley Kepner's people asked me to take her to the premiere, before... before this, before us. I... I should have told you. I tried to cancel it, but Webber and Boom Boom... I told them about us."

My heart beat faster in my chest. I knew Dillon was

private, and I knew from Choo that Webber and Boom Boom were all about selling him to the world as a sexy single young star. "I'm not going with Kiley to the premiere," Dillon said. His gaze found mine. "But they want me to wait on going public with us until two weeks after *Mission Ranger* opens."

I felt better knowing that Dillon wasn't going to the premiere with Kiley, but he wasn't going with me either and two weeks after the opening of *Mission Ranger* I would be back in school.

"In two weeks I'm going to tell the world about us." He pulled me tighter. His arm wrapped around me. "The box office will be so big by then that who I'm seeing won't matter. It won't matter that I'm not a single guy. It won't matter to the studios that I've found my girl."

I forced a smile to my face. It might not matter to him, but somehow it mattered to me. He hadn't heard me, didn't want to hear me. I was going home. Webber and Boom Boom were right—I wasn't the right girl for Dillon. I would never be the right girl for Dillon. He did need someone like Kiley Kepner, someone who would help his career, not someone who could do nothing for him.

Hours later, the room was dark when Dillon pressed a kiss to my lips. We'd slept curled around each other. "Baby, I have to go," he said. "I have to be on set in three hours."

I nodded as he slipped from my side and left me alone in bed. This would always be his life. He needed someone who could be good with that.

CHAPTER 22

DILLON

"THE DEAL FOR THE STEVE LEGEND FILM IS closed," Webber said. He jumped from behind his desk and reached out to slap my hand.

"Awesome," I said and smacked his palm. "Nice job." I grabbed for my water bottle that sat on the table in front of the couch in Webber's office at the agency. "How much?" I took a large gulp. I'd watched Webber negotiate all the details of my latest deal for the last half hour and I was parched just sitting and listening.

A sly smile edged up over Webber's face. "Seven figures."

I couldn't help but smile. Even after Webber took his fifteen percent and the IRS took their thirty percent, Choo and I would be good for a long time. I could pay for the rest of college and if Choo kept doing so well at CTA and wanted to, he could work here.

"Choo!" Webber yelled. I turned and saw my brother pop around the doorway of Webber's office. "I know you were listening to the whole negotiation, don't even pretend you weren't."

Choo smiled. He slapped Webber's hand in a high five.

"Nice work," Choo said. "You were awesome. I didn't think there was any way you were going to get the box-office bonuses."

"You got me box-office bonuses?" I asked.

Webber nodded with his huge Cheshire grin. "Revenue stream, my man, first step to first-dollar gross, which is what we want on the next deal." He turned to my brother. "Go grab some Veuve from the kitchen. This deal plus your premiere tonight"—Webber pointed his finger into my chest—"means we get to start celebrating now."

"Yes, it does," Choo said.

I was flying so high. I had three movies in the can. One was premiering tonight, and my agent had just closed my next film. I took a deep breath. The panic that had raced through my chest ever since our parents kicked us to the curb because Choo was gay started to unlace in my chest.

"You feeling good?"

"I am," I said.

"You know the reason you got this is you are smokin' hot. The young chicks, they dug that billboard, and they are going to dig you in this film. You want them to keep on digging you."

Choo walked back into the room with the bottle of open champagne. He held three glasses and Webber poured.

"You have your whole life to settle down man. Why not have some fun now?" Webber asked.

He raised his glass and clinked it against mine. I met his gaze and then looked at my little brother who cocked his eyebrow. We all took a drink of champagne.

"Gentlemen," Choo said. "I'm out. I've got to go get ready for tonight."

"Can you believe this kid," Webber shot his thumb toward Choo and smiled. "Thinks it's something special that his brother has a premiere tonight. Go on," Webber said with a playful grin, "get out of here."

Choo left and Webber and I settled in for another glass of champagne.

"Man," I said and sighed, "I am having fun, but I have totally just hit the jackpot and met the girl of my dreams." I shook my head and settled back into the couch. Webber didn't understand, I saw the doubt in his eyes.

"With a reader from Kansas?" He leaned back in his chair and propped his feet onto his desk.

I sat forward. "Lay off."

Webber had found me when I was a model and he'd gotten me my first gigs and I thought his opinions were important, but I hoped my tone and the look on my face let him know that Lane would never be just a reader from Kansas.

"Okay, okay," Webber said and held up his hands as if he surrendered. "I mean, you've banged so many of them before, I didn't realize this one was so special." He looked over the rim of his champagne glass.

I scowled. "She is."

"Great. Looks like we have some repackaging to do," he muttered around the rim of his glass. His gaze met mine. "Boom Boom isn't happy. She's spent the last six months creating this carefully crafted image in the media that you're the next bad-boy on the block. Single. Unget-table. Part of why the tabs were salivating over the leak that you and Kiley were sleeping together."

"Screw the tabs," I said.

"Right," Webber said. "Here's the thing, part of why I could get you the deal I got you is because of what Boom Boom has crafted. I have to tell you Kiley's people weren't happy about you deciding not to arrive on Kiley's arm tonight."

"You tell them why?"

Webber shook his head no. "That's Boom Boom's department not mine. Man, I couldn't have closed today if they knew the real deal. Kiley is meant to play opposite you in *The Legend Returns* and if she thought she'd gotten the boot tonight because of a girl from Kansas—"

"Lane," I said, my tone terse. "Her name is Lane."

"Right. If Kiley, the biggest star in the world, thought she'd gotten the boot to be your date at the premiere tonight—you know, after Boom Boom spent the last four months trying to make this happen—because of a girl... I mean Lane, from Kansas, the deal wouldn't have closed."

I swallowed a bitter mouthful of champagne.

"Because as big as you are going to be in three months thanks to these films you've got in the can, right now, Dillon, my man, nobody knows who the hell you are and studios usually don't pay seven figures for 'nobody knows who the hell you are.' They are banking on what they've seen in the can, who Steve Legend wants, and the fact that Kiley's people have hinted that you two would be pretty smokin' hot together."

A knot tightened in my throat. "But it's closed, right?"

"Yeah," Webber said and tilted the glass of champagne.

"The deal is closed, but you know this town, it's fickle. Say if *Mission Ranger* tanks or Kiley decides she's pissed with you and decides to put two other films into her next two slots, well, then we could be screwed. You could be screwed."

My stomach clenched. The fear that was my constant companion rooted deeper in my belly. Choo and I weren't nearly as safe as I'd thought, even with the next film deal closed. Everything could still be yanked away from us. I could lose my career. He could lose his college education. We could still be out on our asses trying to scrape by— with Choo again trying to decide if he'd let our parents "rehabilitate" his gayness just so we could have something to eat and a place to sleep.

"But that won't happen," Webber said. "Probably." He took a long breath and his eyes watched me. "So, what about this girl? The one you want to let the world know that you're involved with? The one you're going to kill your image for. Doesn't she have to go back to school? In like a week?"

I rolled my eyes toward the ceiling and nodded my head. "Yeah, we haven't discussed that," I said. "I... I have to convince her not to go."

"Convince her? Hell, I'd think she'd have her claws so deep into the next biggest star in the world you wouldn't be able to shake the bitch loose."

I glared at Webber.

"Sorry, the girl, Lane... you wouldn't be able to shake her loose what with the two of you finding each other and your imminent success."

"She's not like that," I said. "I don't think it's going to

be an easy sell. She's independent and wants her own career and wants to finish school—"

"Plenty of schools out here," Webber said.

"Don't I know it," I said. "But for her, her finding her way on her own, her breaking in on her own and people knowing it happened for the right reasons... Man, those are some pretty important things for her."

"Gotcha," Webber said. He lowered his glass to his desk. His phone started to ring.

I stood. The celebration was over.

Webber reached for his Bluetooth. "Limo at four," Webber said.

I gave him a thumbs-up and headed for the door. I had some good news to share with Lane and some desperate begging about her changing her permanent location.

LANE

"HERE IS THE THING," AMANDA SAID. "YOU'RE riding with me, Choo, and Jackson." She waved her Diet Coke can toward herself and toward Choo, who was wearing cucumbers on his eyes. A woman massaged his feet and another massaged his hands.

The woman massaging my toes lifted my foot and stuck it into a bag filled with hot wax.

The extra bedroom had been converted into a spa for the premiere. Amanda's pedicure was finished and now the woman was painting her fingernails a flaming red.

"And my brother," Amanda said. "Sterling isn't taking

a date, so he's riding with my dad. Taylor is in Vermont riding his bike, so it will be just us four."

I rested my head against the cushion of the portable pedicure throne. An ache drifted through me, followed by a wave of guilt. I was happy that I was getting to attend the *Mission Ranger* premiere. I was happy I was going with Choo and Amanda, my two closest friends in L.A. I was happy Dillon wasn't arriving with Kiley Kepner. I was happy for all these reasons, but a thick block of disappointment had settled in my belly, and I knew it was because I wanted to go to the premiere with Dillon.

I understood the reasoning. Dillon would arrive alone in his own limo with Webber, his agent, to promote the single, sexy star brand they'd created for him. I understood this. I did. I was in the business. My friends were in the business. My boyfriend was in the business. My brain understood that this movie, this moment in Dillon's career, was meant to be the movie and the moment that launched him. I got that how this launch took place had been decided long before I'd arrived on scene and would determine the trajectory of his career for the next couple of years. I was grateful that Dillon had put the kibosh on going to the premiere with Kiley, but neither he nor Webber nor Boom Boom had come out and said that the hints that Dillon and Kiley were involved, the leaked stories on *Tattler* and *TMZ* by someone "close to them" were untrue.

I knew that I was the only girl in Dillon's life, but I still didn't like being smacked in the face with the tabloid rumors that Dillon and Kiley were a couple each time I went to the grocery or the pharmacy or flipped on the TV or my phone or my computer. Even the *Huffington Post* had run a story about the possibility of Kiley and Dillon dating and what "this coupling" could mean for the Steve Legend film they were scheduled to film together this fall.

My life was private. Dillon's was not. I had to sit through the lies knowing the truth, knowing I was the girl Dillon was with, and even though I felt like it should have been enough knowing that Dillon wanted me, was faithful to me… it wasn't. I wanted the world to know too, or at least not to think he was with Kiley Kepner. I pressed my toes through the hot paraffin. The muscles in my feet relaxed. I exhaled and tried to savor this moment of luxury.

"Your rack of dresses is upstairs," Amanda said. "The stylist came by while you were out with"—she cocked a disapproving eyebrow—"the wolf pack."

Amanda couldn't understand how now that Dillon and I were together that I was still reading scripts and walking dogs, but here was the thing—I loved walking the dogs. I loved Runyon Canyon and the way that Kong and Bernie loped up the hill while Scorsese and Spielberg bounded to the top every morning. And the script reading? Well, I still intended to get a job in the business, and I would have read close to two hundred scripts by the time my summer was finished. I'd definitely read everything that was green lit and everything that was cast-contingent. All this reading put me in a good place for when I started at CTA next spring.

"The stylist gets back at two," Amanda said. She wore flip-flops since her toenails were still wet. "I'm going home to get ready there. Makeup and hair gets to my place in twenty minutes." She bent down and air-kissed my cheeks. "This is called pampering." She sighed. "Okay? Enjoy it."

Choo lifted the cucumber from his eye. "Don't worry. I will force her to love every moment."

They both liked to tease me about how low maintenance I was. When I'd first met with the stylist Dillon had hired for me for the premiere, I'd been not only intimidated but absolutely terrified. I'd stood there and nodded and not said a word about what I liked or what I wanted. After I told Amanda about our meeting, Amanda had made Marni the stylist return. That time Amanda and Marni had gone through a look book with me and picked out the gowns that were now waiting for me upstairs. I didn't even want to think about the cost of the stylist or the gowns—so luxurious, so expensive. Everything was so plush; I was nearly overwhelmed with the luxury of it all.

"Okay, my mani-pedi is complete," Choo said. He sat up and tossed the cucumber slices in the trash. "Also this facial. I am going to get myself glorious, then I will be down to your room to supervise hair and makeup for you, *tout suite!*" He bent down and gave me a peck on the cheek. My heart swelled. I was lucky to have found these people for my life—I loved Choo and I loved Amanda. I was going to miss them when I had to go home.

Hair and makeup took two hours, but picking my dress for the premiere from the rack of gowns was nearly instantaneous. I knew immediately which one I wanted.

"You look amazing," Marni said. "I wasn't sure when I pulled this one, but it's perfect for you."

I twirled in front of the three way mirror she'd set up in my room. The dress was a pale nude color with gold threads woven throughout the fabric. The front had a deep

V-neck and the back plunged low. Dillon loved my legs, so I wanted them bare. The hem was above my knees. I wore a pair of extra-high heels, my first set of Loubies and they weren't on loan. I thought back to the day at the beginning of summer, that most horrible day when CTA had given away my job. I'd had no work. I'd had nowhere to live. I'd had no money. I remembered that girl in HR who had been wearing her pair of Loubies and how I'd thought that wasn't in the cards for me.

This was more than a fantasy—all of this was nearly surreal. I was wearing a designer dress that cost more than my final year of college tuition. A makeup artist had just completed my hair and makeup. I had a stylist futzing over my wardrobe so that I could go to the premiere of my boyfriend's first film.

Boyfriend. Was Dillon my boyfriend? The word didn't even seem accurate. When I considered the one high school boyfriend I'd had and the couple of dates in college I'd gone on—Dillon was so much more. He was my everything.

My heart trembled in my chest. The idea of Dillon being my everything terrified me. I knew he cared for me. I knew that I was important to him, but I wasn't his everything. I doubted I could ever be everything for him. His career meant so much and taking care of his brother— making certain that Choo got through school and didn't have to deal with their parents—those were the things most important to Dillon.

"What do you guys think?" I looked over at the pack on the bed. Four sets of ears perked up with my voice. Kong stood and barked but the other three just rolled their eyes toward me.

"Damn!"

I turned to the doorway where Choo stood.

"Girl you clean up good!"

"I could say the same thing." I smiled. He looked so handsome in his black Armani suit and tie. "Going for the Hollywood glam look tonight?"

He nodded. "Jackson is wearing a similar suit and I am certain will look amazing. We pick him up after we get Amanda." Choo circled me and checked out my dress from top to toe. He glanced over at Marni. "You did an amazing job. She looks perfect."

Marni smiled. "I didn't think this would be the dress tonight," Marni said. "But it totally works. Looks like it was made for her."

His phone chimed and he pulled it from his pocket. "Meet me downstairs in five? I'm going to introduce the fellas to their pet-sitter for the night. Come on guys," Choo called and patted his legs. Kong leapt off the bed. Scorsese and Spielberg were next. Bernie lifted his head, examined Choo, sighed, yawned, and put his head back down, hopeful, I gathered, that everyone would leave without him and he could just sleep.

"Bernie, come on!" Choo said and gently nudged the big guy with his hand. The dog finally stood and lumbered off my bed. He looked back at me and jerked his head as if to say I looked good.

I walked toward the backyard balcony while everyone who was there to make me look beautiful packed up their things. I searched the view. The Big Risk had been magnificent. I had two more weeks before I needed to go back to Kansas. Dillon's movie wrapped soon, then he had two weeks off before he started his next film with Amanda's dad, Steve Legend, and the director Hunter Fabian. We hadn't discussed what was going to happen to us when I went back to school for my last year. We hadn't even really talked about there being an us after the summer. All I knew was that when I left, if I left without an "us," I would be devastated, completely heartbroken. But leaving alone, without a commitment from Dillon, without a relationship, was what I expected. I would take with me the most amazing memories. Memories of falling in love with the soon-to-be biggest star in the world.

"I..."

I turned at Dillon's voice. My room was empty of the makeup artists and stylists and all their paraphernalia. Only Dillon stood just inside my doorway. His eyes were wide. My heart beat harder in my chest. His gaze locked onto me.

My heart slammed into my ribs. He was every bit the exquisite male model. He wore a suit cut to perfection. A hint of shadow tugged on his jaw. His jet-black hair curled over the edges of his crisp white shirt. My breath whooshed from my lungs. The sight of him was like being kicked in the chest. He was so beautiful. I wasn't sure how, but I'd become used to his beauty, not oblivious to it, but used to it, until a moment like this, when he wasn't wearing jeans and a T-shirt. A moment like this, where he looked like he'd stepped of the cover of *Esquire* magazine. He was, quite simply, the most gorgeous guy I'd ever seen. And he was mine... at least for a while longer.

"I don't think you should wear that dress," he said.

"What? Why? I love... you don't like it?"

A sly smile broke across his face. "No, I love it, and I think every guy at the premiere tonight is going to love it too." He walked across the room to me and his fingertips grasped my arm. "I'm going to go nuts thinking about what every guy in that room tonight is going to want to do to you."

He was so close. His breath was hot on my face and I could smell the mint on his breath. His touch, his possession, sent a deep thrill through my body.

Heat started in my chest and worked up my neck. "But there is only one guy who gets to," I whispered.

His hand grasped the back of my neck. His lips were so close to mine. The fingers of his other hand traced down my neck and slowly into the open spot between my breasts. My breath gasped out and heat pooled in the V of my legs.

"You already have on your makeup," he whispered to me, his lips so close to mine they almost touched. "That's really too bad."

He pulled me as close as I could be and I felt his hardness press into me. I didn't care about my makeup I didn't care about my dress with his hand on the nape of my neck and his fingers circling my nipple. All I wanted was for him to kiss me, to be inside me.

"You look too pretty to mess up," Dillon whispered in my ear.

His hand drifted down the side of my dress and found the edge of my skirt. His fingertips slipped up my thigh and my breathing grew short. His blue eyes lined with silver were locked onto mine. His tongue traced over his lips. His fingertips brushed from the edge of my thigh to the obscenely expensive lace panties that covered me. I gasped.

"How'd you get so wet already, baby," he asked His

lips had the wickedest smile. His fingertips reached under my panties and he slipped his fingers between my cleft and pressed against the hot spot between my legs.

"Does it feel good, Laney?"

I bit my bottom lip and nodded. A low moan escaped over my lips. His palm grasped the back of my neck and steadied me. With his touch between my legs, my hips began to roll. He had complete possession of me. His touch controlled me.

He leaned forward, his lips beside my ear and whispered, "You want me to fuck you?"

I couldn't even answer. My want was desperate. I wanted him inside me, to fill me. I couldn't even form words. He slipped two fingers into me and his thumb continued to press across my nub, which throbbed for him. He spun me around and pressed into my back as his hand reached around and his fingers pumped into me. My head pressed back into his chest. My legs were weak and my knees nearly buckled.

"Come for me, baby," he whispered into my ear. "Watch yourself come for me."

I opened my eyes and looked into the three-way mirror that was still in my room—Dillon's face was shadowed with lust, me with my dress hitched up high around my waist, his hand wrapped around me and in between my legs, his fingers pumping into me as his thumb massaged me. My breath shallowed with his.

"That's right, baby, come around my fingers, come for me. I want to watch you come for me."

I pressed my head back and my hips forward. His other hand played with my now-exposed nipples that hung out the top of my dress. The heat built as I watched him play with all the sensitive parts of me.

"Dillon, baby, baby..." I wailed. "I'm going to come, baby..."

"Yes, you are, sweet Lane, you're going to come. I'm going to make you come." His lips sucked my neck and his kiss nearly burned. The heat rose and built and rolled through me as I thrust myself against his hand, unable to control my body, my need, my want.

"Dillon!" I screamed his name—it sounded like a plea across my lips. I arched back and his fingers continued to tease my pussy.

The orgasm rolled through me, over and over and over until the last shudder rushed through my body. Dillon slipped his fingers from me. He slipped both into his mouth. "So sweet, Lane, you taste so sweet."

I bit my lip, knowing that he was tasting me. "I can't kiss you until after." He gently repositioned my panties and pulled the skirt of my dress down. He slipped his hand over it, settling it. He touched my breasts and a hot shock rushed through me as he repositioned my breasts back into my bra and back into my dress. "Damn, baby, that face, that half-lidded, freshly fucked face... I don't even want to let you out of the house."

I glanced into the mirror. He was right. I looked flushed and deeply satisfied, a satisfaction I hadn't known until Dillon.

"That's just the warm-up." He leaned in close to me. "Just wait until we get home tonight. I can't wait to peel that dress off you. But the shoes"—his gaze ventured down my legs toward my heels—"the shoes I want you to keep on."

I bit my bottom lip. Even just after an earth-shaking orgasm, I still wanted to have sex with Dillon right this moment.

"Hey, I got you something," Dillon said. He slipped his hand into his pocket and came out with a rectangular box. "To celebrate my big night." He turned the box to me.

My eyes widened and my heart beat so fast in my chest I thought it might explode. I took the velvet box from him and slowly opened it.

"Oh, Dillon," I gasped. A long line of diamonds glittered inside the box.

"You have the most beautiful neck—this will look amazing on you."

He lifted the strand of diamonds and stood behind me. He clasped it and I stood in front of the mirror, my fingertips dancing over the diamonds.

"It's... oh my God, it's beautiful, but it's too much it's…"

He turned me around to face him. "Nothing is too much for you." He ran his knuckles gently along my cheekbone. "I need you to know that, to understand. Nothing is too much for you, Lane." He pressed his forehead to mine and sighed. "You are becoming my everything."

My heart bounced in my chest. I felt this way about Dillon, but for some reason I still couldn't trust that he felt the same about me.

He was so close to me. "I want to kiss you so bad." A frustrated smile slipped over his lips.

"I have lipstick in my bag," I said and wiggled my eyebrows.

"Thank God." He pressed his lips to mine.

CHAPTER 23

DILLON

"THE SCREAMING IS INSANE," I SAID TO Boom Boom.

"Soon, darling, all those screams will be for you." She stopped in front of the bank of photographers. "Step and repeat."

Webber stood behind me and off to the side. Ryan was flying high. He had slammed back six drinks and snorted lines of blow in the car. He threw his arm around my neck. The photographers, as well as the fans, went wild. Flashes burst around us.

"Is that your girl up ahead?"

I slid my eyes to the left. Ahead of me on the red carpet was Lane with Amanda. Amanda Legend was a photo magnet. Her father was *the* biggest action star in the world, and her brother was a producer. She didn't want anything to do with the industry, but she'd agreed to come for Lane's sake so that Lane didn't have to face this evening alone. The photogs flashed pics of Lane and Amanda together. Lane looked amazing.

A flame of want burned through my chest. I took a long deep breath. I wanted to be the person standing beside Lane. Choo and Jackson ambled behind Amanda and Lane. My brother and his date weren't chum for the photogs... yet. They quickly slid by the bank of photographers and into the theater.

Lane glanced my way and flashed me a smile. A warmth lit through me. I wanted to walk over, grab her around the waist, and slip a huge kiss onto her lips. Boom Boom would freak and Webber might stroke out. I'd agreed to let them keep the bad-boy sexy single guy routine alive until the movie opened and the box office was solid.

"It's Kiley Kepner!" a shutterbug shouted.

Ryan slipped his arm from around my neck. He rolled his eyes skyward. "What a pain in the ass," he muttered.

Every photographer turned to their left. The sound of camera clicking increased.

"Kiley!"

"Over here!"

"Kiley! Come take a picture with your boyfriend!"

"They don't mean me," Ryan said. He patted my lapel and slipped away from me. Soon Boom Boom had me by the arm. She shoved me beside Kiley, who turned and pressed her breasts into my side.

My heart lurched in my chest.

"Don't they make a spectacular couple?" Boom Boom called to the salivating photographers.

I looked over my shoulder. Lane stood in the doorway

to the theatre. Her mouth was open and her eyes widened. She watched as Kiley's arm snaked around my neck. Kiley pulled me closer and with her other hand she took my chin and turned my face to hers.

"Smile," she whispered. "I'm giving you more press than you could ever buy."

My tight smile locked onto my face. I slid my eyes toward Boom Boom, who wouldn't meet my gaze. Kiley looked away from the photographers and back to me. I felt her lips press onto my cheek. They felt like plastic. I pulled back with a surprised look on my face, I did my best to maintain my nonchalance like I got kissed by superstars every day while the girl I loved stared at me slack-jawed from five feet away.

Lane. This was going to hurt Lane.

I slipped my arm from Kiley's waist and had started for the theater door when Kiley grabbed my wrist.

"Not so fast," she hissed around her fake smile. "I have on heels."

"I don't care if you're wearing stilts," I said. "I have to get inside."

She wouldn't let go of my arm and there was no way I could jerk free in front of a hundred photographers and not look like the biggest asshole in the world. I let her hold my arm and we walked through the doors into the theater.

"For somebody who wants to pretend to be my boyfriend," Kiley said, "you sure are in a hurry to get away."

"I don't want to pretend," I said. I scanned the room, looking for any sign of Amanda or Lane. I needed to find Lane, she would be hurt and upset and—

"Dillon, man, come on," Hunter Fabian called from the door between the lobby and the theater. Beside Hunter stood Steve Legend—the biggest action star in the world and my costar on my next film. Steve flashed me his box-office-winning smile. I hadn't known he was coming to the *Mission Ranger* premiere. He nodded toward me and held out his hand to Kiley. She slipped from my side and grasped Steve's hand.

"Can't start the film without you, mate," Hunter called.

I let a smile break out over my lips as I did one more fast check of the theater lobby. Where was Lane? Kiley whispered in Steve's ear and then released his hand. She disappeared into the darkened theater. I walked toward Hunter and held out my hand to Steve Legend. Right now, they were the two most important men when it came to making my career.

LANE

"I DON'T KNOW WHY I'M CRYING," I SAID AND sniffed. I shoved a tissue under my eye. "I knew what they wanted to do, how they wanted to sell Dillon, what he needs to do for his career. It's not like I didn't know."

"Knowing about something doesn't make it hurt any less," Amanda said. "Believe me." She took my crumpled tissue, tossed it in the trash, and handed me another tissue. She leaned against the sink. "Look, the business sucks. It messes with people's heads. I've never met anyone who comes out of the industry normal."

I blew my nose. I didn't want to hear this. I looked down at my toenails, painted bright red and peeking out of my pretty shoes. I'd ruined my makeup, not from having sex with Dillon, but by crying my eyes out because the entire world now believed he was sleeping with Kiley Kepner.

"Even if you want to be in the business, it doesn't mean you have to let the business control your life. Find something that isn't about the industry," she said. "A hobby. A friend. A boyfriend—someone who is normal or sane." She pulled a strand of hair that had fallen into my face away from my tear-soaked cheek. "Like I did you."

I looked at Amanda.

"But then you had to go and mess that all up by falling in love with the next big action star, didn't you?" A small smile flickered across her face. "He loves you." Her voice was soft and her eyes were sincere. "And you may not want to, but you love him too. It's completely obvious when you two are together. And yes, it's totally messed up that he has to pretend to be seeing that hellacious bitch, Kiley."

"I thought you liked her," I said.

"Like her? You mean the way everyone in the business likes everyone?" Amanda turned and set her clutch on the vanity. "We grew up together. We were best friends until she slept with one of my boyfriends. I do *not* like her." Amanda leaned forward and adjusted her false eyelash. "I am polite to her. I do what I've been trained to do. I am on friendly terms with her. Who knows when my father or my brother or someone else I care about may need something from her? I keep my personal feelings personal and I am nice to her, but I definitely don't like her."

Something shifted in my chest. How hard would that have been for Amanda? Her entire life she had to keep every personal feeling locked deep inside because of her family's business.

"I don't know if I can do that," I said and wrinkled my brow.

"You already have," Amanda said. Her gaze shifted in the mirror from examining her makeup to me. "Did you like Dillon when you first met him?"

I thought back to that very first day when Dillon had humiliated me in front of the entire crew of *Offend and Defend*. "No."

"But you were polite to him and you took a job from him and now what?"

"Now I'm in love with him," I whispered.

I looked into the mirror. I searched my own eyes. He'd humiliated me that day and then today… today I felt like… even though I understood why… I felt like he'd just denied me, denied our love to the entire world. I wanted to be okay with it. I wanted to love him enough so that the things that Dillon had to do for his public image didn't bother me. I wanted to love him enough so that I didn't feel jealous and hurt and abandoned and every other bad feeling that careened through my chest.

"And tonight," Amanda said and turned back to me. She crossed her arms over her chest and settled her gaze on to mine. "You'll do it again. You'll walk out there to the premiere, you'll go to the party, and you'll pretend. You'll pretend none of this bothers you. You'll pretend you're having a great time. You'll follow Dillon and his team's lead and you'll even pretend you aren't sleeping with him and you aren't in love. And you'll do it for his career. For the *business*." Amanda picked up her clutch. She took the final tissue from my hand.

A cold bitterness wove through her words. I wondered how many times in her life as the child of the world's biggest action star she'd had to pretend—pretend to be happy, pretend to have the perfect life, pretend to have the perfect family. Maybe Amanda was finished pretending and that was why she wanted to get as far away from entertainment and the industry as she could.

Amanda dusted her fingertips under my cheek and wiped away a tiny piece of white fuzz. "You'll do all this for Dillon. You'll do it for love." She turned toward the door and pulled it open. "Welcome to Hollywood."

DILLON

"DUDE, I WOULD TOTALLY TAP EITHER ONE OF those," Ryan said. His breath was hot with whiskey and he hung his arm around my neck.

He pointed his drink first toward Kiley, who stood a few feet to my right, and then he swung his arm back to his left where Lane stood chatting with Amanda and Amanda's dad, Steve Legend. I hadn't gotten to Lane yet. We'd texted after the film when Webber, Ryan, and I took the limo to the premiere party. Then there'd been mobs of people. I hadn't been able to fight the crowd to get to her. This moment was the closest I'd been to Lane since the red carpet and now my drunk costar was hanging off my neck like he was ready to pass out on the floor.

"Pull it together, buddy," I said. I looked around the

room. Top-level executives and producers milled around. This wasn't the place you wanted to collect a reputation for not holding your liquor. "Ryan, you're wasted."

"Man, I'm fine," he slurred and then jammed his glass of whiskey to his lips.

"Oh yeah," I said and steered him away from the president of production of Worldwide Pictures. "You're A-okay." I walked toward Webber with Ryan hanging off my side.

"Webber, man, we've got to get him home," I said.

Webber took a deep breath and nodded. "This is becoming too regular of an occurrence. Come on, guy, let's get you home."

Ryan liked to party and drank a ton of booze, but I didn't think I realized just how massive a habit his drinking had become.

"Dude, I am not going home yet," Ryan slurred. H pulled himself up and shook his head. "This is my premiere too and I'm staying. Got me?"

Webber and I looked at each other. I wasn't going to knock Ryan's ass down and drag him to the car.

"Got you,' I said and patted him on the shoulder. "Then you better slow down with that stuff." I nodded toward his drink.

"Dude, I'm all good as I long as I have this stuff"—he patted his pocket and I knew he had coke in there—"to go with that stuff." He lifted his glass and upended his drink. He was balancing the downer effects of the liquor with the upper effects of the coke—it was a good ride as long as you kept the ratio right.

I looked across the room to where Lane stood between Choo and Amanda. That was where I wanted to be, with her. Not with some horribly atrocious, entitled bitch. I'd wanted the press and the prestige that came with being linked to the biggest star in the world. I'd thought my reasons were legitimate... to protect my brother... but right now... Shit, I definitely didn't want any of it bad enough.

Kiley walked up to me. "It's time to go." Her gaze followed mine. She was beautiful, but she was mean and shallow and broken to her core. "Look," she whispered, "I get that you think you're in love with her, and I am completely A-okay with that. As soon as tonight is over, our deal is finished. But let's get through tonight." She reached up and grabbed each lapel of my jacket.

"I want to call this deal off," I said, my voice barely above a whisper.

A smile lit up Kiley's face. "Oh, Dillon." She sighed and patted one of my lapels. "You are so cute. You have to be a much bigger star to control a situation such as this." Her gaze locked on mine. "You don't decide when this faux relationship is finished, we do." She leaned close and whispered, "And by 'we,' I mean me and my very powerful boyfriend." She nodded her head toward where Lane stood beside Amanda and Steve Legend. Steve lifted his drink in a salute to us and nodded.

My stomach lurched. I was being used as a cover story for the sex fest that Kiley Kepner and Steve Legend were having. I'd just signed on for their next film—this whole charade could go on for months.

From across the room, Lane's eyes skimmed over me and Kiley and how close Kiley now stood beside me. My gaze remained on Lane she tried... she tried like hell... I could see pain shimmer across her face as she looked first at me and then at Kiley touching me. Lane's gaze dropped to the floor and she turned her body away from us.

"So," Kiley whispered, "if you do want to be the next big action start and eventually call the shots, you'll figure out who is in charge." She placed her palm on my lapel again, and with a wicked smile stared into my eyes. "And Dillon, the guy in charge?" She shook her head. "It isn't you."

My chest tightened. This whole PR facade could go on much longer than just tonight. Kiley with Steve could get my offer pulled. Her people could leak stories about her and me on set for months—stories that wouldn't need any kind of confirmation—stories that would be printed on the covers of countless magazines just because of Kiley's team making innuendos. I could deny each one, but how could I expect Lane to live with all the rumors? How long before she simply didn't believe me and left?

Kiley turned and linked her arm through mine. "Let's go," she said. "The after-party at my place awaits."

I looked over my shoulder at Lane. Her lips were pulled tight in a thin line, and Amanda had her arm around her shoulders. My heart ached because of the shattering pain I knew I was causing her.

LANE

I DIDN'T CRY AT THE PREMIERE PARTY. I WAS better than that. I was more professional. Besides, I'd already cried in the bathroom at the actual premiere—how big of a baby could I be? Instead, I waited until Amanda and I were in the limo. Choo was going home with Jackson.

"I am such a baby," I said and dabbed at the corners of my eyes. Amanda handed me another tissue.

"No," Amanda said, "you're not. It's just a big mess. But a big mess that will end soon. Right? Dillon's meant to pretend for tonight and then the whole thing with Kiley is finished."

I curled my lips upward in a sad, soppy smile. The mess with Kiley would end soon. I sniffled and nodded.

"I can't go to her after-party," I said without meeting Amanda's gaze. "I just can't." I pressed my lips together. I had wanted to go to the premiere and the premiere party and I had hoped that I would get to spend a tiny bit of time with Dillon, but that hadn't happened. He had been too busy with his agent and Kiley and Ryan and we'd barely said two words to each other.

"You can drop me at my place, and then you can go to Kiley's," I said.

I didn't know what time Dillon would get home. He'd left with Ryan and Kiley. My heart had shattered with his departure with them. Of course I'd known that he had to leave with them. I got that Boom Boom and Webber needed to brand Dillon and that by dating Kiley they could do that. My head understood, but my heart... Well, my heart hurt like hell. I wanted to run up to Dillon and yank Kiley's hand from his arm. I wanted to plant the most amazing kiss on his lips. I wanted him to claim me in front of the world, PR plans be damned.

"I'm not going to Kiley's," Amanda said. "No way." She pulled a compact from her purse, flipped it open, and examined her still-perfect makeup. "I'm going with you."

She clicked closed the compact. "We'll have a girlfriend gabfest. After we stop for cheeseburgers. Isn't that what girlfriends do?"

"Yeah," I said. "I even have some pajamas and some popcorn."

"Sounds perfect."

"And ice cream."

"Ice cream?" Amanda slid her eyes toward me. "You know I haven't had ice cream since the summer I was eleven. When my mother sent me to a fat camp in Switzerland."

"Seriously?"

"Seriously," Amanda said. "But I think I definitely need some ice cream tonight."

DILLON

"I'm out," I said and leaned over to Webber. He had his lips pressed to the neck of a girl straddling his lap. The time was closing in on four a.m. and I needed to get home. Kiley's party was filled to capacity with rock stars and actors and directors and TV stars—there were tons of people crammed into her house. This wasn't my scene. At least not anymore.

"You gonna get him home?" I asked Webber.

Webber pulled his lips away from the girl's neck and looked toward Ryan, who was passed out facedown on the couch. He was totally okay with sleeping it off right in the middle of this Hollywood bash.

Webber nodded. "I got him," he said. He pressed his

lips to the girl's and his hand cupped her ass as he pulled her tighter onto his lap.

I walked toward the front door. I was exhausted. Even with the bevy of eye-candy pulsing through this party, the only place I wanted to be was home, in my own bed, with Lane. I opened the door and walked out onto the front step.

Silence thrummed through the night. The quiet felt like a caress after all the noise and music and high-pitched giggles of inside. I took a long, deep breath and pulled my phone from my pocket and texted Bob. He replied he'd be in the drive in two minutes.

"Hey, you're leaving?"

I looked toward the familiar voice. Kiley stood just outside the front door. She'd changed from the dress she'd worn to the premiere of *Mission Ranger* into a nearly see-through dress. Her legs went for miles, and while admittedly one of the most beautiful women in the world, she wasn't Lane.

I couldn't blame Kiley entirely. I had agreed to the entire charade. Tomorrow the tabs would print pics of us out on the town together. I clenched my hand. Steve Legend film be damned, next week I was having Boom Boom leak that Kiley and I were only friends and would remain only friends. I simply couldn't see that look of pain on Lane's face again, even if I had to give up a film with Steve Legend.

"Not your scene?" Kiley purred. She stepped closer to me.

"I'm kind of done with all that." I forced my anger deeper into my gut. I was a professional and in this town, you didn't ever want to wipe out a bridge. "Look, Kiley," I said with an even tone. "Thank you for everything—I mean, you're right. You and Steve offered me a huge opportunity both with *The Legend Returns* and all the publicity. I don't want to seem ungrateful."

She moved closer to me, her body skimming the front of mine. "Dillon, don't worry about it. We can't help who with or when we fall in love. Believe me, I know." She placed her hand on my arm. "You really helped me out, and I'm looking forward to working with you on *The Legend Returns*."

"Thanks," I said. I wasn't sure Kiley would be so excited about working with me on *The Legend Returns* once I told Boom Boom to leak the story that Kiley and I weren't involved, but I didn't want to get into details with Kiley tonight. I simply wanted to go home.

Kiley stood too close. I smelled the hot whiskey on her breath. Her lips were close to mine. Any guy in the world would have read the signs and pressed their body into hers. But I didn't want Kiley. I wanted Lane, I needed Lane, I was in love with Lane.

"Good night, Dillon," Kiley said. Her lips were on mine and she pressed her body into me. For a fraction of a second, my body, my mind, and my lips were completely confused. I grabbed her arms and jerked back.

"Yeah, Kiley, good night," I said. My tone was terse. Lip-lock was not part of our deal. Not in any way. I turned toward the Escalade. Bob jumped out from behind the wheel and opened the back door.

"Get me out of here," I said and Bob slammed the door.

LANE

DILLON'S FOOTSTEPS WOKE ME. THE DOGS WERE sacked out around me on the bed. Each pup stood, stretched, and bounced to the floor. I glanced at my phone. Five a.m. My breath hitched in my chest. Amanda had said that Kiley's late-night after-parties often lasted well into the next day. I'd wanted Dillon to come home and be with me.

"Hey, baby," he said. He'd already undressed and he slipped into bed wearing nothing. He slid his hands across the bed and under my body, then wrapped his arms around me. The pain from this night disappeared.

I loved his touch.

He pressed his body against mine and his hardness pressed against my backside. He cupped both my breasts in his hands. Heat swirled through my body and swept away my fatigue. My skin grew warm and a throbbing desire pulsed between my legs. He pressed his lips to my neck.

"God, I missed you tonight," he whispered into my ear.

The scent of whiskey decorated his breath beside the lingering scent of something floral, something feminine. My stomach pitted with fear. He'd been out until five a.m. with one of the world's most beautiful female stars, at her home, drinking. I pressed my lips tight and willed away my thoughts of doubt. Dillon would never be with another woman and then come home to me. Would he? Hadn't he proved over and over and over that he only wanted me? His lips roamed along my neck and his hand slid down my belly and slipped into my panties.

My body responded to his touch. I anticipated the pleasure I'd receive and my hips pressed backward into his hardness. His fingers slipped between my moist folds and pressed against the spot between my legs, the spot that caused heat to lick every inch of me.

Dillon stroked me. I gasped for air. I pushed hard against him while his fingertips circled the nub between my legs.

"God, Lane." His plucked at my nipple with his other hand. "Baby, I missed you."

A deep, sensual moan coursed out of my mouth. I bit my bottom lip. I wanted him. Even when I was confused, I wanted him. His touch sent me spiraling. He slipped his fingers deep inside me and I gasped. I wanted to be filled by him.

"Lane, I want you."

"Dillon, please, please," I whispered. I wanted to feel him inside me, I wanted to know that he was mine, I wanted his body, our bodies together to take away these doubts, and these fears, and this pain I felt over tonight and Kiley and that I had to leave to go back to school. I wanted all those thoughts washed away by the physical pleasure his body gave me.

"What do you want, sweet Lane?" His voice was deep, like a possessive growl. His lips pressed to my ear and his fingers pleasured me. His fingers made my body writhe with a hot desire over which I had no control. "Tell me, sweet Lane, tell me."

I bit my bottom lip. I knew what he wanted; he wanted

me to talk dirty to him, he wanted me to say words that I never said. "I…"

He pressed his fingertips harder to my nub and I felt his penis bumping along my backside. I wanted him. I wanted him to…

"I want you to fuck me," I gasped.

A deep growl came out of Dillon's mouth. His fingers slid from inside me and his cock jammed upward, slicing into me with a hard heat that made my body explode with pleasure.

"I'll fuck you, sweet Lane. I'll fuck you."

My body was all heat as Dillon pushed up and into me, and I pressed back into each of his thrusts. His fingertips still moved on my nub as he thrust up and into me from behind.

"You are mine, Lane. You are mine," he growled with each thrust. "Tell me you are mine."

"I'm yours, all yours," I wailed. My body and my mind fought to hold on, to ride the edge of pleasure.

"Baby, I'm going to come," Dillon said as his thrusts grew harder and deeper and my body clasped around him. I fell over the edge and he shattered with me as we both came.

CHAPTER 24

LANE

THE NEXT DAY, DILLON HAD TO LEAVE TO DO some final pickup shots for *Offend and Defend*. I was walking the dogs when my phone beeped. I slid it from my pocket. The number was CTA.

"Lane?" the semi-familiar voice said. "This is Nancy from CTA, HR."

"Nancy!" I said. "How are you?" I scrambled to the edge of the trail at Runyon Canyon and did my best to catch my breath.

"Good," she said. "Is this a bad time? You sound… you sound a little winded."

"No, I mean yes. It's a good time, but I'm walking the dogs. You know that job you found for me? Well, part of it is walking four dogs."

"Yes," Nancy said with a small laugh. "I have heard a great deal about that job."

My stomach twisted. I hoped she hadn't heard about me sleeping with my employer. That part I had kind of wanted to keep to myself.

"Listen, Lane, one of the agents here who is in charge of the trainee program that you'll enter next spring wondered if you'd come in and meet with him. You know, before you head back to school."

Kong traced a figure eight around my legs, and since he was on his leash, the leather strap tightened around my thigh. "Sure!" I said and tried to extricate my legs without doing a face-plant into the dust. "When?"

"He wanted you to come by today," Nancy said. "This afternoon, if that isn't too soon for you?"

"Today?" I pulled the leash above my head and twisted. "Sure, no problem."

"Great," Nancy said. "I'll tell him. Does two thirty work?"

"Okay." I pressed Off and looked at the time. "Come on guys, we gotta run," I said to the pack. "I have to go and discuss my future."

DILLON

THE ESCALADE PULLED TO A STOP ON THE tarmac. I hopped out before Bob pulled open the back door. This trip to the desert was a surprise and completely unscheduled. Hunter Fabian stood beside the jet steps wearing a Dodgers baseball cap and aviator sunglasses. He walked toward me with his hand outstretched and a giant smile on his face.

"Mate!" Hunter said and swung an arm around my shoulder. "I can't thank you enough. I just got the call and they said we could get those shots tonight. Ryan's already on board."

"No problem," I said and forced what I hoped look like a real smile onto my face. I didn't want to be a pain in the ass. Lane would have to understand. It was a military base and if they said we had to do the shot tonight then we had to do the shot tonight. There wasn't really a way around it. Tonight I'd made big plans for us. I wanted to discuss how we were going to do the long-distance thing. I'd wanted to try to figure out a way to convince Lane to transfer to UCLA or USC to finish her last year of college in Cali. I couldn't imagine being without her. I would understand if she felt like she had to finish up school where she'd started, but if she was determined to stay in Kansas, then I was moving my home base. I'd go do my films, but then I would come back to her. I'd made my decision; I couldn't be without her. Not for any period of time. I needed Lane to make me feel grounded and sane, to help me feel like I was a real person in this crazy world.

Hunter leaned in close. "This is exactly why I'm so happy you're doing the Legend film with me, Steve, and Kiley." He tapped me on the shoulder. "You're a team player. You completely get it."

I wasn't sure Hunter would believe that I "got it" once I kicked Kiley and our fake love story to the curb.

Hunter released my shoulder and walked toward the jet steps. "Wheels up in ten!" he called to me.

I nodded and waved. I slipped my phone from my pocket. This "team player" had to readjust some personal plans. I punched the button and after two rings Boom Boom picked up.

"Boom Boom?" I said.

"My favorite client, how are you?" she asked.

"Listen, I need your help. I've got some last-minute pickup shots tonight. Can you reschedule some dinner plans for me? I got the reservation through your office and I was wondering if you could try to reschedule it for tomorrow night?"

"Consider it done, my love," she said. "For two, yes?"

I nodded. "Yeah."

"So how are the little lovebirds?" Boom Boom asked. Her voice held an edge.

"Lane's good," I said.

"You know, Kiley's people called me today," Boom Boom said.

I took a deep breath. I didn't want to hear anything that Kiley's people had to say. I'd struck a deal with the devil when I'd agreed to the charade.

"They'd like to postpone making the breakup announcement until you begin to film *The Legend Returns*," Boom Boom said.

"No way," I said. I crossed my arms over my chest. "There is no way—that is like what? Two months from now?"

"Three, darling, but who's counting? Look, I know it's hard, but here's the thing: Kiley is the one who got you that role and—"

"I can't do it, Boom Boom. I can't do it to myself and I definitely can't do it to Lane." I couldn't ask Lane to keep our relationship hidden.

"I didn't want to tell you this, but Kiley's people are

intimating that if you won't do this for her, they will ask Worldwide to withdraw your offer on *The Legend Returns*."

Heat rolled through my belly and climbed to my chest. Of course they would. Webber and Boom Boom had warned me that if I didn't do what Kiley asked that the offer for *The Legend Returns* could disappear. And now I knew why. She and Steve Legend were using me to hide their affair—from the public and from Steve's wife.

"Darling, I told them I didn't think that there was any way at all that you would agree to it."

"Absolutely not, I said.

"Right," Boom Boom said. "So I just got off the phone with Webber, and he'd gotten a phone call from Worldwide Business Affairs."

My heart clutched in my chest. My gut felt as though I was falling down a never-ending hole.

"And they're putting a tiny hold on your deal," Boom Boom said.

I pressed my fingertips to my temple.

"You should definitely give Webber a call. Worldwide has some concerns about how well you and Kiley are getting along. They don't want to walk into any problems. It would seem that Kiley's agent might have called the president of production at Worldwide and mentioned that Kiley wasn't sure she wanted to work with you on the film. The studio is giving us forty-eight hours to work this out."

My heart careened in my chest. There was nothing to work out. Nothing at all. I loved Lane. I wanted to be with her.

"Call Webber," Boom Boom said. "I'll change the ressy for a different night."

LANE

I FOLLOWED WEBBER'S ASSISTANT INTO Webber's office. Pictures of the biggest stars in the film industry, each standing beside Webber, lined the walls. Some of the women had their lips pressed against his cheek. I examined a picture of Webber standing beside Jennifer Lawrence who was holding the Academy Award.

"Lane, thanks for coming into the office."

I spun around. I'd seen Webber a couple of times. He always seemed too slick for words. I somehow felt like less when I was in his presence. He was so put together with his perfect looks, his perfect suit, and his perfect shoes. He was as good-looking as any of the celebrities he represented, but where Dillon had a naturalness to him and openness once you got past the barriers, Webber seemed to have a sharp and callous edge. I wondered if it was possible to get past that with Webber or if this was simply who he was.

"No problem," I said.

He sat in his desk chair. "You enjoying L.A.?"

I sat in the chair opposite his desk and nodded.

"I bet," Webber said.

I flushed. His words seemed to hold some kind of judgment. Shame cascaded through me.

Webber's desk was giant and made of black wood. Nothing but a laptop, one pen, and a water glass decorated the surface. No papers, no files, no scripts, no pictures—nothing. His desk was completely devoid of any other object. I wasn't sure why that struck me.

"I feel like I know you," I said. "Dillon talks about you all the time."

"He does?" Webber tilted forward in his chair. "That's good to know."

"He trusts you," I continued. "He believes in you and what you're doing for his career."

Webber's eyes widened with interest in what I had to say about Dillon and Dillon's feelings toward him. "He's going to be a gigantic star." Webber leaned back in his chair and settled his feet onto the corner of his desk. "*If* he plays his cards right."

Webber's assistant walked in, put an envelope on Webber's desk, and set a bottle of water in front of me.

"Thank you," I said.

She nodded, scurried from the room, and pulled the door shut.

"I wanted to have you in to thank you for doing such an amazing job for Dillon this summer."

Heat burst up my neck and bloomed on my face. Embarrassment trickled through me. Webber knew that Dillon and I had more than a work relationship. I still remembered Webber's words of wisdom the first time that we met: Don't sleep with Dillon. Well, I had. I had not only slept with Dillon MacAvoy, but I'd fallen in love with him too. Webber picked up the envelope that his assistant had placed on the edge of the desk.

Webber's eyes raked over me and I felt a sick twist in my gut. "This," he said and nodded at the envelope, "is your bonus for the summer."

What was he paying me for? What did he *think* he was paying me for?

"As well as the letter from CTA offering you a job in the agent-trainee program after you graduate next spring."

"Thank you," I stammered out. I took the envelope and set it in my lap. I looked down at the white rectangle that lay on my suit skirt, the same suit I'd worn to CTA the first day of this summer. So much had changed between then and now. I was a different person. I wasn't just a girl from Kansas who knew no one in L.A. and very little about the industry. Now I had friends, a job offer for a future career, a boyfriend... I looked at the picture on the wall of Dillon and Webber. Dillon's smile was gigantic—he looked as though he was laughing about something Webber had just said. Dillon looked happy. He and Webber, they looked like friends.

Webber stood and walked around his desk. He rested his long frame on the edge of his desk. His gaze settled on me. His look was stern, serious, as though he had important words to say.

"Here's the thing," Webber said. He crossed his arms over his chest, tilted his chin, and looked at me. "Dillon has a huge opportunity right now." Webber's eyes softened. "After this summer, I'm sure you've figured out how hard the entertainment business is?"

I nodded. Breaking into entertainment either on the executive side or the acting side was nearly impossible.

"We've worked so hard... Dillon's worked so hard to have this moment. This moment where he has a chance. An opportunity to maybe become a big star."

Webber stood and walked to the chair next to me. He sat.

"Lane," Webber's voice was softer. "I am sure you are a wonderful girl. I mean, it is obvious that Dillon cares for you. I think he believes that he even loves you and that is beautiful." Webber leaned back into his chair. "But that's not what we're selling, and it's definitely not what the studios are buying." He scrubbed his hand over his mouth. "Right now, with Dillon, they are buying an image. An image that is going to create a giant fan base, and that image is the single, bad-boy star who dates the world's most beautiful women." Webber's gaze locked onto mine. "Not a girl from Kansas."

The lump in my throat that had started growing when Webber had handed me the envelope was now lodged so firmly in my throat that I could barely breathe. I knew what Webber was said was true.

"In six months, once Dillon's opened three films and his fan base is secure and his career is launched, that might be the right time for him to be in love, but now?" Webber shook his head and a grimace scrawled over his face. "Now after all these months of building this image and developing this thing with Kiley. Now would be the worst time. You know her people want the studio to pull the offer for *The Legend Returns* because of you?"

My heart floundered in my chest. I closed my eyes for a second.

"I haven't told Dillon yet. I haven't told him because I'm afraid I know what he'll say."

I pulled at my hands. I knew what Dillon would say too. He'd say forget them. I was pretty sure that at this point, Dillon might just jettison his career for me. He might say forget the PR game and the Hollywood scene and everything else and choose me. I looked up at Webber and my eyes were slick with tears.

"He'll pick me," I whispered.

Webber nodded. "He'll pick you."

The silence weighed heavy in the room. I knew what Dillon wanted, I knew what he'd worked so hard to obtain, I knew why he wanted to feel safe and why he wanted Choo to feel safe. I knew that he was on the cusp of superstardom and he wouldn't get this moment again.

"You have a job here when you graduate, no matter what you decide." Webber pressed his fingertips together. "I will say, that in nine months... that might be the perfect time, but not now. If you two happen now, I can't guarantee him a career or success. Hell, I can't guarantee him success anyway, but right now, with the track I've laid and Boom Boom has laid, I know he has a real shot if he stays on this path. If we can close this next deal with Worldwide and give them what they want as far as a supposed romance between Dillon and Kiley, then he'll be in a great spot professionally."

I ran my fingertips around the edges of the white envelope.

"He's in Moab until Thursday," Webber said.

I nodded. I knew Dillon was gone until then. I stood. My heart hurt. My eyes were slick with tears. I wouldn't cry. I couldn't cry here. I wouldn't cry in Webber's office— I didn't want him to see my pain. I turned and walked out the door.

❧

I WAS HALFWAY THROUGH NEVADA WHEN THE

texting started. I'd walked the pups, kissed each one good-bye, written a note to Choo, and taken off. My stuff was piled into the back of my Jeep. I knew it was the coward's way out, I knew that I owed Dillon more than this, I owed Choo more than this, I owed Amanda more than this, but I also knew that if I tried to explain to Dillon why I had to go, why I was leaving, then I would absolutely never go. I couldn't look in his eyes and see the love and the pain and still have the strength to walk out the door. I wasn't strong enough, I wasn't big enough, to surrender everything I wanted for the good of his career if he was the one standing there telling me not to leave.

I pulled off for gas and checked my phone. Text after text from Dillon. Twenty-four missed phone calls. I couldn't listen to them. I needed more miles between us. I had to get home, I had to get back in school, I needed to be in the reality of my Kansas life, the life I'd lived forever, and not the glamour of L.A. before I spoke to Dillon, before I tried to explain what I'd done and why.

I closed my eyes. He had to understand. Please let him understand why. Hadn't he said time and time again to me that his career meant everything to him? That Choo's future and college meant everything to him? This was his chance, this was his shot. I couldn't be the reason that all his hard work and planning failed. If we were meant to be, then he would understand what I was doing and why. I knew I couldn't ask him to wait for me. I knew that his team's game plan included setting him up with the most beautiful actresses and models in the world. I'd surrendered any hope that in nine months when I returned to L.A., after him dating the most gorgeous women in the world, that Dillon MacAvoy would even remember my name. I'd be a long-ago, faded memory.

I wandered into the gas station and grabbed a Diet Coke and some Cheetos. I walked to the front of the gas station to pay.

My eyes roamed the tabs next to counter. My heart jumped in my chest and a thread of ice slithered down my spine. There, on five tabloid covers, was a picture I would never forget. A picture that broke what remained of my heart. I recognized the suit Dillon wore and the girl to which his lips were locked. My heart pounded in my chest.

I'd been a fool, a complete and utter fool. I lifted the magazine from the rack and my fingertips nearly burned. My eyes watered. I bit my bottom lip. I'd believed Dillon that nothing was going on, that Kiley meant nothing to him, that there was no attraction, nothing but the PR factory spinning wish-filled tales for fantasy-obsessed fans. I was wrong. Dillon had lied. This picture was taken the very night he'd come home and gotten into the bed we shared. The very night he'd touched me and kissed me and I'd begged for him to sleep with me. The night he'd made me scream his name over and over again.

My bottom lip trembled and I clenched it with my teeth. Anger settled into my chest. I was the stupid little girl from Kansas. I slipped the magazine back into the rack. I didn't want it. I didn't want a reminder of Kiley, of Dillon, of how stupid I'd been.

"Some beautiful babies those two are gonna make," the woman behind the cash register said. She pushed her smudged eyeglasses up the bridge of her nose. I handed her my money.

I climbed into my Jeep. I craved the mind-numbing miles ahead of me, hundreds of miles, the sound of rubber slapping pavement killing the thoughts in my head. My entire summer had been a lie. I was simply like every other reader that Dillon MacAvoy had ever had. The words Dillon had said to me were untrue. I'd forced myself to ignore my doubts and I had believed him. My phone rang. I looked down. It was Amanda. The tears streamed down my face and I answered my phone.

CHAPTER 25

<u>DILLON</u>

I BURST THROUGH THE FRONT DOOR OF THE house. "Where is she?"

The pitter-patter of toenails on wood greeted me. My heart pounded, but I gave each dog a quick pet. Fear beat through me, a low thrumming in my veins.

"She's gone." Choo stood in the doorway between the TV room and the foyer. His eyes were narrow and his arms were crossed over his chest.

"Lane!" I yelled and bounded toward the stairs. I couldn't believe what my brother had just said. I couldn't believe it. Panic thundered through my body. I took the steps two at a time, and the pack bounded up the staircase around me.

"Laney!" I yelled. She had to be here. She couldn't have left. She wouldn't have left. I stopped first in the doorway of my room. Nothing. No Lane. I bolted down the hall to her room and threw open the door.

Stillness hit me. Light pummeled through the windows. The room felt empty and untouched. My belly felt hollow and cold grasped my insides. My eyes darted around the room.

"No." My heart started to rip in my chest. "No, no, no." I walked to the closet and yanked open the door. "No!"

I stared at the empty shelves, the empty hangers, the empty floor where her battered duffel bag used to be. Hope slid from my body. Any hope that I could explain, that I could catch her, that I could pull Lane into my arms and convince her that this whole thing was a colossal mistake. A huge mistake that I would do anything to fix.

"She's not here." Choo's voice was heavy with sadness.

I turned to him. His eyes were slick and his face pale. He hadn't looked this sad since the day Mom and Dad had tossed him into the street. Choo held a tiny slip of paper in his hand. I walked to him and he held the paper out to me.

I'M SORRY. I HAD TO GO.
    Lane

PAIN RIPPED THROUGH MY HEART.

"What the hell were you thinking?" Choo whispered. "She was the best thing to ever happen to you. To me. To us. How could you go and mess this up?"

I ran my hand over my face. "I didn't, I didn't—"

"You kissed Kiley Kepner," Choo said. "It's all over the tabs and every other foul place you can imagine. How could you do that? There is no way Lane could possibly stay after that."

"It wasn't what it looks like," I said.

"Then what the hell was it, because I have to say it looks pretty bad."

"When did she leave? Where did she go? Have you heard from her?"

Choo shook his head no. "I got home yesterday and the note was here. She must have taken off while I was at the agency."

I dashed toward the door. I had to find her. I needed her. I had to explain and she had to listen.

❦

"YOU ARE A COMPLETE DUMB ASS."

I deserved that comment. I deserved that and more. Amanda leaned back into the lounge chair next to the pool and took a long, slow sip of her water. She set it on the table in front of her.

"Please, I know you've spoken to her—she won't answer my calls, she won't respond to my texts, she won't—"

"That's right," Amanda said. "Because she doesn't want to talk to you right now. She doesn't want to see you. She wants to be alone."

I paced along the edge of the pool. I scrubbed my hand along my face. "I need to explain what happened, how that happened. I didn't... it wasn't... fuck!" I balled my hands into fists. The muscle in my jaw clenched as my teeth ground. "It wasn't what it looks like."

"Right," Amanda said. She crossed her legs and glared at me through slitted eyes. "It looks bad."

I closed my eyes.

"More press for you," Amanda said. "Isn't that what you wanted?"

Air whooshed from my lungs. What I had wanted. I tilted my head toward the ground. I stared at the slate tiles on Amanda's patio. What had I wanted before Lane? I couldn't remember. I could barely remember life before meeting Lane, before being loved by Lane, actually living before Lane.

"Yeah," I whispered. "I guess it *was* what I wanted." I lifted my head and looked at Amanda. "What everyone wanted, but that, that moment, that picture it wasn't… it's not real."

Amanda raised her eyebrow. "Are you trying to tell me that the photo is fake? That it isn't you with your lips planted against Kiley's lips the night of the premiere?"

"No, that's not what—"

"Then what are you saying Dillon?"

"What I'm saying is that Kiley kissed me! That she came in fast, that I jerked away, that it had to be a setup—I didn't know anyone was there, I wasn't into it, I didn't want it and—"

"And that's why you didn't tell Lane about it?"

My heart stopped beating. The blood drained from my face and a tingling scrummed over my fingertips. I dropped into the chair beside Amanda. I couldn't breathe and my stomach clenched.

"You remember that night? How you stayed out until five a.m.? How you came home to Lane? How you... well I'm just guessing on the rest. But you didn't tell Lane that Kiley kissed you." She tilted her head to the side. Her tone said all that I already knew: I was an idiot. A complete moron. "You failed to mention this kiss that meant nothing."

"Because it meant nothing."

"Right," Amanda said. "While I might believe you, and Lane might even choose to believe you, can you see how these pictures, the humiliation of seeing the man you are sleeping with on the cover of every tabloid magazine, kissing a huge celebrity, might be enough to cause a girl to run?"

"What am I going to do? I have to find her, I have to go get her, I have—"

"You have to leave her alone," Amanda said.

I shook my head no. "Amanda, I can't I can't just let her run away and not tell her and not try to explain and not let her know that I... that I love her."

"She knows," Amanda said. "That's the saddest part. She knows, and she loves you too. But Dillon, I'm telling you that right now she does not want to see you. You have got to give her some time and some space to work through this. She thinks she's doing something noble for you. She believes all that shit about your brand and you launching your career and how important this moment is for you. She really believes that if you don't go through with this charade with Kiley that you are going to lose your opportunity for success. Lane doesn't want to be the reason why you don't get your shot."

"But she's not, she won't be, she can't... I can't—"

"Really? You really believe that? That Kiley is going to

just let some no-name little girl from Kansas swoop in and steal the limelight from her? That won't happen, not in a million years, and especially when she's sleeping with my father."

"You know about Kiley and your dad?"

Amanda nodded. "Just found out. The hard way." She twirled a lock of black hair between her fingers. "I'm nearly certain they'll be married before the end of the year."

"I can't be their beard. Even if I lose the role in *The Legend Returns*." I settled my elbows onto my knees and leaned toward Amanda. "You have to help me. Please, help me tell Lane. I know she'll take your call." My voice was on the edge of a plea, but I didn't care. I didn't have any pride when it came to Lane. I couldn't survive this hollow feeling that was carving a hole in my belly. "Lane is everything. Everything I want. Everything I need. Everything."

Amanda pressed her lips together. Her eyes flicked over me and I saw compassion and empathy flash through them. She knew that I loved Lane and she knew that Lane loved me. She had to help me; she had to help me reach Lane.

She turned her head away, the muscle in her jaw pulsed, and then she turned her eyes back to me. "Dillon," she said, "nobody gets everything they want all the time, not even a celebrity."

LANE

I ANSWERED MY PHONE IN COLBY, KANSAS. I couldn't take the number of calls racking up. My heart couldn't take that his heart was breaking like mine. I couldn't pretend that Dillon would leave me alone if I just ignored him. I didn't want to see him and I didn't want him showing up on my doorstep at school, and I knew he would. I knew if I ignored his texts, his calls, him... that he would hop on a plane and be at school waiting for me. I also knew what I had known when I left Los Angeles—that I didn't have the courage, the strength, the ability to leave Dillon if I had to see him. I couldn't look into his eyes and turn away. I loved him. I loved him even though I was angry with him. I loved him and I knew... after a thousand miles rolling it over in my mind... in my heart I knew that Dillon hadn't kissed Kiley. I knew that something had to have happened. But I also knew that he hadn't told me about the kiss and that broke my heart.

I wanted Dillon to find his success. I wanted him to feel the security that he would feel with his success. I wanted that for him and for Choo, and if that meant I had to have one final phone call with Dillon so that he would leave me alone forever, then I would have it.

I pulled into the parking lot of a restaurant and parked. It was hot in western Kansas. The phone rang and I took a long, deep breath and finally, after repeated calls and texts from the guy I loved, I answered my phone.

"Lane?" His voice was breathy and short, as though he couldn't believe I'd picked up. "Oh my God, Lane. Laney, are you okay? Where are you? Oh God, please don't hang up. Don't hang up..."

I swallowed the sob that choked in my throat and

wanted to burst from my chest with the pain and the love I heard in his voice. I could do this. I had to do this.

"I won't hang up," I said. "I… I want to talk to you."

"Oh, baby, Laney, please, baby, I want to talk to you too. Are you okay? Are you home? Can I come get you?"

"I'm in Colby, Kansas."

"Where the hell is Colby, Kansas?"

The tiniest smile curved around my mouth with his words. "It's really far away from Los Angeles," I said. "I'm almost home."

He paused then. He took a deep breath. "Baby, I want home for you to be where I am."

My heart broke… again. How many times could one heart break? I closed my eyes and took a long, deep breath. If I cried… If he heard me cry it would be over—he had to know that this was my decision, and he had to believe there was no way to change my mind.

"Home for me is Kansas," I said.

"Baby, the photo, I'm so sorry, the photo it wasn't… I mean… it didn't…"

"I know," I said. "I mean, it hurt so bad when I saw that picture. I can't even begin to tell you how bad it hurt, but I know, Dillon. I know you and I know it wasn't how it looks."

"Oh, Lane." His voice cracked. "Baby, I love you so much."

Hot tears rolled down my face with his words. "I… I can't be with you." I covered my mouth with my finger-tips. I muffled the choking sound that threatened to come out.

"What? Baby, you have to come back. I can't… this won't work without you. I can't do this. Choo can't do this. We need you, baby. You have to come back. I need you... Please, baby."

"No, Dillon. I have to be here. Please. Don't call me again. Don't text. Leave me alone. I have to be here and I have to be here alone."

"Lane—"

He called my name as I pressed the Off button. I couldn't speak anymore. I could barely breathe. I turned off my phone and drove.

I rolled into Lawrence at eleven a.m. after two days on the road. My body ached and I needed a shower. I drove down Massachusetts toward my apartment. A giant billboard screamed to the world the release of *Mission Ranger* with Dillon in the lead. He and Ryan stood well-armed, looking sweaty and dirty and sexy as hell. The film would make a gazillion dollars, I was sure. And Dillon would be a star. A huge star. My heart hurt as I glanced at his giant face. A face I'd kissed and that had kissed me. A face I would never get to kiss again.

I pulled into the parking spot in front of my apartment and slid from my Jeep. I'd thought about what Amanda said, that the business was messed up and that she was certain that the kiss had been manufactured. She'd watched Dillon with me and she knew Kiley and that there wasn't any way he'd want to be with her.

But she was so hot. And she was so Hollywood, and she was everything that he would want in a girl—everything that I would never be.

Emma pulled open our apartment door. She had a giant smile on her face and clasped me into a big hug. I was so happy to be home. I'd forgotten how much I missed her. I held tight to the tears that wanted to break free from my eyes.

"You look tired," she said. She had her white-blond hair pulled up into a ponytail. Her blue eyes crinkled with concern and hints of sadness.

I smiled weakly. I'd called her from the road and filled her in on the drama and told her I'd be home early from California. She was a good friend, and like any great friend, talking to her and now, seeing her—it was like I'd just seen her yesterday. She'd gotten to Lawrence before me and had cleaned up our place from the emptiness of the summer and filled it with food and flowers.

"Go take a shower," Emma said. "I fixed us some lunch."

My throat tightened with the idea of food, but my stomach growled. Classes didn't start for another week, but I had plenty to do. I was already enrolled, and I needed to check on when my work-study job would start. I needed to buy books and everything else that went with school. It was so strange to be back in Kansas.

I threw my duffel onto my bed and slumped down beside my bag. I wanted to cry. I'd shed tears across four states on the way home. Serious tears that could have filled buckets— I thought I was all cried out. I lay back on my bed. This summer hadn't been anything like I'd expected. Everything had been different, everything had changed. I was different inside and out. I'd taken the Big Risk and I'd gotten what I'd wanted—a job offer for next spring—but suddenly that job offer didn't seem to matter to me, because I'd lost something that meant more to me than any job could.

I'd lost my heart and the love of a lifetime.

I peeled my clothes from my body and wandered into my shower. I turned the shower to hot. I wanted to wash the dirt, the grime, the tears, wash all of it from my body. I wanted to feel clean and freshly scrubbed, I wanted to begin school and pretend that I hadn't lost my heart to Dillon MacAvoy, to pretend that I'd never even met him, never even known him, never been a part of a life with him. I stepped under the water and let the heat sear into my skin. The thought of Dillon in the shower with me, his body pressed against mine, entered my brain. Hot tears spilled over my cheeks and mixed with the hot water pouring over my body.

I had known this pain would come at the end of my summer, would be a result of my time with Dillon. I'd known this would be the bitter heartbroken end. That day, standing on the beach, for the first time when I'd stared at the infinite ocean—I'd known. I'd made a deal with myself that day. I would trade a lifetime's worth of memories for a lifetime of pain. I pressed my hands to the tiles of the shower. Sobs choked upward and wracked my body. Had I realized then what this pain—this soul-crushing heart-break—would be? Tears rolled from my eyes. Even if I'd known what the pain of this moment would feel like, the pain I was certain would forever be trapped in my heart next to my memories of Dillon—even then I wouldn't have traded one minute of Dillon's love for peace.

I straightened my spine and pushed my head under the shower. The water washed the tears from my face. Dillon was meant to be a memory I left in California, a memory that I kept throughout my life. A memory I would take out and cherish and look at with melancholy and a smile, but Dillon was never meant to be mine. Our worlds were too different, we were too different—I didn't fit into his life. His life was planned out and his success was imminent if I left him alone. And now, whether the kiss was real or fake... it didn't really matter. Kiley and Boom Boom and Webber and Worldwide—they would all get what they wanted, what they needed for Dillon, they would get the world's next big star the next big actor, the next big heart-throb, and I was definitely not going to stand in the way of all that. Not me, not a little girl from Kansas with a broken heart.

CHAPTER 26

Dillon

"DUDE, GET YOUR LAZY ASS UP."

Bright light poured into my bedroom. I covered my eyes with my hand and looked toward the windows where sunlight burst in from the outside.

"Have you taken a look at your fat ass? Filming starts on *The Legend Returns* in two weeks." Choo pushed open the balcony doors. "You stink, you know that?" He stood with his hands on his hips and stared down at me. "What would all the women in America think if they could see their latest heartthrob looking like this pile of shit?" He picked up an empty Jack Daniels bottle from the floor. "Really?" He shook his head. "I know you miss her, but this is a little cliché, even for you, big brother."

I rolled onto my back and covered my face with my hands. I didn't want to get out of bed, and I didn't want to film *The Legend Returns* with Steve Legend. I didn't even care that *Mission Ranger* had opened huge and broken box-office records. I was suddenly the hottest commodity in town, and I didn't care about any of it. I didn't want anything but Lane. The four-pack burst through the open bedroom door and bounded onto my bed. Bernie gave me a giant lick up the side of my face.

"Go take them to Runyon," Choo said. "Run some of that liquor off your belly."

The dogs pranced around my bed and Kong barked at the word Runyon.

"Seriously, dude, you lost her so you could do the Steve Legend film, now don't lose the film because you look like a pile of shit."

"Fuck off," I growled at Choo.

He had no idea the heartache that tore at me. The fact that no matter what I did I could never fix this, never change what had happened, that I would never again be with Lane. She'd made that clear.

The paps had broken the story about Kiley Kepner sneaking around with Steve Legend, and I was off the hook. Hunter Fabian had left me a voice mail saying Steve couldn't wait to get to set so he could get away from his soon-to-be ex-wife's divorce lawyer.

"Why don't you go get her," Choo said.

I picked my forearm up off my eyes and peered at him. "Have you talked to her?"

He didn't answer. I suspected that even though Lane wouldn't answer my calls or my texts, she was still speaking with my brother.

He stone-faced me. "I'm just saying, what use is it being the newest biggest star in Hollywood if you can't use some of that hard-won glamour to get the girl you want?"

"The girl I want doesn't want me, remember? I screwed that up." The muscles in my jaw clenched.

"Yeah, and I've been pretty much wrong when it comes to Lane since the beginning, haven't I?" Choo said and grabbed three beer cans off my dresser. "Fine, don't listen to me, your brother, the person in this family who actually still has a relationship with the girl you love."

"Love." I sighed. I rolled to sitting. "Man, I *do* love her."

"Like that was any kind of secret." Choo grabbed the garbage can from under my desk and started tossing empties into it. "I am sending Mathilde in with a flamethrower and a gas mask. Seriously, brother, this is some sorry shit."

My gaze darted around my room. With the shades open and the sun pouring into my room, it did look pretty rank. "I'm not even sure how long I've been in here."

"Too long," Choo said. "You know you're a big star now, though, right?"

I nodded. Some big star. I didn't want to leave my room. I didn't want to act. All I wanted was a girl I couldn't have.

"Do you really think…" I couldn't say the words. The idea of going to get Lane and her saying no made the pain inside my heart throb. She could rip it out again by saying no, by turning her back on me, by deciding I wasn't worth the risk.

"You won't know for sure unless you try."

I nodded. I yanked back the covers and planted my feet

on the ground. Lane was worth the world. She was worth every single attempt to try.

LANE

FOR WEEKS ALL I DID WAS DRAG MYSELF TO MY classes, then to my work-study job at the registrar's office, then I fell into bed at home. I barely read for class. I didn't eat. I did shower because after the first week I'd started to smell and Emma had finally mentioned that I was scaring her. I lay on my bed. Today was Saturday. No classes and no work-study. I didn't want to go anywhere. I didn't want to do anything. I lay curled in my bed with the shades drawn. My body wanted to sleep. Sleep was so peaceful. Sleep was the only time I didn't completely ache, the only time my heart didn't throb with pain and when I didn't have to fight the desire to cry.

There was a gentle tap on my door.

"Come in," I called out.

Emma opened the door. "Hey," she said. She smiled and slipped into my room. "I brought you a coffee." She reached out her hand just far enough so I had to sit up. "It's almost eleven." She moved toward my bedroom window. I didn't stop her. I knew me wallowing was completely unhealthy, and she was just trying to be my friend.

"So, some of us are going to a matinee at the Second Run. Want to go?"

I closed my eyes. I didn't want to go. I wanted to stay in my room. I didn't want to see anyone or hear their murmurs to each other as to whether I was okay and would ever get over Dillon. I bit my bottom lip.

"Then we're going to get lunch at the Taproom," Emma said.

"Sure," I said.

"Great!" Her smile took over her face. "Get up and get dressed—the movie starts in an hour."

I pulled the blanket off my legs. "Emma," I said as she got ready to leave my bedroom.

She turned back to me. "Yeah?"

"Thank you. I know that... Well, I know that I'm an emotional basket case and not any fun to be around and well... Thank you for being such a good friend."

"Oh, Laney, you have a broken heart. And sweetie, yours got broke real bad. I mean..." She looked up at the ceiling of my room. "You took this amazing risk and I am so proud of you, but this happened." Her eyes settled back on me. "I mean, I know you got that great job waiting for you out there at the end of the year, but maybe, maybe this was meant to happen so you know how much we love you back here."

My bottom lip quivered. She was saying what I had been thinking for the last couple of weeks. Ever since I drove into Lawrence and felt the warmth of being home. Maybe I wasn't meant to move to Los Angeles, maybe I simply wasn't an L.A. type of girl. I had great friends here, a great city a half hour away.

"I know you can still get a job at Core Tech," Emma said. "My daddy can totally get you in. They were so impressed by the way you went out there all by yourself and got that job and when I told him you came back with an offer for next spring—I mean, he was just blown away."

I nodded. The things that Emma said made perfect sense. They did. I would have a wonderful life here with all my friends from college who knew me, and I'd be in a sane sort of industry. The type of industry that didn't force you to lie and pretend you were someone that you weren't.

"Thanks Emma," I said.

She nodded and smiled. She was my best friend in the world. "Now get ready!" she said and pulled my door shut.

❧

THE SECOND RUN WAS CHEAP AND ALWAYS filled with kids from school. Movies ran there a couple of weeks after they ran at the big theaters. You couldn't beat the price—only five bucks a ticket. I walked up to the theatre beside Emma, Kristin, and Laurie.

"We're going to the Sandra Bullock film," Emma said.

I stopped. I froze. There he was. Right in front of me. A poster of *Mission Ranger*. My stomach swirled and the world tilted. Dizziness zipped through my brain. The picture of him. I'd been there when they took these one-sheet photos. Ryan had been drunk and cracking bad jokes. Dillon had wanted to get the whole damn thing finished so that he and I could go to dinner in Malibu.

"Honey? Lane, you okay?" Emma asked and nudged my arm.

My bottom lip quivered. I wasn't okay. I felt sick. I wasn't ready to go to the movies. The movies would always remind me of Dillon. He was in the movies. I couldn't yank my eyes from the poster.

"I'm sorry," I said. I just…" Three pairs of eyes looked at me, each containing a varying shade of sympathy.

"I just don't feel good," I said. "I'm going to go home, okay?" My eyes pleaded for Emma to understand. I didn't want her to make a scene or ask me to stay. I already felt like the biggest loser in the world that a poster of a guy whom I had dated had stopped me in my tracks and sent me scurrying back to my room.

"Sure," Emma said and glanced around at Laurie. "Let me come with you."

"No!" I said. I closed my eyes and took a long breath. "I don't want to ruin the day. I just… I don't feel very good. I'm fine—the fresh air will be good for me."

Emma tilted her head. Concern still filled her eyes. "Okay," she said slowly, "but you'll text me if you need me."

I nodded. I wouldn't need her. What I needed was to get Dillon's face out of my brain. What I needed was for this pain to stop throbbing through me. I needed to move on with my life and make my heart realize what my brain already knew: Dillon wasn't mine. He belonged to the world now—he was the next big thing.

Since *Mission Ranger* had come out, people couldn't stop talking about Dillon MacAvoy and how much they loved Dillon MacAvoy and how sexy was Dillon MacAvoy. His success made healing from the heartbreak more diffi-cult. I knew Dillon in a different way, I knew the true Dillon, I had loved the real Dillon and now… now he was gone, lost to me forever. I knew I wouldn't love like that again, I couldn't. I wouldn't want the risk of feeling this way. My heart was gone; it would forever belong to the guy in that poster.

I walked through campus and down the hill toward Memorial Stadium. The trees had started to turn and there were crimson and gold and amber leaves. Normally the colors would look beautiful to me; they had in the past. Now I was so consumed by my pain that not even the fall colors and the crisp chill could boost my spirit.

Could you feel the difference of the seasons in Los Angeles? I'd only been there for one season. If I moved to L.A., I would miss the seasons. I sat on the bench beside Potter Lake. The colors were glorious. I chewed on the inside of my cheek. This was safe. This place was comfort. I was going to stay here. I was going to have a wonderful life. Far from all the glamour, all the games, all the politics of Hollywood. I wanted what was here for me: stability, continuity, friendship. Living here might not make my heart pitter-patter and beat fast, but it would most definitely make me feel safe. This was home.

DILLON

I LOOKED OUT AT ALL OF LOS ANGELES AT MY feet. An empty feeling clawed through me. I had every-thing I thought I wanted. Bernie leaned against my side while Kong did figure eights around my feet. Scorsese and Spielberg sniffed in the bushes at the edge of the path. I was a star. My career was solid. I was in the next Steve Legend film. I had all that—all I had wanted—and I felt empty inside. Completely and utterly empty. My cell phone rang.

"Hey man," Webber said.

"What's up?" I kept the edge out of my voice.

"Good to hear your voice," Webber said. "Steve and Hunter want to have a read-through next week at Steve's new house. Whole cast will be there."

"Send me the deets," I said.

"Hey... uh... you okay? I mean, I heard you were kind of... well, you were kind of off the radar."

If having a shredded heart because of losing the girl I loved was off the radar, then it was true. "Yeah, man, it's been a rough couple of months."

"Well, it's good to have you back. Boom Boom has a ton to talk to you about. Magazines are clamoring for photo shoots and interviews. Man, you are smokin' hot. We need to take advantage of all this while we can."

I nodded. This is what I'd wanted, what I'd worked hard to get, and even with it right here at my fingertips, I still felt empty and shallow.

"Sure," I said. I kicked a rock across the path. I couldn't get excited about this without Lane.

"She wanted you to have this," Webber said. His voice was softer.

"What?"

"Man, I shouldn't even tell you this." He sighed. "But I... look." He paused, a pause where I knew he was making a decision.

"Are you talking about Lane?"

"She came in to pick up her letter of intent for her job here, for after she graduated."

My heartbeat grew faster. The words, I knew whatever words Webber said next wouldn't make me a happy man.

"And I told her… I explained to her about where you were in your career and the opportunity you had right now, and how it would only come once and sometimes it never came at all for some actors. And she got it. It broke her heart, but she got it."

I clenched my jaw. I wanted to beat Webber's ass. I wanted to beat Boom Boom's ass. I even wanted to kick my own ass. This wasn't Webber's fault—hadn't I told Lane that nothing was more important to me than my career? Hadn't I proved that nothing was as important to me as my career by seeing Kiley—even if only for press? Yeah, it'd been my very actions that proved my career was important, even more important than Lane.

My heart hitched. A sour feeling slimed through my gut. Of course she thought and believed that I wanted my career more than her.

"That's why she left, man," Webber said. "Not that she couldn't hack the glamour and the publicity, but because she thought she'd be taking the career opportunity from you. That she'd be stealing your big break. The opportunity to be in a Steve Legend film."

I shook my head. I snapped my fingers and Kong, Scorsese, Spielberg, and even Bernie trotted to my side. "I gotta go," I said.

"Sure, man. Where you goin'?"

"The place I should have gone two months ago," I said. "I'm going to Kansas."

CHAPTER 27

LANE

AFTER MY FILM HISTORY CLASS ON TUESDAYS, I headed straight to Strong Hall to work five hours at the registrar's office. I pulled my coat tighter around my body as the wind whipped down Jayhawk Boulevard. I ducked my head and tried to stay warm. I hadn't slept much last night. I kept dreaming of Dillon. Our first time together had kept replaying in my mind: every touch, every kiss, every moment that he made my body ache for him. Then I'd wake up, realize I was alone in my bed, and cry. Cry for what I'd had. Cry for what I'd lost. Cry because I knew I would never find a love like Dillon ever again.

I would fall back to sleep and the same scene would replay in my dreams. I hated this. Now I wasn't even safe from memories of Dillon when I slept. I braced myself against a blast of cold air and pressed my lips tight. I couldn't go through this pain in the daytime and then have to face our intimate moments together when I slept. I had actually felt his hands on my body, rubbing me and touching me. I woke up and the sheer pain of the aloneness and the thought of never touching Dillon again created a horrible empty hollowness inside me.

I wove around the edge of a crowd that was forming across from the humanities building. Sometimes freshmen gave stump speeches on campus. If you were brave enough to do it, you got an automatic A for the semester in Freshman Speech. I edged around the growing group, crossed the street, and climbed the steps to the door of the admin building. My fingers touched the metal handle of the giant glass doors.

"Stop that girl!"

I froze. My heart jolted in my chest and my throat thickened. I tried to swallow. Tears started in the back of my eyes. Finally, after what felt like a forever moment, I turned my head and looked over my shoulder.

Standing on a stone bench with students milling around him was Dillon.

"Yeah, that one," he said.

My eyes danced around the crowd. I felt incredibly embarrassed and exposed.

"I love that girl," Dillon yelled. "I love Lane Channing."

He jumped from the stone bench and the crowd parted before him. He walked toward me, his gaze never leaving mine. It was like we were alone, as though there weren't a couple hundred students watching the newest big star in the world walk toward me, a no-name girl at the University of Kansas. His eyes were locked on mine. In his gaze I saw all my pain, all my loss, all my hope reflected in his eyes.

I reminded myself to breathe. I couldn't swallow. A lump choked closed my throat. My mouth dropped open. The cold was gone. The wind was gone. The crowd was gone. All there was in this world was Dillon and me. He stopped on the step just below where I stood.

Blood thundered through my head. I still couldn't move. As much as I wanted to reach out and grab him, to pull him into my arms, I was frozen. I could barely believe that this moment was real, that this moment was happening, that the man I loved now stood before me. Dillon knelt in front of me.

I pressed my fingertips to my open mouth.

"Lane, I'm sorry. I can't live this life without you... I won't live this life without you. Please let me spend the rest of my life proving to you that nothing, nothing in this world has meaning without you." He reached into his jacket and pulled out a black velvet box.

I heard a collective gasp from the crowd.

"Lane Channing..." Dillon's bright blue eyes, filled with hope, filled with love, filled with promises I knew he would keep, locked onto my eyes. "Will you marry me?"

My heart leapt. I couldn't speak. Worry clouded Dillon's eyes with my silence. "Lane, baby, please, baby... I..."

"Yes," I whispered. "Oh my God, yes," I said and dropped my books to the ground.

He jumped up and Dillon's lips were on mine. He pulled me so tight, so close. "Oh, baby, you made me the happiest man in the world. I love you, Laney. I can't live without you." He grasped both sides of my face and stared into my eyes.

I saw forever in his eyes. The forever that went with his words. There would be only us.

"I'm so sorry baby. Nothing is more important than you. No film, no career, nothing... You're the most important thing in my world."

The crowd burst into cheers. Dillon turned and waved to his fans, to the world. I buried my face into his jacket, embarrassed with all the attention. The campus police stopped their patrol car, and Bob walked up beside Dillon.

"Okay, you two lovebirds," Bob said. "I think it's time to get you to a secure location."

EPILOGUE

LANE

"You ready for this?" Dillon asked.

He squeezed my hand and his eyes ate me up. I wore a gown that was cut low. Sitting beside him in the town car, my dress rode high on my hip. His fingertips danced around the edges of my thigh. I looked up at him through my eyelashes.

"We don't have time for that right now," I purred.

Spirals of heat swept through my body. The last six months had been the best six months of my life. I lived with Dillon. I attended USC with Amanda. I was surrounded by people I loved and I worked in an industry, that even with all the crazy, I adored.

"I can ask Bob to drive around the block a couple of times," Dillon whispered in my hair.

"We're already late," I gasped as his fingers slipped farther up my thigh. "Besides, I think we're here."

"Damn," Dillon said. A wicked smile flashed across his face. "After..." He nuzzled my neck. His hand straightened my skirt over my legs. "You're amazing. I can't wait to call you Mrs. MacAvoy."

My heart hammered harder. Warmth slid through my belly. "If you'd stop saying yes to movies, we could get married."

"We are getting married. I have the date in my calendar. A place. A bride." He pulled me close and gave me a long hot kiss.

I wanted to sink into him and relax into that giant, gorgeous chest, but I knew what waited for us on the other side of the door. Bob now stood outside the car. He tapped on the glass of the window. A warning and a signal worked out between him and Dillon.

Dillon raised his eyebrows and looked at me. I nodded. Dillon tapped the window with his knuckle. I took a long, deep breath.

The door swung open and Dillon jumped out. The roar was nearly deafening, and the flashes blinded me. Dillon turned back to the car and reached for my hand. Our fingertips touched and I knew I was okay; I knew I was safe.

I slipped one foot and then the other out of the car. My eyes grew accustomed to the flashing lights. My ears were ready for the cheers and the shouted questions. Dillon clasped me close, pulled me into his side with his arm around me like he always did. We walked down the red carpet, hand in hand, toward his shining star and our future together, forever.

The End

Keep reading for a SNEAK PEAK at the NEW Glamour Series book, *Vicious Glamour*...Coming soon!

CHAPTER 1

CHAPTER 1

"Kiley, you are such a bitch." Harv's shit-brown eyes hold a threat that his sixty-plus year-old doughy body can't follow through on.

"Not the first time I've heard those words." *And if I get what I want, it definitely won't be the last.*

"You may be the most vicious bitch I know," he growls.

"Vicious bitches come from somewhere," I say. "We're usually built from the ground up." I nod toward the giant flat screen on the wall in Harv's swank Century City office. "Keep watching."

I don't watch the video, because I was there the day it was shot. I can still smell the come and the scent of vanilla lotion that lingered on Tatiana's skin. On screen I'm the blonde with my head between her thighs. She moans and writhes and pulls my hair.

"That's my fucking wife," Harv says.

"You mean that's your wife that I'm fucking." I lift my

whiskey in a salute to Tatiana's moans of pleasure. The amber liquid barely burns as I sip. "It gets better, much, much better."

I sit on the brown suede couch in Harv's office and his face contorts. Harv's at war between his natural Y chromosonal proclivity to find the visual of two hot women fucking a turn-on, versus the fact that I'm fucking his wife in a clandestine encounter- – an affair as it were – to which he was not invited.

"You could've at least asked me," he mumbles. Because that's the type of guy Harv is. An utter narcissist He's not nearly as upset that I'm fucking his wife, as he is that we didn't ask him to join us while we fucked.

He tightens his grip on the remote and his knuckles whiten. The bulge in Harv's pants grows. His wife, Tatiana, a Victoria's Secret model from Russia, has that effect on most men. She makes their dicks bulge.

"Ohhhh...."

I remember this moment. Tati loved my tongue between her thighs and the pleasure I delivered.

"There's a reason why we didn't invite you," I say, with a not-so-subtle hint of wickedness in my voice. Because now, here comes the revenge, served up hot with a hard cock and a young man's model-perfect body. Unlike the schlubby pile of goo Harv inhabits.

I glance at the screen. This sexy-ass motherfucker is too good not to look at; the main reason we didn't invite Harv. The hard-ass hottie walks into the frame.

"No," Harv says. "No fucking way."

I bite my bottom lip. My toes curl. Because even though I was there in the room giving Tati the best head of her life, I did not partake in the pleasure of the male stud getting ready to fuck her.

"That's....that's....." Harv clutches his hand over his heart.

Harv can't believe what he's seeing, and really, who can blame him? This scene, on screen before him, must be every sixty-something-man with a hot twenty-something wife's nightmare. And I made the nightmare even worse. Yes, I did. Because I knew exactly how to drive the final stake through Harv's heart.

"Your son." I finish Harv's sentence for him. "But I mean come on Harv, Tatiana's closer in age to Harv Junior than she is to you."

Yes, there is Harv junior, flipping his twenty-eight year old step-mommy onto all fours and getting right up behind her thick-as-fuck ass. His long, hard cock is smooth and gorgeous; the camera angled on just the point of entry.

Smack.

A swift smack to step-mommy's ass.

"Oh, Harv!" step-mommy shrieks. "Please, please, yes, give it to me!"

I smile and take a long pull on my bourbon. There are no words necessary because revenge is a vicious bitch and I am serving up a giant heaping helping today.

The twenty-four year old man now on screen is—aside from the part of his gene pool that is abhorrent and standing beside me—sexy as hell.

At this point, I've removed my mouth from Tatiana's sex and also my body from the frame, and am standing to the side of the room outside of the shot and near the camera.

The entire scene is so clear both onscreen and in my memory. So. Fucking. Hot. My toes curl inside my Louboutin heels and my breath shortens, even now, as I watch Harv Junior's hard, perfect cock slide into Tatiana's sex.

Harv clutches his chest. "I...." His gaze locks on me. His mouth drops open. "How could you do this?"

I laugh. Like glass shattering against a marble floor, so sharp is the sound of my own horrible laughter. I stand and walk toward Harv. I'm close to him, so close that I feel the heat rolling off him, and again he is at war with his desire to grab my hair and fuck me, or bitch-slap me. Torment is in his eyes.

"How rich is that question?" I set the crystal tumbler, now empty of bourbon, on the settee. "Really Harv? I could ask you the same question? How could you have slipped into the bed of a sleeping fourteen-year-old girl?"

Harvey stares at me. Crimson rolls up his neck and colors the pallid skin of his face. Maybe he'll stroke out here, in his office.

"What do you want?" His voice hovers just above a whisper.

A wicked smile crosses my lips. *What do I want? What I want, Harv can't give me. What I want was stolen from me at a young age, and now, I've got to find a way to get it back.*

"You are a sick fuck. A sick and perverted fuck that did bad and depraved things to more young girls than just me." My blood red fingernail drags along Harv's cheek. He doesn't move. My lip curls. "What I want, you can't give me."

Harv swallows.

Maybe he never realized how much I remember; all the

sad, sick details. The weight of his body on mine. The smell of him. His stinking flesh.

"We've known each other a long time, haven't we Harv? Ever since all those *parties* my parents used to throw."

The red drains from his face because he remembers. The sick, twisted fucking memory comes back to him. Maybe he convinced himself that I didn't remember or maybe somehow he managed to tell himself the lie that I wanted what he gave. I mean, I might have been fourteen, but I definitely didn't look it.

I lean forward and my lips are close to his ear. "You remember those parties, don't you Harv? The ones where my mom would pass out, my dad would leave with some actress, and sometimes you'd spend the night?"

He jumps away from me with his mouth hanging open. His chest heaves up and down. *That's right you sick, horrible fuck, let's see how you like being the prey. See how fear feels.*

"I....I...." He scrubs his hand through his hair and turns away from the screen. "That was....a different time, I was a different man. There were parties and drugs and the booze and, my God...really? This? Because of what happened a decade ago?"

My victory is short-lived because in this moment, with that one sentence, Harv minimizes what happened to me, a fourteen year old girl, a decade ago.

"Yeah. This. Because you know what, Harv? As bad as what you're seeing right now is, it's not nearly as bad as how I've felt for the last ten years."

I turn toward the door. My heart pounds and rage-y tears prick my eyes. A lump thickens in my throat, because even with the revenge, I still feel damaged and dirty and foul. No matter how bad I manage to make Harv feel, him feeling bad doesn't make me feel better.

I turn on my heels and I'm nearly out the door, my stomach oily and sick. Fuck Harv. Fuck Momager. Fuck Dad. Fuck them all, because everyone got exactly what they wanted. Well, everyone but me.

But I *will* get what I want. No matter what I have to do to get it.

CHAPTER 2

CHAPTER 2

Am I searching for a ghost that doesn't want to be found? I press my phone closer to my ear to hear the voice on the other end. The re-shoots for *Dead Men Die* are close to the 405 and standing outside it's tough to hear the voice on the other end of the line.

"Mr. Turner, we've searched the greater Indianapolis area and the surrounding counties and there is no trace of your mother."

I've hired Greystone [LINK Beck], the best security agency in LA, and if Greystone can't find Mom then there's no way that she's going to be found. *Fuck.*

My chest tightens. What do I tell Trevor? How do I tell my little brother that our mother has disappeared? Again. For what may be the final time.

"We did get a possible lead in Columbus—"

"Go!" I bark into the phone. Hope claws into my frontal lobe. "Check it out. Find her. I don't care how long it takes or what it costs." The tightness in my chest relaxes because as long as there is a lead, a possibility, I don't have to tell my brothers what I really fear to be true. Especially not now.

"Hey Jackson, they're ready for you." A PA stands in front steps of the house where we're doing reshoots.

I nod. "Look," I say into the phone, "I need to know where she is. Follow every lead and find her."

"You got it," King [LINK **] says into the phone.

I've met him twice. King is all business and since he's with Greystone, I know he's not only doing his job, but he's the best guy for it.

The phone clicks off and I turn toward the house. Time for me to go be the Jackson Turner that millions of people watch on screen, and not the guy who is searching for his mom. I turn my phone over and Lyle's number pops onto the screen.

My heart flips in my chest. My brother knows I'm on set today filming reshoots and there is no way he'd call unless— "Hey, what's up?" I ask, before my brain can even start with the fear and the questions and the—

"You need to meet us at the hospital."

My stomach clenches. Lyle just said two dreaded words; *us* and h*ospital* in the same fucking sentence.

"It's bad."

"How bad?" I glance at the PA still standing on the steps, now tapping his foot. If he's tapping his foot out here, I can only imagine what the director is doing inside. Zymar isn't known for being an easy-going guy to work with.

"Bad enough that the words 'medically induced coma' are being thrown around."

Fuck. Fuck, fuck, fuck.

"I'll be right there." I dash toward the front steps of the house. "Fifteen minutes, I'm on my way." Who needs to be in an action-movie when my real life is filled with this much drama?

***

I HATE HOSPITALS. I'VE SPENT HOURS UPON hours in hospitals. First with Mom. Then myself, and now, the last year, with Trevor.

Shit.

Lyle sits in Trevor's room. He's out. Asleep, but not comatose. I don't know what they gave him because the nurse took the chart. I pace at the foot of her bed.

"Sit the fuck down," Lyle says. "You won't fix anything pacing."

For once I listen to my brother. Most times I don't. "How was he before?"

"Like he always is. Fine. Great. Doing his thing, and then he's on the ground convulsing." He crosses his arms over his chest and takes a deep breath.

"Did you talk to Dr. Chalmers?" I ask.

"She was here. Said she'd be back in a couple hours. What took you so long?"

His face darkens with the question. I shrug. Admitting that I actually finished my two scenes before I left the set is fucking embarrassing. What kind of asshole does two scenes of reshoots before coming to see his brother in the hospital?

This asshole.

"You finished your scenes for the re-shoot." Lyle

shakes his head and rolls his eyes toward the ceiling. "Wow, you're almost as bad as Mom."

"Fuck you," I whisper. "I'm nothing like Mom. If I was, I'd be long gone."

He says nothing because he knows I'm right. There's no good reason to ride down our sick and sordid familial memory lane.

I walk to the head of the bed and peer at Trevor. Is he even in there? Where does he go when this shit happens? After a bad seizure his body's a husk, completely uninhabited. I've asked him if he remembers anything from when he's out and he says no, but there's this hint of something in his eyes that he's not telling me. I don't push because who the fuck wants to talk about their seizures?

"Hey guys." Dr. Chalmers enters the room. Her skin is the color of midnight and her eyes are a warm brown, shot through with gold. She's always cool and calm and completely at ease in a hospital.

Lyle flashes me a look and there is panic and fear behind his eyes. We're both wondering the same thing: Is this the time that the Trevor we both know and love doesn't return to us? Is this the time they tell us there is permanent brain damage? Is this the time Trevor has to stay and they take out the blob in his brain?

Hope claws over the desperation commandeering my brain. I silently will Dr. Chalmers to give me something good to cling to. *Please say anything that lets me hold onto the hope.*

"I think it's time."

My heart careens through my chest, upended like a boat in a typhoon. I glance at Lyle and his gaze catches mine. The words we've anticipated and dreaded have finally been said.

"We have to remove the tumor. Trevor's quality of life has deteriorated to the point that we can't wait anymore. Plus it's gotten bigger. I'm certain this is why his seizures have accelerated."

"Is he going to wake up before the surgery?" I ask.

Dr. Chalmers looks over at Trevor and I follow her gaze.

"We'd like for him to wake up," she says. "But regardless, we need to schedule the surgery."

I nod and close my eyes. Yeah, now I'm also going to be the asshole that attends a movie premiere the night he finds out his brother needs brain surgery.

CHAPTER 3

Momager's home office is black and white and gold and purple. Her desk is glass and there are mirrors hanging both behind her desk and the wall across from it, because really, for Momager, she can't look at herself enough: A wicked black widow on a mirror, spinning a web that allows her to eat and kill anyone unfortunate enough to get trapped.

Right now, the most deeply ensnared is me. Daddy is in Asia and Chloe is in Switzerland, or she was. At least the last I heard, that's where she was. A boarding school for the rich and privileged. But now? Who knows? Chloe's whereabouts are Momager's secret. Daddy is too busy to care, and I want the information so desperately that Momager guards Chloe's whereabouts like it's the nuclear codes.

I drop into the black leather chair across from Momager's desk. She doesn't look up but continues to flip through the Vogue in front of her. Her manicurist works on her nails, sharpening them into fine points that will soon be blood red, Momager's favorite color. Her nails are filed so sharply she could shiv you in the kidneys if she didn't shred you with her words first.

"Why aren't you with your trainer?" Her soulless black eyes glance away from the Vogue and lock onto to me.

A chill crushes my spine. "Nice to see you too."

"Seriously, why aren't you with Raoul? You've gained four pounds and it's showing in your ass. You haven't locked down the role in Cici's next film. Now is not the time to get sloppy."

Ah, the warmth and love of Momager dearest. There isn't any love from Momager, because she has no love to give. The woman hasn't a maternal bone in her body. My birth was required to lock my rock star father into position, plus I was the cute accessory to our fake happy home until I became another revenue stream for Momager.

"I did my work-out early," I say. Would it kill Momager to ask me how I am? It might. In all the years that I've been with Momager, and truly it's been since I was in utero, I've never heard her utter any endearment toward me.

"Where've you been?" Momager isn't interested in me or my life, but more about controlling what I do, who I see, and where I go.

"Century City." I leave out the part about terrorizing pedophiles by sleeping with their wives and sons. Harv is a long-time friend of Momager and a very powerful man in H-town. She'd despise the idea that I've humiliated him, which only makes what I've done all the more pleasurable for me.

She flips another page, much more interested in the

magazine than she'd ever be in me. "You have the *Silver Swords* premiere tonight. The car will be here at four."

"I'm not going."

Momager lifts her gaze from the magazine and drills her viper-like stare into me.

My stomach folds over itself. A blast of Momager rage is imminent. My lazy I don't care expression is a sad ruse. My deepest desire is that 'I don't care about Momager' could be my truth—that I could actually *not* fucking care what Momager does or says or thinks, but right now, that laissez-faire attitude and the piece of me that Momager controls....owns....extorts me with, makes nonchalance an impossibility.

"You know," she says with an affected lilt in her voice that feels like a steak knife shoved into the base of my skull, "Chloe is supposed to come home from school next month"—Momager's eyes slice through my bravado like a scalpel through flesh—"maybe I should just have her stay at school."

"No," Want seeps into my voice.

A gleam in Momager's eyes and her lips turn upward into a wicked smile. "Then you'll go," she says. "Tonight."

She knows I will. While Momager controls Chloe, she also controls me. With one horrible little flick of her wrist she can crush me in an instant by destroying the only thing I love.

"And you'll drop the four pounds."

Anger rises in my throat like a living thing. I want to scream and smash and snap her neck, but instead I simply nod. She controls me through my one vulnerability, but isn't that how we survive life? By never being vulnerable?

"Stacia will be here in an hour to dress you. Drex gets here at four."

Pimping me out is Momager's primary means of income. Her luxe office in her Hidden Hills manse comes from a combo of Daddy and me working the entertainment world while she sits and flips through her Vogue.

I cross my legs and suck in my cheeks. Who needs enemies when you've got a Momager and an entire industry set to capitalize on your youth, beauty, and desire for love. Momager reaches over and lifts a stack of papers and drops them in front of me. "Your divorce papers came."

Another sad road I traveled in my quest to find love and a life without Momager dearest. Although Steve Legend tried to be good to me, unlike the beast that gave birth to me, we simply couldn't make our marriage work.

Momager examines her nails.

"I set up an appointment for you with Choo. I think you're image is in need of a little repair. The video from Tahiti with you screaming at the cabana boy, and now the divorce? I know *you* don't care about your brand, but I do. There are a lot of failures the public will forgive in a woman, but coming across as a bitch isn't one of them, no matter what the reason. You need to clean up your act. Find a charity you want to work with or—"

"A child I'd like to adopt?"

Her eyes lock onto mine and her lips thin for a millisecond.

My heart stops in my chest and I can barely breathe. I know this look. I've seen it before. It happens every time she takes something that I love away. I've gone too far.

I've almost mentioned the unspoken filthy lie that rots between us, the one thing we will not and do not discuss.

"You know there's no place in this house for children," she says. "Remember what happened to you?"

"Remember?" I whisper. "I've spent a lifetime trying to forget."

Momager pretends not to hear me and flips another page of her Vogue. "Your father called from Asia. Five more dates have been added to his tour."

We aren't really a family, more like a multi-national entertainment conglomerate.

"I'm flying over at the end of the week and I'll be there for the rest of the tour. You'll be here on your own," she says.

My heart skips a beat. On my own? Even at twenty-four and divorced, Momager hardly ever lets me 'be on my own.' She's got the perfect extortion piece to control me and she wields that leverage freely.

On my own. Dream words. Perhaps a little room to maneuver and maybe even put more of the building blocks in place that I need for my freedom. *Our* freedom.

"Heard anything from Connor about *Bitter Hearts?*" Momager asks. Now *she's* trying to seem oh-so-nonchalant. But she's not an actress. Her entire day, month, perhaps year, hinges on me getting the part in Lydia Albright and Cici Solange's next film. Momager has tried for a decade to crack into their Hollywood Girls Club [Hollywood Girls Club Link] without success. Me getting this role in their film is Momager's access point, or so she thinks.

"I should hear soon."

"I thought you nailed the audition. Did you shit the bed?"

So much love. So much self-esteem building. So much maternal caring over something that is important to Momager.

"Lydia and Cici will be there tonight," Momager continues. "Maybe I should go too."

I lift an eyebrow. She may be the only person in H-Town who fails to realize just how much Cici Solange loathes her. And if Momager even *thinks* she's getting an invite into the fab-four's friendship circle she is oh-so sadly mistaken. But bad times for Momager could mean good times for me.

"I mean, maybe," I say. "But I did hear from Lydia's stepdaughter that she might want to speak with me....alone."

Momager's dead-soul stare flickers at me. Her gaze travels over my face. "Don't fuck this up," she says. "If Lydia wants to speak to you then—"

The phone on Momager's desk rings. "Get that," she barks to her manicurist, who fishes the receiver from the cradle and places it on Momager's shoulder.

This is my moment to escape. I stand and walk toward the office door. Heat pummels through my chest. The entire reason for my conception was to lock down Daddy dearest and his bank account for a minimum of eighteen years. She's used me and my DNA for the last twenty-four years for her own personal gain. I won't win this war today. No, this is a long battle, which I'm willing to wage, but I've got to be smart to win our freedom.

"Kiley?" She calls.

I turn back. Her hand is over the phone's mouthpiece.

"Yeah?"

"Don't wear the white Versace, it makes your ass look big and not in a good way."

Heat blasts my chest. I walk out of her office and down the hall toward the dressing room. There are reasons I don't call this woman Mom, because I've always been her meal ticket and she's my pimp. But Momager's free ticket to ride is almost up.

PRE-ORDER *VICIOUS GLAMOUR* NOW ON ITUNES!

ALSO BY MAGGIE MARR

The Hollywood Girls Club Series

Hollywood Girls Club

Secrets of the Hollywood Girls Club

Hollywood Hit

Hollywood Girls Club, the Series

The Eligible Billionaires Series

Can't Buy Me Love

One Night for Love

A Christmas Billionaire

Last Call for Love

Running from Love

Eligible Billionaires Books 1–5

Eligible Billionaires: The Travati Brothers

A Forever Love

A Billionaire for Christmas

A Convenient Arrangement

A Forbidden Love

Eligible Billionaires Books 6-9

The Powder Springs Series

Courting Trouble

The Christmas Wish

Candy Cane Lane

The Glamour Series

Hard Glamour

Broken Glamour

Fast Glamour

Easy Glamour

Luxe Glamour

Impossible Glamour

Coming Soon: Vicious Glamour

The Hollywood Hitmen Series

Beck

Coming Soon: Jax

The Wonderful Love Duet

*Wonder F*ck*

Mister WonderFULL

Wonderful Love

ACKNOWLEDGMENTS

First, thank you to, you, my readers. Thank you for buying my books and spending time with the characters.

Thank you to my agent, Kristin Nelson and every person at Nelson Literary Agency. Thank you to Sarah Hansen of Okay Designs for a beautiful cover and her vision for the Glamour Series. Thank you to Lori Bennett who is patient, and determined, and kind. I love working with you! Thank you to Angie Hodapp who creates the interior designs for my paperbacks. Thank you to Anne Victory, my editor, who keeps my words looking good and thank you to her colleague Crystalle, for picking up the errors that my eyes miss. Thank you to Jennifer Brown who is brilliant at proofing my paperbacks.

A special thank you to Amy Zacky for being a beta reader when I needed an extra beta reader.

Thank you to the Los Angeles Romance Authors RWA Chapter and to the Womens Fiction Writers Association.

Thank you to my friends and family who make my writing possible: Margaret Marr, Nancy Veskerna, Lauren

Harrison, Gavin White, Peyton Morgan, Nealie Harrison, Mark Morgan, Peggy Cafferty, Melissa Clark, Garrett Marr, Janet L'Huillier, Gayle Leftwich, Eloise & Dixie Marr, Joyce & Tom Leahy, Dolores Henderson, Lindsy & Mark Henderson, Linda & Bill Henderson, Amy & Brent Zacky, Victoria & Karl Makinen, Sheryl & Steven Ross, Paramount Elite Gymnastics and the entire Paramount family, E. Lockhart, Lauren Myracle, Sara Zarr, Sarah Mylnowski, Maryrose Woods, Jennifer Barnes, Ally Carter, Alan Gratz, Tara Altebrando, and BOB.

Thank you, to my husband and my children for the love, the support, and the joy.

ABOUT THE AUTHOR

USA Today Bestselling Author Maggie Marr is a hopeless romantic with a dirty mind. She writes strong women and the men they love. Maggie got her start in entertainment slinging boxes in the mailroom and eventually became a motion picture agent. Over twenty books later, Maggie still works in entertainment and makes her home in Los Angeles.

Please join her mailing list to get a FREE Maggie Marr starter library and keep up with all things Maggie!

Website: www.maggiemarr.net
   Newsletter: http://eepurl.com/c050yz
   Facebook: Maggie Marr Books
   Twitter: @maggiemarr
   Pinterest: Maggie Marr
   Instagram: Maggie_Marr_Author